Danielle Steel has been hailed as one of the world's most popular authors, with over 530 million copies of her novels sold. Her many international bestsellers include *Loving, Star, Family Album, Golden Moments, To Love Again, Season of Passion* and other highly acclaimed novels.

Visit the Danielle Steel website at www.daniellesteel.com

By Danielle Steel

*published outside the UK under the title PASSION'S PROMISE

DANIELLE STEEL

TO LOVE AGAIN

sphere

SPHERE

First published in Great Britain by
Sphere Books Limited 1980
Reprinted 1985 (twice), 1986 (twice), 1987, 1988,
1989 (twice), 1991, 1994
Reprinted by Warner Books 1994
Reprinted 1995, 1996, 1998, 1999
Reprinted by Time Warner Paperbacks 2002 (twice)
Reprinted by Time Warner Books in 2005
Reprinted 2006
Reprinted by Sphere in 2007
Reissued by Sphere in 2008
Reprinted 2008 (twice)

ISBN 978-0-7515-4138-0

Printed in England by Clays Ltd, St Ives plc

Papers used by Sphere are natural, renewable and recyclable
products made from wood grown in sustainable forests and certified
in accordance with the rules of the Forest Stewardship Council.

Mixed Sources
Product group from well-managed
forests and other controlled sources
www.fsc.org Cert no. SGS-COC-004081
© 1996 Forest Stewardship Council

Sphere
An imprint of
Little, Brown Book Group
100 Victoria Embankment
London EC4Y 0DY

An Hachette Livre UK Company
www.hachettelivre.co.uk

www.littlebrown.co.uk

To Bill, Beatrix and Nicholas,
with all my love.

And to Phyllis Westberg,
with love and thanks.

Chapter One

In every city there is a time of year that approaches perfection. After the summer heat, before the winter bleakness, before snow and rain are even dreamed of. A time that stands out crystal clear, as the air begins to cool; a time when the skies are still bright blue, when it feels good to wear wool again, and one walks faster than one has in months. A time to come alive again, to plan, to act, to be, as September marches into October. It is a time when women look better, men feel better, even the children look crisp again as they return to school in Paris or New York or San Francisco. And maybe even more so in Rome. Everyone is home again after the lazy months of summer spent clattering along in ancient taxis from the piazza to the Marina Piccola in Capri, or they are fresh from the baths in Ischia, the sun-swept days at San Remo, or even simply the public beach in Ostia. But in late September it is over, and autumn has arrived. A business-like month, a beautiful month, when it feels good just to be alive.

Isabella di San Gregorio sat sedately in the back seat of the limousine. She was smiling to herself, her dark eyes dancing, her shining black hair held away from her face by two heavy tortoise-shell combs as she watched passersby walking quickly through the streets. Traffic was as Roman traffic always is: terrifying. She was used to it, she had lived there all her life, except for her occasional visits to her mother's family in Paris and the one year she had spent in the States at twenty-one. The following year she had married Amadeo and become a legend of sorts, the reigning queen of Roman couture. She was by birth a princess in that realm, and by marriage something more but her legend had been won by her talent, not only by acquiring Amadeo's name. Amadeo di San Gregorio had been the heir to the House of San Gregorio, the tabernacle of Roman couture, the pinnacle of prestige and exquisite taste in the eternal international competition between women of enormous means and aspirations. San Gregorio – sacred words to sacred women, and Isabella and Amadeo the most sacred words of all. He in all his golden, green-eyed Florentine magnificence, inheriting the house at thirty-one; she the granddaughter of Jacques-Louis Parel, the king of Paris couture since 1910.

Isabella's father had been Italian but had always taken pleasure in telling her he was quite sure that her blood was entirely French. She had French feelings and French ideas, French style, and her grandfather's unerring taste. At seventeen she had known more about high fashion than most men in the business at forty-five. It was in her veins, her heart, her spirit. She had an uncanny gift for design, a brilliance with colour, and a knowledge of what worked and what didn't that came from studying her grand-father's collections year after year. When at last in his eighties he had sold Parel to an American corporation, Isabella had sworn that she would never forgive him.

She had, of course. Still if he had only waited, if he had known if . . . but then she would have had a life in Paris and never met Amadeo as she had when she set up her own tiny design studio in Rome at twenty-two. It had taken six months for their paths to cross, six weeks for their hearts to determine what the future would be, and only three months after that before Isabella became Amadeo's wife and the brightest light in the heavens of the House of San Gregorio. Within a year she became his chief designer, a seat for which any designer would have died.

It was easy to envy Isabella. She had it all – elegance,

2

beauty, a crown of success that she wore with the casual ease of a Borsalino hat, and the kind of style that would still make an entire room stop to stare at her in her ninetieth year. Isabella di San Gregorio was every inch a queen, and yet there was more. The quick laughter; the sudden flash of diamonds set in the rich onyx eyes; her way of understanding what was behind what people said, who they were, why they were, what they were and weren't and dreamed of being. Isabella was a magical woman in a marvellous world.

The limousine slowed in a vast traffic snarl at the edge of the Piazza Navona, and Isabella sat back dreamily and closed her eyes. The blast of horns and invective was dimmed by the tightly sealed windows of the car, and her ears were too long accustomed to the sounds of Rome to be disturbed by the noise. She enjoyed it, she thrived on it. It was a part of the very fibre of her being, just as the mad pace of her business was part of her. It would be impossible to live without either one. Which was why she would never leave her business life entirely, despite her semi-retirement of the year before. When Alessandro had been born five years before, the business had been everything to her, the spring line, the threat of espionage from a rival house, the importance of developing a boutique line of ready-to-wear to export to the States, the wisdom of adding men's wear and eventually cosmetics and perfume and soap. All of it mattered to her intensely. She couldn't give it up, not even for Amadeo's child. This was her lifeblood, her dream. But as the years had gone by, she had felt an ever greater gnawing at her soul, a yearning, a loneliness when she returned home at eight thirty and the child was already asleep, tucked into bed by other hands than hers.

'It bothers you, doesn't it?' Amadeo had watched her as she sat pensively in the long grey satin chair set just so in the corner of the sitting room.

3

'What?' She had seemed distracted as she answered, tired, disturbed.

'Isabellezza – ' Isa-beauty. It always made her smile when he called her that. He had called her that from the first. 'Talk to me.'

She had smiled at him sheepishly and let out a long sigh. 'I am.'

'I was asking you if it bothers you very much not being here with the child.'

'Sometimes. I don't know. It's hard to explain. We have – we have lovely times together. On Sundays, when I have time.' A tiny tear had crept out of one of the brilliantly dark eyes, and Amadeo held out his arms to her. She had gone to them willingly and smiled through her tears. 'I'm crazy. I have everything. I . . . why doesn't the damn nurse keep him up 'till we come home?'

'*Alle dieci?*' At ten o'clock?

'It isn't, it's only . . .' She had looked at her watch in irritation and then realised that he was right. They had left the office at eight, stopped to see their lawyer at his home for an hour, stopped for yet another 'minute' to kiss their favourite American client in her suite at the Hassler, and . . . ten o'clock. 'Damn. All right, so it's late. But usually we're home at eight, and he's never awake.' She had glared at Amadeo, and he had laughed gently as he held her in his arms.

'What do you want? One of those children that movie stars take to cocktail parties when they're nine? Why don't you take off more time?'

'I can't.'

'You don't want to.'

'Yes, I do . . . no, I don't.' They had both laughed. It was true. She did and she didn't. She wanted to be with Alessandro, before she missed it all, before he was suddenly nineteen and she had missed her chance. She had seen it

4

happen to too many women with careers – they mean to, they're going to, they want to, and they never do. They wake up one morning and their children are gone. The trips to the zoo that never happened, the movies, the museums, the moments they meant to share, but the phones were ringing, the clients waiting. The great events. She didn't want that to happen to her. It hadn't mattered so much when he was a baby. But now it was different. He was four and he knew when he didn't see her for more than two hours in three days, he knew when she was never there to pick him up at school, or when she and Amadeo spent six insane weeks planning the next collection or the line for the States.

'You look miserable, my love. You want me to fire you?' To Amadeo's astonishment as well as her own she had nodded. 'Are you serious?' Shock registered in his eyes.

'Partly. There must be a way for me to work part of the time and be here a little bit more too.' She had looked around the splendour of their villa, thinking of the child she hadn't seen all day.

'Let's think about it, Bellezza. We'll work something out.'

And they had. It was perfect. For the past eight months she had been chief design consultant to the House of San Gregorio. She made all the same decisions she had always made, she had her hand in every pie. The unmistakable hand of Isabella was still recognisable in every design San Gregorio sold. But she had removed herself from the mechanics of the business, from the nitty-gritty of the everyday. It meant overburdening still further their beloved director, Bernardo Franco, and it meant hiring another designer to carry out the interminable steps between Isabella's concepts and the final product. But it was working perfectly. Now Isabella came and went. She

5

sat in on major meetings. She pored over everything with Amadeo during one marathon day each week. She stopped in unexpectedly whenever she had an appointment nearby, but for the first time she felt she was truly Alessandro's mother now too. They had lunch in the garden. She saw him in his first school play. She took him to the park and taught him nursery rhymes in English and funny little songs in French. She laughed with him, ran with him, and pushed him on the swing. She had the best of all possible worlds. A business, a husband, and a child. And she had never been happier in her life. It showed in the light that danced in her eyes, in the way she moved and laughed and looked when Amadeo came home. It showed in the things she said to her friends as she regaled them with tales of Alessandro's latest accomplishments: 'And my God, how that child can draw!' Everyone was amused. Most of all Amadeo, who wanted her to be happy. After ten years of marriage he still adored her. In fact, more than he ever had. And the business was thriving, despite the slight change of regime. Isabella could never absent herself totally. It simply wasn't her style. Her presence was felt everywhere. The sound of her echoed like a perfectly formed crystal bell.

The limousine stopped at the kerb as Isabella caught a last glimpse of people on the street. She liked what women were wearing this year. Sexy, more feminine. Reminiscent of her grandfather's collections in years before. It was a look that pleased her very much. She herself stepped from the car in an ivory wool dress, perfectly draped into a river of tiny, impeccably executed pleats. Her three long strands of enormous pearls hung from her neck at precisely the right depth of the softly draped neckline, and over her arm was a short chocolate mink jacket, a fur that had been designed just for her in Paris by the furrier once employed by Parel. But she was in too much of a hurry to slip it on.

6

She wanted to discuss some last-minute details of the American line with Amadeo, before meeting a friend for lunch. She glanced at the faceless gold watch on her wrist as a sapphire and a diamond floated mysteriously on its face, indicating only to the initiated the exact time. It was ten twenty-two.

'Thank you, Enzo. I'll be out five minutes before noon.' Holding the door with one hand, he touched his cap with the other and smiled. She was easy to work for these days, and he enjoyed the frequent trips in the car with the little boy. It reminded him of his own grandchildren, seven of whom lived in Bologna, the other five in Venice. He visited them sometimes. But Rome was his home. Just as it was Isabella's despite her French mother and her year in the States. Rome was a part of her, she was born there, she had to live there, she would die there. He knew what every Italian knew, that a Roman was meant to live nowhere else.

As she walked decisively across the sidewalk toward the heavy black door in the ancient facade, she glanced up the street as she always did. It was a sure way to know if Amadeo was in. All she had to do was look for the long silver Ferrari, parked at the kerb. The silver torpedo, she called it. And no hands touched that car, except his. Everyone teased him about it, especially Isabella. He was like a small child with a toy. He didn't want to share it. He drove it, he parked it, pampered it, and played with it. All by himself. Not even the doorman at San Gregorio, who had worked there for forty-two years, had ever touched that car. Isabella was smiling to herself as she approached the impressive black door. At times he was like a little boy; it only made her love him more.

'*Buon giorno, Signora Isabella.*' Only Ciano, the grand-fatherly doorman in black-and-grey livery, called her that.

'*Ciao, Ciano, come sta?*' Isabella smiled widely at him, displaying teeth as beautiful as her much celebrated pearls. '*Va bène?*' It goes well?

'*Benissimo.*' The rich baritone rolled musically at her as he swept the heavy door open with a bow.

The door shut resoundingly behind her as she stood in the entrance hall for a moment, looking around. As much as the villa on the Via Appia Antica, this was her home. The perfect pink marble floors, the grey velvets and rose silks, the crystal chandelier that she had brought from Parel in Paris after long negotiation with its American owner. Her grandfather had had it made in Vienna, and it was almost beyond price. A sweeping marble staircase rose to the main salon above. On the third and fourth floors were offices done in the same greys and pinks, the colours of rose petals and ashes. It was a combination that pleased the eye as much as the carefully selected paintings, the antique mirrors, the elegant light fixtures, the little Louis XVI love seats tucked into alcoves here and there where clients could rest and chat. Maids in grey uniforms scurried everywhere, their starched white aprons making crisp little noises as they brought tea and sandwiches to the private rooms upstairs where clients stood through arduous fittings, wondering how the models survived entire shows. Isabella stood for a moment, as she often did, surveying her domain.

She slipped quietly into the private elevator, pressing the button for the fourth floor, as she began to go over the morning's work in her head. There were just a few things to take care of; she had settled most of the current business yesterday, to her satisfaction. There had been design details to work out with Gabriela, the chief designer, and administrative problems to discuss with Bernardo and Amadeo. Today's work wouldn't take her long at all. The door slid silently open and revealed the long grey carpeted hall. Everything about the House of San Gregorio was downplayed. Unlike Isabella, who was anything but. She was obvious and splendid and eminently visible. She was a woman one saw and wanted to see, a woman one wanted to be seen by. But the House of San Gregorio was a showcase for beauty. It was important that what they had to show there was not overwhelmed by the house itself. It wasn't, it couldn't be. Despite the beauty of the seventeenth-century building that had once been the home of a prince, the wares of San Gregorio were too resplendent to be overwhelmed by anything or anyone. Isabella had created a perfect meshing of remarkable models, extraordinary designs, and incredible fabrics and brought them together with women who wore them well. She knew that somewhere, in the States, in Paris, in Milan, the women who wore their boutique line, their ready-to-wear, were not anything like the women who came to this address. The women who came here were special – countesses, princesses, actresses, literary figures, television personalities, notables and nobles who would have killed or died for San Gregorio's designs. Many of them were women like Isabella herself – spectacular, sensual, superb.

She walked silently towards a pair of double doors at the end of the long hall and pressed down on the highly polished brass handle. She appeared like a vision in front of the secretary's desk.

'Signora!' The girl looked up, startled. One never quite knew when Isabella would appear, or just what she would have on her mind. But today Isabella only nodded, smiled, and walked immediately toward Amadeo's office. She knew he was in. She had seen the car. And unlike Isabella, he rarely strayed to the other floors. He and Bernardo kept mainly to their upstairs offices. It was Isabella who prowled, who wandered, who appeared suddenly in the mannequins' room, in the corridors outside the private fitting rooms, in the main salon with the long grey silk runway, which had to be constantly replaced. That was a source of constant irritation to Bernardo, ever practical in his directorship of the house. It was on his shoulders that the budget fell. As president and chief of finance, Amadeo designed the budget, but Bernardo had to live with it, seeing that the fabrics and beads and feathers and wondrous little ornaments fell within the limits Amadeo had set for them. And thanks to Bernardo they always existed well within that budget. Thanks to Bernardo the house had been carefully and at times brilliantly run for years. Thanks to Amadeo's investments and financial acumen they had prospered. And thanks to Isabella's genius with design they had gloried as well as flourished. But it was Bernardo who bridged the world of design and finance. It was he who calculated, speculated, weighed, and pondered what would work, what wouldn't, what would cost them the success of the line, or what was worth the gamble. And thus far he had never been wrong. He had a flair and a genius that made Isabella think of a matador, proud, erect, daring, flashing red satin in the face of the bull, and always winning in the end. She loved his style and she loved him. But not in the way that Bernardo loved her. He had always loved her. Always. From the first day he had met her.

Bernardo and Amadeo had been friends for years and they had worked together in the House of San Gregorio before Isabella had appeared on the scene. It had been Bernardo who had discovered her in her tiny atelier in Rome. It had been he who had insisted that Amadeo come to see her work, meet her, talk to her, and perhaps even convince her to come to work for them. She had been remarkable even then, sensationally beautiful and in- credibly young. At twenty-two she was already a striking woman, and a genius with design. They had arrived in her little studio that day to find her wearing a red silk shirt and a white linen skirt, little gold sandals and not much else. She looked like a diamond set in a valentine. The heat had been crushing, but even more so moments later when her eyes met Amadeo's for the first time. It had been then that Bernardo realised how much he cared too and that it was already too late. Amadeo and Isabella had fallen instantly in love, and Bernardo had never spoken up. Never. It was too late, and he would never have been treacherous to his friend. Amadeo meant too much to him; for years he had been like a brother, and Amadeo was not the kind of man one betrayed. He was precious to everyone, beloved by all. He was the one person you wanted to be like, not a man you'd want to hurt. So Bernardo didn't. He knew also that it saved him the pain of finding out that she didn't love him. He knew how much she loved Amadeo. It was the governing passion of her life. Amadeo actually meant more to her than her work, which in Isabella's case was indeed remarkable. Bernardo couldn't compete with that. So he kept his pride and his secret and his love and he made the business better; he learned to love her in another way, to love them both with a passion of his own, and a kind of purity that burned like a white fire within him. It created enormous tension between him and Isabella, but it was worth it. The results of their encounters, their rages, and their wars were always splendid: extravagantly beautiful women to parade down their runways . . . women who occasionally paraded into Bernardo's arms. But he had a right to that. He had á right to something more than his work and his love for Amadeo and Isabella. He burned with a kind of bright light all his own, and the women who drifted through the house, models or clients, were drawn to him by something they never quite understood, something never fully revealed, something Bernardo himself no longer consciously thought about. It was merely a part of him now, like his infallible sense of style, or his respect for the two people he worked with, who in their own way had become one. He understood perfectly what they were. And he knew that he and Isabella could never have been like that. They would have remained two, always two, always in love, always at war; had she even known his feelings, they would have met like colliding constellations, exploding in a shower of comets across the heavens of their world. But it was not like that with Isabella and Amadeo. It was gentle, tender, strong. They were soldered as one soul. To see Isabella look into Amadeo's eyes was to see her disappear into them, to move into a deeper part of herself, to see her grow and fly, her wings stretched wide. Amadeo and Isabella were as two eagles soaring across their private sky, their wings in perfect harmony, their very beings one, their unison complete. It was something Bernardo no longer even resented. It was impossible to resent a pair like that. They were beautiful to see. And now he had grown confortable with what was a fiery working relationship with a lady he loved from afar. He had his own life. And he shared something special with them. He always would. They were an indestructible, inseparable threesome. Nothing would ever come between them. The three of them knew that.

As Isabella stood outside Amadeo's office door for a moment, she smiled to herself. She could never see that door without thinking of the first time she had seen it and these halls. They had been different then. Handsome but not as strikingly elegant as they were now. She had made them something more, as Amadeo had made her something more. She grew in his presence. She felt infinitely precious, and totally safe. Safe enough to be what she was, to do what she wanted, to dare, to move in a world with no limits at all. Amadeo made her feel limitless, he had shown her that she was, that she could be everything she wanted to be and do everything she wanted to do, and she did it all with the power of his love.

She knocked softly on the door few people knew about. It led directly into his private office. It was a door only she and Bernardo used. And the answer came quickly. She turned the handle and walked in. For a moment they said nothing, they only looked as the same thrill swept through her soul that she had felt since she had first seen him. He smiled in answer. He felt it too. There was unfettered pleasure in his eyes, a kind of gentle adoration that always drew her to his arms like a magnet. It was the gentleness in him that she loved so much, the kindness, the compassion he always had. His was a different fire from hers. His was a sacred flame that would burn forever, held aloft for the sad and weary, a proud light, a beacon to all. Hers was a torch that danced in the night sky, so bright and beautiful that one almost feared to approach it. But no one feared to approach Amadeo. He was eminently welcoming. Everyone wanted to be close to him, although in truth, only Isabella was. And Bernardo too, of course, but differently.

'*Allora*, Isabellezza. What brings you here today? I thought we settled everything yesterday.' He sat back in his chair, one hand held out to her, as she took it.

'More or less. But I had a few more ideas.' A few. . . . He laughed at the word. A few with Isabella meant thirty-five, or forty-seven, or a hundred and three. Isabella never had a few of anything, not a few ideas, or a few jewels, or a few clothes. Amadeo smiled broadly as she bent for a moment to kiss his cheek and he reached out and touched her hand.

'You look beautiful today.' The light in his eyes bathed her in sunshine.

'Better than this morning?' They both laughed. She had been wearing a new cream on her face, her hair tied up

13

high on her head, a comfortable dressing gown, and his slippers.

But Amadeo only shook his head. 'No. I think I liked you better this morning. But . . . I like this too. Is it one of ours?'

'Of course. Would I wear anything not ours?' For a moment the dark eyes flashed into his green ones.

'It looks like one of your grandfather's designs.' He studied her carefully, narrowing his eyes. He had a way of seeing and knowing all.

'You're very smart. I stole it from his nineteen thirty-five collection. Not totally, of course. Just the flavour.' She grinned. 'And the pleats.'

He smiled at her in amusement and bent toward her again for a rapid kiss. 'The flavour is excellent.'

'It's a good thing we don't work together full time anymore, we'd never get anything done. Sometimes I wonder how we ever did.' She sat back in her seat, admiring him. It was impossible not to. He was the Greek god of a hundred paintings in the Uffizi in Florence, the statue of every Roman boy, long, lean, graceful, elegant; yet there was more. The green eyes were knowing, wicked, wise, amused. They were quick and certain, and despite the golden Florentine beauty of his genes, there was strength there as well, power and command. He was the head of the House of San Gregorio, he had been the heir to a fairly major throne, and now he wore the mantle of his position well. It suited him. He looked like the head of an empire, or perhaps a very large bank. The neatly tailored pin-striped suit accentuated his height and narrow figure, yet the broad shoulders were his own. Everything about Amadeo was his own. There was nothing fake or flawed about him, nothing borrowed, nothing stolen, nothing unreal. The elegance, the aristocratic good looks, the warmth in his eyes, the quick wit, the sharp mind, and the

14

concern he had for those around him. And the passion for his wife.

'What are you doing down here all dressed up today by the way? Other than sharing a "few" ideas with me, of course.' He smiled again as their eyes met, and Isabella broke into a smile.

'I'm having lunch with some ladies.'

'Sounds terrible. Can I lure you to a room at the Excelsior instead?'

'You might, but I have a date with another man after lunch.' She said it smugly, and laughter danced in her eyes, as well as his.

'My rival, Bellezza?' But he had no cause to worry and he knew it.

'Your son.'

'In that case, no Excelsior. *Peccata*.' A pity.

'Next time.'

'Indeed.' He stretched his legs out ahead of him happily, like a long, lazy cat in the sun.

'All right. Shut up. We have work to do.'

'*Ècco*. The woman I married. Tender, romantic, gentle.'

She made one of their son's horrible faces, and they both laughed as she pulled a sheaf of notes out of her handbag. In the sunlight in his office he saw the sparkle of the large emerald-cut diamond ring he had bought her that summer for their tenth anniversary. Ten carats, of course. What else? Ten carats for ten years.

'The ring looks nice.'

She nodded happily as she looked down at it. It looked good on her long graceful hands. Isabella wore everything well. Particularly ten-carat diamonds. 'It does. But you look nicer. I love you by the way.' She pretended to be flip, but they both knew she was not.

'I love you too.' They shared a last smile before plunging into work. It was better now. Better when they weren't together every day. By the end of the afternoon he was always hungry for her and anxious to get home. And there was something special now about their meetings, their evenings, their lunches, their days. She was mysterious to him again. He found himself wondering what she was doing all day, where she was, what she was wearing, as the thought of her perfume filled his mind.

'You don't think the American line is too subdued? I wondered about that last night.' She squinted at him, not seeing him but the designs she and Gabriela had gone over the day before.

'I don't. And Bernardo was ecstatic.'

'Shit.' She returned her eyes to his with genuine concern. 'Then I'm right.' Amadeo laughed at her, but she didn't smile. 'I'm serious. I want to change four of the fabrics and add one or two of the pieces for France to that line. Then it'll work.' She looked certain, as she always did. And she was rarely wrong. That absolute certainty of hers had won them fashion awards for ten years. 'I want to bring in those purples, and the reds, and the white coat. Then it will be perfect.'

'Work it out with Bernardo and tell Gabriela.'

'I already did. Tell Gabriela, I mean. And Bernardo's new soap for the men's line is all wrong. It hung in my nose all afternoon.'

'That's bad?'

'Terrible. A woman's perfume should stay with you. The smell of a man should only come to you as you go to him and leave you with only a memory. Not a headache.'

'Bernardo will be thrilled.' For a moment he looked tired. Occasionally Isabella and Bernardo's wars exhausted him. They were essential to the business though, and he knew it. Without the fierce pull of Isabella and the stern anchor of Bernardo the House of San Gregorio would have been very different than it was. But as the axle that kept the two wheels from flying off in separate directions, he felt the strain on him was at times more than he enjoyed. But as a threesome they were a miraculous team, and all three of them knew it. And when all was said and done, somehow they always managed to stay friends. He would never understand it. With Isabella raging and calling Bernardo names that he had never even dreamed she knew, and Bernardo looking as though he might at last commit murder, he would then find them after hours in one of the private fitting rooms, drinking champagne and finishing a plateful of the day's sandwiches like two children at their own tea party after the grown-up guests have gone home. He would never be able to figure it out; he was just grateful that it worked that way. Now, with a sigh, he looked at his watch. 'Do you want me to call him in?' He never had to deliver messages for Isabella. She always delivered them herself. Straight from the hip. To the groin.

'You'd better. I have to be at lunch at noon.' She looked at the unreadable watch. That had been a present from him too.

'God. We're playing second fiddle to ladies' lunches now.' But there was laughter in his eyes. He knew that in Isabella's life that would never be true. Other than himself, and Alessandro, it was the business that Isabella lived for, that kept her breathing and kicking and eight hundred per cent alive.

Amadeo picked up the phone and spoke briefly to his secretary. She'd call Mr. Franco at once. Which indeed she did, and he came at once as always. He strode into the room like an explosion, and suddenly Amadeo could feel Isabella tense. She was already preparing for battle.

'Ciao, Bernardo.' Isabella smiled casually at him as he walked into the office in one of a hundred dark suits that he owned, all of which looked exactly the same to Isabella. He wore the same gold pocket watch on each one of them, the same impeccably starched white shirts, and ties that were usually dark with tiny, tiny white dots. Or when he felt very outrageous, tiny red ones. 'I love your suit.' It was their standing joke. She always told him that his suits were excessively boring. But the simplicity of his suits was part of his style.

'Listen, you two, don't start today. I'm not in the mood.' Amadeo looked ominously at them, but as always his eyes laughed even when his lips did not. 'Besides, she has to be at lunch in forty minutes. We're only second best to her lunches now.'

'That figures.' Bernardo squeezed out a small smile and sat down. 'How's my godson?'

'Alessandro is perfect. The dining room curtains, however, are not.' Amadeo started to grin as Isabella told the tale. He loved the boy's mischievousness, the fire in the dark eyes so much like hers. 'When I was here yesterday, solving your problems for you' – she raised an eyebrow, waiting for Bernardo to take the bait, and was clearly disappointed when he did not – 'he borrowed my manicure scissors and "fixed" them, as he put it. He cut off roughly a metre which, he tells me, got in his way every time he drove his favourite truck along the window. He couldn't see the garden. Now he can see the garden. Perfectly, in fact.' But she was laughing too, as was Bernardo. When he smiled like that, twenty of his thirty-eight years fell away from him and he was barely more than a boy himself. But he had worked too long, and when he wasn't being amused by tales of Alessandro, he often looked austere. Much of the weight of the House of San Gregorio was on his shoulders and it often showed. He had worked hard and well for them, and it had taken its toll. Never married, childless, too much alone, and too often at work, late at night, early in the morning, on Saturdays, on holidays and holy days and days when he should have been somewhere else, with someone else. But he lived for what he did, he wore his responsibilities like his dark suits; they were a part of him, like his hair, almost as dark as Isabella's and his eyes, the colour of the Roman summer sky. His was the face the models fell for. But they meant little to him. They amused him for an evening or two, not more. 'Your new soap doesn't work.' As usual she gave it to him straight, and Amadeo almost winced, waiting for the battle to begin.

Bernardo sat very still. 'Why not?'

'It gave me a headache. It's too heavy.'

'If someone cut my dining room curtain in half, I'd get a headache too.'

'I'm serious.' Her eyes levelled ominously into his.

'So am I. Our tests all show it's perfect. No one else felt it was too heavy.'

'Maybe they had bad colds and couldn't smell it.'

Bernardo rolled his eyes and burrowed back into his chair. 'For God's sake, Isabella, I just told them to go ahead on production. What the hell do you want me to do now?'

'Stop it. It's wrong. Just like the cologne was wrong at first, and the same reasons.' This time Amadeo closed his eyes. She had been right about that one too, but it had been a battle Bernardo had lost with pain. And fury. He and Isabella had barely spoken to each other for a month.

Bernardo's lips tightened, and he dug his hands into the pockets of his vest. 'The soap has to be strong. You use it with water. In the bath. You rinse it off. The scent goes away.' He explained it to her through narrowed lips.

'*Capisco*. I've used soap before. Mine doesn't give me a headache. Yours does. I want it changed.'

'Goddamn it, Isabella!' He slammed a fist on Amadeo's desk and glared at her, but she was unmoved.

She smiled victoriously at him. 'Tell them at the lab to work overtime on it, and you won't be held up in production by more than two or three weeks.'

'Or months. Do you know then what happens to the ads we've already run? They're wasted.'

'They'll be more so if you go ahead with the wrong product. Trust me. I'm right.' She smiled slowly at him then, and Bernardo looked for a moment as though he might explode.

'Do you have any other pleasant surprises for me this morning?'

'No, just have a few additions to the American line. I already talked to Gabriela about them. They don't present a problem.'

'My God, why not? You mean it will be easy? Isabella, no!' But suddenly he was smiling again. He had a vast capacity for fury and forgiveness.

'You'll let me know about the soap?' She homed in on him again.

'I'll let you know.'

'Good. Then that takes care of everything, and I don't even have to run off to lunch for another twenty minutes.' Amadeo grinned at her, and she ensconced herself on the arm of her husband's chair and gently touched his cheek with her hand. And as she did so the anniversary diamond caught the bright sunlight and dashed it in a shower of rainbow reflections against the far wall. She saw Bernardo watch it with a look of sudden displeasure and she looked amused. 'What's the matter, Nardo, one of your girl friends giving you a bad time again?'

'Very amusing. As it so happens, I've been chained to my desk for the last week. I'm beginning to feel like the house eunuch.' Amadeo's brows knit with a sudden frown. He was worried they were working him too hard, but Isabella knew that Bernardo's sudden look of woe stemmed from something else. She knew him too well to believe he minded being overworked any more than she did. And she was right in thinking that he did not. They were all three tremendously overworked, and they loved it. Bernardo was only a trifle more compulsive than his two friends. But he was now looking genuinely disturbed as he glanced from Isabella's large diamond ring to her pearls. 'You're crazy to wear that, Isabella.' And then with a meaningful look at Amadeo: 'I told you that last week.'

'What's all this about?' Isabella looked from one to the other in amused consternation, and then her eyes settled on her husband's kind face. 'He's trying to get you to take back my ring?'

'More or less.' Amadeo looked suddenly very Italian as he shrugged.

But Bernardo was not enjoying their game. 'You know damn well that isn't what I meant or what I said. You know what happened to the Belloggios last week. It could happen to you.'

'A kidnapping?' Isabella looked stunned. 'Don't be ridiculous, Nardo. The Belloggio brothers were the two most important political men in Rome. They knew everyone and they wielded an extraordinary amount of power. The terrorists all hated them as capitalist symbols.'

'They also knew they were worth a bloody fortune. And their wives trotted around this town looking like an ad for Van Cleef. You don't think that had anything to do with it?'

'No.' Isabella looked undisturbed, and then she stared at Bernardo again. 'What's gotten into you? Why should you suddenly start worrying about that? Are you having trouble with your ulcer again? That always makes you peculiar.'

'Stop it, Isabella. Don't be childish. That's the fourth major kidnapping this year, and contrary to what both of you seem to think, not all kidnappings happening in Europe these days are political. Some of them just happen because people are rich and they let the whole damn world know it.'

'Ah, and so you think I walk around advertising what we've got. Is that it? My God, Bernardo, how incredibly vulgar.'

'Yes, isn't it, though?' His eyes suddenly blazed, as he grabbed a newspaper off Amadeo's desk. His eyes were on the pages as he leafed quickly through it and the other two watched him. 'Yes, terribly, terribly vulgar, Isabella. I'm so glad you wouldn't do anything as coarse as that.' And with that he flipped the paper open to a large photograph that showed them both walking into a large palazzo the night before. It had been a party to celebrate the opening of the opera, and Isabella was wearing a strikingly beautiful beige moiré evening dress with a matching coat, lined in a breathtaking blanket of sable, that fell all the way to her feet. And around her neck and on both wrists were ropes of diamonds that glittered in unison with the large rock on her hand. 'I'm glad you're so simple.' And then he looked ominously at Amadeo. 'Both of you.' The chauff-eured Rolls Amadeo only brought out for state occasions was visible just behind them, and the small studs in the shirt under Amadeo's evening jacket glittered much like the small diamonds at Isabella's ears. They both looked at the photograph blankly as Bernardo glared accusingly at them from where he stood.

'We weren't the only ones there, you know.' Isabella said it softly. It touched her that he cared, and the subject wasn't entirely new. He had brought it up before, but now with the Belloggios being kidnapped and murdered there seemed a dogged determination about his concern. 'Darling, you really don't have to worry about us.'

'Why? Do you think you're so sacred? You think no one

22

will touch you? In these times if that's what you think, you're mad! Both of you!' For moment he seemed close to tears. He had known one of the Belloggios and gone to the funeral the week before. The kidnappers had, insanely, demanded fifteen million dollars and the release of half a dozen political prisoners. But the family had been unable to accede to their demands, and the government unwilling to. The results had been tragic. But although Isabella and Amadeo looked sympathetic, they remained unmoved. Bernardo was obviously seeing ghosts.

Isabella stood up slowly and walked to where Bernardo stood. She reached up, hugged him, and smiled. 'We love you. And you worry too much.' Amadeo was frowning, but out of concern for Bernardo, not fear for himself.

'You don't understand, do you?' Bernardo looked at them both in growing despair.

But this time it was Amadeo who answered as Isabella sat down in a chair with a sigh. 'We understand. But I think there's less reason for concern than you think. Look at us' – he waved humbly from Isabella to himself – 'We're no one. We're dress merchants. What can anyone want from us?'

'Money. What about Alessandro? What if they take him?' For an instant Amadeo almost shuddered. Bernardo had scored.

'That would be different. But he's never alone, Bernardo. You know that. The villa is closed. No one could get in. You needn't be so worried. He is safe, and we are safe.'

'You're wrong. No one is safe anymore. And as long as you both run around looking like that' – he waved unhappily at the newspaper picture again – 'you're courting disaster. I saw that this morning and I wanted to kick you both.' Amadeo and Isabella exchanged a quick look, and Bernardo turned away. They didn't understand.

They thought he was crazy. But it was they who were mad. Naive and simple and stupid. Bernardo wanted to shout at them both but he knew there was no point. 'Dress merchants' . . . the biggest couture house in Europe, one of the largest fortunes in Rome, two spectacular-looking people, a vulnerable child, a woman covered with jewels . . . dress merchants. He looked from one to the other again, shook his head, and walked to the door. 'I'll see about the soap, Isabella. But do me a favour, both of you.' He paused for a moment, looking agonised again. 'Think about what I said.'

'We will.' Amadeo said it softly as Bernardo closed the door. And then he looked at his wife. 'He may be right you know. Perhaps we should be more careful about you and Alessandro.'

'And about you?'

'I'm hardly an object of great interest.' He smiled at her. 'And I don't go around in diamonds and furs.'

She smiled at him for a moment and then pouted. 'You can't take back my ring.'

'I don't intend to.' He looked at her tenderly.

'Never?' She was a petulant child as she sat down on his lap and he grinned.

'Never. I promise. It's yours. And I'm yours. Forever.' He kissed her then, and she felt the same rising fervour in her that he had aroused in her since they'd met. Her arms went around his neck, and her mouth came down hard on his.

'I love you, *carissimo* . . . more than anything in this world . . .' They kissed again, and she felt tears sting her eyes when at last she pulled away. That happened sometimes. She was so happy, she wanted to cry. They had so much together, so much history, so many victories, not only the awards and the kudos, but the tender memories, the birth of their son, the days they had spent alone on an island in

Greece five years before when they felt the business was suddenly too much for them; it had been then that Alessandro had been conceived. A thousand moments stood out in her mind and made Amadeo infinitely precious to her once again.

'Isabellezza . . .' He looked down at her with a smile in his deep emerald eyes. 'You have made my life perfect. Have I told you that recently?'

She smiled back. 'You've done the same for me. You know what I'd like to do?'

'What?' Whatever it was, they would do it. There was nothing he would deny her. Others would perhaps say she was spoiled, indulged by her husband. But she wasn't. She equally spoiled him. It was something they did for each other. A reciprocity of generous loving that they both enjoyed.

'I'd love to go to Greece again.' Bernardo's words of warning were already forgotten.

'When?' He smiled again. He wanted to go too. It had been one of the most beautiful times of his life.

'In the spring?' She looked up at him, and he found her unbearably sexy.

'Shall we make another baby?' It was something he'd been thinking about for a while. This seemed a good time. They had only wanted one before Alessandro. But he was such a joy that lately Amadeo had been thinking of broaching the subject with Isabella again.

'In Greece?' Her dark eyes opened very wide, and her mouth seemed rich and full as he bent to kiss her again. After he did, she smiled at him. 'We don't have to wait until Greece, you know. People make babies in Rome all the time.'

'Do they?' He whispered it into her neck. 'You'll have to show me how.'

'*Ecco, tesòro.*' And then suddenly she laughed at him and

25

looked at her watch. 'But not until after lunch. I'm late.'

'How awful. Perhaps you'd best not go at all. We could go home to the villa and – '

'*Doppo* . . .' Later. And then she kissed him once more and walked slowly to the door, turning for an instant with her head cocked to one side as her hand touched the handle. She looked back over her shoulder at him with a question. 'Did you mean it?'

'About your not going to lunch?' He smiled, amused.

But she shook her head and laughed at him. 'No, you lecherous beast. I mean about the baby.' She said the last very gently, as though the idea meant something to her too.

But he was nodding his head as he looked at her. 'Yes, I did. What do you think, Bellezza?'

But she smiled at him mysteriously from the door. 'I think we should keep it in mind.' And then with a kiss she was gone as he stood watching the door. He wanted to tell her just once more that he loved her. But it would have to wait until tonight. He was surprised too at what he had just said about wanting another baby. He had thought about it but not yet put it into words. Now suddenly he knew that he meant it. And it didn't have to interfere with her career. Alessandro didn't, and they both had a great deal to give the child. In fact the more he thought about it, the more he liked the idea. He went back to his desk and picked up a sheaf of papers with a smile.

It was almost one o'clock when Amadeo finally stood up and stretched. He was pleased with the figures he had been pursuing. The American deals they had made that autumn were going to bring in a tidy price. Very salutary indeed. He was about to take himself for a solitary lunch of congratulation when he heard a soft knock on the door.

'*Si?*' He looked surprised. His secretary usually buzzed him, but she was probably already out to lunch. He turned toward the door and saw one of the under secretaries peeking timidly around the door.

'*Scusi, signore, mi dispiace* . . . I'm sorry but . . . ' She smiled at him. He was so unbearably handsome that she never quite knew what to say. She hardly ever got to talk to him anyway.

'Yes?' He smiled back. 'Is there something I can do?'

'There are two men here to see you, sir.' Her voice trailed off as she blushed.

'Now?' He dropped his eyes to the appointment book, open on his desk. There was nothing penned in until three. 'Who?'

'They . . . it's about your car. The -- the Ferrari.'

'My car?' He looked surprised and confused. 'What about it?'

'They – they said there was . . . an accident.' She waited for an explosion but none came. He looked disturbed but not angry.

'Was anyone hurt?'

'I don't think so. But they're here . . . just outside . . . in Miss Alzini's office, sir.' He nodded gently and walked past her through the outer office to find two men looking awkward and embarrassed. They were wearing neat but simple clothes, their hands were large and brown, their faces red; he was not yet sure if it was from mortification or the sun. And it was very clear that they were in no way used to such surroundings. The shorter of the two seemed afraid to even stand upon the carpet, and the taller clearly wished that he might disappear instantly through the floor. A butcher perhaps, maybe a baker, working men, labourers perhaps. And when they spoke, their voices were coarse but awed and respectful. They were aghast at what had happened. They were beside themselves to learn that the car was his.

'What happened?' He continued to look confused but

27

his voice was gentle and his eyes were kind, and if he felt any dismay about his car, he betrayed it not at all.

'We were driving; it was very crowded, your honour. You know, lunch.' Amadeo nodded patiently as he listened to the tale. 'A woman and a little girl were running across the street; we swerved so as not to hit them, and . . .' The shorter man grew redder still. '. . . we hit your car instead. Not too bad, but it hurt the car a little. We can fix it. My brother has a shop, he does good work. You'll be pleased. And we pay. Everything. We pay everything.'

'Of course not. We'll work it out between our insurance companies. Is there a great deal of damage?' He tried not to show the unhappiness he felt.

'*Ma* . . . We are so sorry. Not for all the world would we have hit your honour's car. A Fiat, a foreign car, anything, but not so fine a car as yours.' The taller man wrung his hands, and at last Amadeo even smiled. They were so absurd, standing there in his secretary's office, probably more demolished than his car. He found himself having to suppress a burst of nervous laughter and was suddenly glad that Isabella was not around to look mischievously at him with her mock-serious gaze.

'Never mind. Come, we'll go and look.' He led them to the tiny private elevator, inserted his key, and stood with them as they descended toward the first floor, the two men with heads bowed in humiliation and Amadeo attempting to engage them in some ordinary banter.

Even Ciano had gone to lunch when Amadeo stepped outside and looked up the street toward the car. He could see their car still double-parked beside it. It was a large, awkward, antiquated-looking car and might in fact have been heavy enough to inflict some serious damage. With a look of masked concern he strode up the street, the two men walking nervously behind him, clearly terrified by what he'd see. As he reached his car, walking along the

28

sidewalk, he noticed that a third companion was still waiting in the ancient Fiat, looking unhappy as he saw Amadeo approach. He inclined his head in brief salutation, and Amadeo stepped around his car into the street to inspect its injured left side. Slowly his eyes swept along the side as he stooped over slightly, the better to see the damage they had done. But as he hovered there, bending over, his eyes suddenly narrowed in confusion; there was no damage, no dent, no injury to the beloved car. But it was too late to ask them further questions. As his eyes widened in surprise an object of immeasurable weight swept down brutally on the back of his neck, and sagging instantly, he was pushed and then pulled unceremoniously into the back of the waiting car. The entire matter took less than an instant and was neatly handled by Amadeo's two innocent-looking morning callers. The men slid calmly into the Fiat beside their friend, and it pulled sedately away from the curb. Within two blocks of the House of San Gregorio, Amadeo was neatly bound and trussed, a gag and blindfold secured, and his motionless form lay silently, barely breathing on the floor of the car as his kidnappers drove him away.

Chapter Two

The sun had just set with a bright flow of orange and mauve as Isabella stood resplendent in green satin in her living room. Delicate brass and crystal wall sconces cast a soft light around the room. She glanced at the deep blue Fabergé clock on the mantelpiece. She and Amadeo had bought it years before in New York. It was a collector's item, a priceless piece, almost as priceless as the emerald-and-diamond necklace carefully clasped around her neck. It had been her grandmother's and was said to have once belonged to Josephine Bonaparte. It held her long white neck in its delicate grasp as she spun slowly on one heel and began pacing the room. It was five minutes to eight, and they were going to be very late for the Principessa di Sant'Angelo's dinner. Damn Amadeo. Why tonight, of all nights, couldn't he be on time? The princess was one of the few people who actually unnerved Isabella. She was eighty-three years old with a heart of Carrara marble and eyes of steel, a long-ago crony of Amadeo's grandmother, and a woman Isabella frankly abhorred. She gave regular command performances, cocktails at eight, dinner precisely at nine. And they still had to drive halfway across Rome and then out into the countryside to the Palazzo Sant'Angelo, where the principessa held court in ancient yet startlingly beautiful ball gowns, brandishing her gold-handled ebony cane.

On edge, Isabella caught a glimpse of herself in a mirror over a delicately ornate French table and wondered if she should have done something different with her hair. She studied her reflection with dismay. Too simple, too severe.

She had swept her hair high on her head in a perfectly plain knot so as not to detract from the necklace and the matching earrings Amadeo had had made. The emeralds were exquisite, and her dress was precisely the same shade of green. It was from her own collection of that year, a perfect shaft of green satin which seemed to fall straight from her shoulders to the floor. Over it she would wear the white satin coat she had designed for it, with the narrow, tightly fitting collar and broad cuffs lined in an extraordinary fuchsia silk. But perhaps it was too striking, or maybe her hair looked too plain, or . . . dammit where the hell was Amadeo? And why was he late? She glanced at the clock again and began to purse her lips as she heard a breathless, soft whisper from the door. Surprised, she turned and found herself staring into the wide brown eyes of Alessandro, in sleepers, hiding behind the living room door.

'Sh . . . Mamma . . . *vieni qui* . . .' Come here.

'*Ma cosa fai?*' What are you doing? She was instantly drawn into the conspiratorial whisper, a broad grin spreading across her face.

'I escaped her!' The eyes were afire with the same flame as hers.

'Who?'

'Mamma Teresa!' Maria Teresa, of course. The nurse.

'Why aren't you sleeping?' She was already beside her son, kneeling carefully on her high heels. 'It's very late.'

'I know!' A giggle of pure five-year-old glee. 'But I wanted to see you. Look what I got from Luisa!' He held out a handful of cookies lovingly bestowed by the cook, the crumbs already squeezing through the chubby fingers, the chocolate chips nothing more than a brown blur in his hand. 'Want one?' He shoved one rapidly into his mouth before proffering the hand.

'You should be in bed!' She was still whispering, restraining her laughter.

'Okay, okay.' Alessandro gobbled another cookie before his mother had a chance to decline. 'Will you take me?' He looked at her with eyes that melted her soul, and she nodded happily. This was why she no longer worked eleven hours a day at the office, no matter how much she sometimes regretted not spending every waking moment at Amadeo's side. This was worth it. For that look, that shining mischievous smile.

'Where's Papa?'

'On his way home, I hope. Come on.' Alessandro slipped his clean hand carefully into hers, and they made their way down a long dimly lit parqueted hall. Here and there were portraits of Amadeo's ancestors and a few paintings they had bought together in France. The house looked more like a palazzo than a villa, and occasionally when they held very grand parties, couples waltzed slowly down the long mirrored hall to the strains of an orchestra.

'What'll we do if Mamma Teresa finds us here?' Alessandro looked up at his mother again with those melting brown eyes.

'I'm not sure. Do you think it would help if we cry?' He nodded sagely, then giggled, hiding his mouth with his still crumb-covered hand.

'You're smart.'

'So are you. How did you get out of your room?'

'Through the door to the garden. Luisa said she'd make cookies tonight.'

Alessandro's room was done in bright blues and filled with books and games and toys. Unlike the rest of the house it was neither elegant nor grand, it was simply his. Isabella let out a long elaborate sigh as she marched him towards the bed and grinned at the boy again. 'We made it.'

32

But it was more than Alessandro could stand. He collapsed on his bed with a small whoop of glee, pulling the rest of the cookies out of a pocket – he had only carried the excess in his hand. He set about gobbling them as Isabella urged him under the covers.

'And don't make a big mess.' But it was a useless caution, and she didn't really care. That's what little boys were about – cookie crumbs and broken wheels, headless soldiers and smudges on walls. She liked it that way. The rest of her life was silken enough. She liked the nubs and crumbs and textures of her times with her son. 'Will you promise to go to sleep as soon as you finish?'

'I promise!' He looked at her solemnly with admiring eyes. '*Tu sei bella.*'

'Thank you. So are you. *Buona notte, tesòro.* Sleep tight.' She kissed him on the cheek and then on his neck. He giggled.

'I love you, Mamma.'

'I love you too.'

As she stepped back into the hall she felt tears fill her eyes and felt foolish. To hell with the Principessa di Sant'Angelo. She was suddenly glad Amadeo had been late. *But good Lord, what time must it be now?* Her heels clicked rapidly as she hurried back to the living room for another look at the clock. It was eight twenty-five. How was that possible? What was going on? But she knew all too well what was probably going on. A last-minute problem, an urgent call from Paris or Hong Kong or the States. A fabric that couldn't be delivered, a textile mill on strike. She knew all too well how easily one could be delayed. Crises like that had kept her from Alessandro every night for far, far too long. Now she decided that it was probably wise to give Amadeo a call, meet him at the office, with his dinner jacket over her arm.

She walked back to her tiny pink silk boudoir and picked

33

up the phone. The number was part of her fingers, part of her soul as well as her mind. A last exhausted secretary picked up the phone. '*Pronto*. San Gregorio.'

'*Buona sera*.' She identified herself quickly and unnecessarily and asked the woman to find Amadeo and put him on the line. There was a pause, a rapid apology for the delay, and then a pause again as Isabella tapped her foot and began to frown. Maybe something was wrong. Maybe he'd driven that damned too-fast car of his into a tree. She suddenly felt too warm in the heavy green satin, felt her heart seem to stop as Bernardo took the phone.

'*Ciao. Cosa c'e?*' What's up?

'Where the hell is Amadeo, dammit? He's almost two hours late. He promised he'd come home early tonight. We're dining at the gargoyle's house.'

'Sant'Angelo?' Bernardo knew her well.

'Who else? Anyway where is he?'

'I don't know. I thought he was with you.' The words escaped him too quickly as his brow furrowed into a frown.

'What? Isn't he there?' For the first time Isabella was frightened. Maybe something really had happened to him with the car.

But Bernardo was quick to answer, and there was nothing unusual in his even tone. 'He's probably here somewhere. I've been slaving over that damn soap you don't like. I haven't been in his office since noon.'

'Well, go find him and tell him to call home. I want to know if I should meet him at the office or if he still wants to come here to dress. The old bitch will probably kill us. Now we'll never make it to dinner on time.'

'I'll go check.'

'Thanks. And, Bernardo? You don't think something's wrong?'

'Of course not. I'll find him for you in a minute.'

34

Without saying more, he hung up. Isabella stared uneasily down at the phone.

Her words rang in Bernardo's ears . . . *something wrong*. *Something wrong*. That was precisely what he did think. He'd been trying to find Amadeo himself all afternoon to discuss a new possibility with that bloody soap. They would need more money for testing, quite a lot of it, and he had wanted Amadeo's okay. But Amadeo had been out. All day. Since lunchtime. Bernardo had consoled himself with the thought that Isabella and Amadeo had probably disappeared for an afternoon rendezvous. They did it often, as only he knew. But if Amadeo wasn't with her, then where was he? By himself? With someone else? With another woman? Bernardo cast aside that thought. Amadeo didn't cheat on Isabella. He never had. But where was he then? And where had he been since noon?

Bernardo began to comb the offices, prowling all four floors. All he could discover was a young, trembling secretary, still pounding away at the typewriter on her desk, who explained that two men had come to see Amadeo to explain that they had accidentally smashed up his car. Signore San Gregorio had left then, she explained. Bernardo felt himself turn grey as he hurried out to the street and slipped nervously into his car. As he shoved the Fiat into gear and pulled away he saw the Ferrari where he had seen it since that morning, in its parking space at the curb. He slowed for a moment as he drove past it. There was no damage. It hadn't been touched. His heart began to race. He drove much too quickly toward Isabella and Amadeo's home.

True to his word, Bernardo had obviously found him. Isabella grinned to herself as she hurried across the living

35

room to return to her boudoir to answer the phone. Idiot, he had probably forgotten the principessa and her dinner, as well as the time. She'd give him hell. But without much conviction. She was roughly as capable of giving Amadeo hell as she was of forbidding Alessandro his chocolate cookies. The vision of his chubby, crumb-covered smile came to mind again as she picked up the phone.

'Well, well, darling. A little bit late coming home tonight, aren't you? And what the hell are we going to do about the principessa?' She was already smiling, spoke before waiting for his first word. She knew it would be Amadeo.

But it wasn't. It was a strange man.

'*Pronto, signora.* I don't know what you are going to do about the principessa. The question is what are we going to do about your husband?'

'What?' Christ. A crank call. Just what she needed. And briefly she felt like an ass. A secret admirer perhaps? Despite their unlisted phone number, now and then some stranger called. 'I'm sorry. I think you have the wrong number.' She was about to hang up when she heard the voice again. This time it sounded more harsh.

'Wait! Signora di San Gregorio, I believe your husband is missing. Isn't that right?'

'Of course not.' Her heart was racing. Who was this man?

'He's late. Is that right?'

'Who is this?'

'Never mind that. We have your husband. Here . . .' There was a sharp grunt, as though someone had been pushed or struck, and then Amadeo was on the line.

'Darling, don't panic.' But his voice sounded tired, weak.

'What is this? Some kind of joke?'

'It's not a joke. Not at all.'

36

'Where are you?' She could barely speak as panic gripped her. Bernardo had been right.

'I don't know. It doesn't matter. Just keep your head. And know . . .' There was an endlessly painful pause. Isabella's whole body began to shake violently as she clutched the phone. '. . . know that I love you.'

They must have pulled the phone away from him then; the strange man's voice returned. 'Satisfied? We have him. Now do you want him back?'

'Who are you? Are you mad?'

'No. Only greedy.' There was a cacophony of laughter as Isabella desperately tried to steady her grip on the phone. 'We want ten million dollars. If you want him back.'

'You're crazy. We don't have that kind of money. Nobody does.'

'Some people do. You do. Your business does. Get it. You have the whole weekend to figure it out while we baby-sit for your husband.'

'I can't . . . for God's sake . . . listen . . . please . . .' But he had already hung up, and Isabella stood wracked by sobs in her boudoir. Amadeo! They had Amadeo! Oh, God, they were mad!

She didn't even hear the doorbell ring, or the maid run to answer it, or Bernardo's rapid footsteps as he ran toward her sobs.

'What is it?' He looked at her in horror from the doorway as she stood convulsed by what she had just heard. 'Isabella, tell me, what?' Was he hurt? Was he dead?

For a moment she couldn't speak and then, uncomprehending, she stared at him as tears poured down her face. Her voice was a pathetic croak when she spoke to Bernardo at last. 'He's been kidnapped.'

'Oh, my God.'

Chapter Three

An hour later Isabella was still sitting in her boudoir, ashen and shaking, clutching Bernardo's hand when they got the second call.

'By the way, we forgot to tell you, signora. Don't call the cops. If you do, we'll know. And we'll kill him. And if you don't come up with the money, we'll kill him too.'

'But you can't. There's no way – '

'Never mind that. Just stay away from the cops. They'll freeze your money as soon as the banks open, and then neither he nor you will be worth a damn.' They had hung up again, but this time Bernardo had listened too.

She was crying again after the call.

'Isabella, we should have called the police an hour ago.'

'I told you not to, dammit. The man is right. The police will watch us all weekend and then on Monday they'll freeze everything we've got so we can't pay the ransom.'

'You can't anyway. It would take a year to free up that kind of money. And the only one who could do it anyway is Amadeo. You know that.'

'I don't give a damn. We'll get it. We have to.'

'We can't. We have to call the police. There's no other way. If they do want that kind of money, you don't have it to give them, Isabella. You can't risk making them angry. You have to find them first.' Bernardo looked almost as pale as Isabella as he ran a desperate hand through his hair.

'But what if they find out? The man said – '

'They won't. We have to trust someone. For God's sake, we can't trust them.'

'But maybe they'll give us time to raise the money. People will help us. We could make some calls to the States.'

'Screw the States. We can't do that. You can't give them time. What about Amadeo while you try to come up with the money? What are they doing to him?'

'Oh, God, Bernardo! I can't think . . .' Her voice disappeared into a pale, childlike whine as Bernardo took her into his own trembling arms.

'Please, let me call.' It was only a whisper. And her answer was only a nod. But the police were there in fifteen minutes. At the back door, wearing old clothes, looking like friends of the servants, with old frayed peasants' hats in their hands. At least they had made the effort to conceal who they were, Isabella thought, as Bernardo ushered them inside. Maybe Bernardo was right after all.

'Signora di San Gregorio?' The policeman recognised her immediately. Isabella was looking frozen and regal as she sat glued to her chair still in the emeralds and the green satin gown.

'Yes.' It was barely audible. Tears once again drowned her dark eyes, and Bernardo took a tight grip on her hand.

'We are sorry. We know you are in much pain. But we must know everything. How, when, who last saw him, have there been earlier threats, is there anyone in your business or your household whom you have reason to suspect? No one must be spared. No kindness, no courtesy, no loyalty to old friends. Your husband's life is at stake You must help us.' They looked suspiciously at Bernardo, who met their gaze evenly. It was Isabella who explained that Bernardo had insisted on calling the police.

'But they said . . . they said that if we called . . . that . . .' She couldn't go on.

'We know.'

They made endless inquiries of Bernardo and sat

39

patiently with Isabella during two hours of unbearably painful interrogation. By midnight it was over. They knew all that there was to be told. Bitter firings in the business, intrigues and rivalries, forgotten enemies and grudge-bearing friends.

'And they've said nothing about when they want the money or where or how?' Isabella shook her head miserably. 'It is my suspicion that they are amateurs. Lucky ones perhaps, but nonetheless, they are not professionals. Their second call, to remind you not to call the police, shows that. Professionals would have told you that immediately,' the sombre senior officer said.

'I knew it myself. That was why I didn't let Signore Franco call you.'

'You were wise to change your mind.' The officer in charge spoke again, soothingly and with great compassion. He was the kidnap specialist on the Roman force. And regrettably, he had had a great deal too much experience in recent years.

'Will it help us if they're amateurs?' Isabella gazed at him hopefully, praying that he would quickly say yes.

'Perhaps. These matters are very delicate. And we will handle it accordingly. Trust us, signora. I promise you.' And then he remembered something he himself had forgotten. 'You were going somewhere this evening?' He glanced again at the jewels and the dress.

She nodded dumbly. 'We were going to a – a dinner . . . a party . . . Oh, what does it matter now?'

'Everything matters. Whose party?'

For a moment Isabella almost smiled. 'The Principessa di Sant'Angelo. Will you make inquiries of her too?' Oh, God, the poor gargoyle.

'Only if it becomes necessary.' The inspector knew that name. The most formidable dowager in Rome. 'But for the moment it will be wisest if you tell no one yourself. Do not go out, do not tell friends. Tell people that you are ill. But answer the phone yourself. The kidnappers may not be willing to speak to anyone else. We want to know the rest of their demands as quickly as possible. You have a little boy?' She nodded mutely. 'He stays at home too. And the entire house will be ringed by guards. Discreetly, but definitely.'

'Do I keep the servants at home too?'

'No.' He gave a firm shake of the head. 'Tell them nothing. And perhaps one of them will give himself away. Let them out as usual. We will follow all of them.'

'You think it may be one of them?' Isabella looked ashen but hopeful. She didn't care who it was, just so they found Amadeo in time, before those lunatics did something to him, before they . . . she couldn't think of the words. She didn't want to. It couldn't happen. Not to Amadeo. Not to them. Tears began to fill her eyes again, and the inspector turned away.

'We will just have to see. And for you, I regret, it will be a very difficult time.'

'What about money?' But as soon as she had said it, she regretted the words. The inspector's face went suddenly hard. 'What about it?'

'Do we . . . shall we – '

'All of your accounts and those of your business will be frozen on Monday morning. We will notify your bank just before they open.'

'Oh, my God.' For a moment she looked at Bernardo in terror, and then in fury at him and the cop. 'How do you expect us to run our business?'

'On credit. For a while.' His face looked frozen as well. 'I'm sure that the House of San Gregorio will not have trouble doing that.'

'Then what you are sure of, Inspector, and what I am sure of are two different things.' She stood up quickly, her

41

eyes ablaze with their own angry light. She didn't give a damn about money for the business. She wanted to know that she could get her hands on it if she had to, for Amadeo, if the cops' ideas turned out not to work. Damn them, damn Bernardo, damn . . .

'We'll let you get some sleep.' For the first time in her life, she wanted to shout out loud at him 'Fuck you' but she didn't. She only clenched her teeth and her hands, and in a moment they were gone and she was alone with Bernardo in the room.

'You see, damn you! You see! I told you they'd do that. Now what the hell are we going to do?'

'Wait. Let them do their job. Pray.'

'Don't you understand? They have Amadeo. If we don't come up with ten million dollars, they'll kill him! Haven't you gotten that into your head?' For a fraction of an instant she thought she was going to slap him, but the look on his face said that she already had.

She raged, she stormed, she cried. And he slept in the guest room that night. But there was nothing either of them could do. Not on a weekend, and not with the accounts frozen, and probably not without.

She never went to bed that night. She sat, she waited, she cried, she dreamed. She wanted to break everything in the villa, wanted to wrap it all up and offer it as gifts . . . anything . . . anything . . . just send him home . . . please . . .

They had to wait another twenty-four hours for the next call. And it was more of the same. Ten million dollars by Tuesday, and it was now Saturday night. She tried to reason with them, that it was the weekend, that it was impossible to get money together when the banks and offices and even their business was closed. They didn't give a damn. Tuesday. They figured that gave her plenty of time. They would tell her the location later.

42

And this time they didn't let Amadeo come to the phone.

'How do I know he's still alive?'

'You don't. But he is. And he will be until you screw up. As long as you don't call the cops and you come up with the money, he'll be fine. We'll call you. Ciao, signora.' Oh, Jesus . . . what now?

She looked like a ghost by Sunday morning, her eyes darkly ringed, her face deathly pale. Bernardo came and went, attempting to keep up a semblance of normalcy, and making references to hearing from Amadeo on his trip. It was easy to believe the story that she was sick. She looked it. But none of the servants gave anything away. No one seemed to know the truth. And the police had found out nothing. By Sunday night Isabella felt sure she would go mad.

'I can't, Bernardo, I can't anymore. They're not doing anything. There has to be another way.'

'How? Apparently even my personal account will be frozen. I'm going to have to borrow a hundred dollars from my mother tomorrow. The police tell me I can't even cash a cheque at my bank.'

'They're going to freeze you too?' He nodded silently. 'Damn.'

But there was one thing they wouldn't have frozen by Monday. One thing they couldn't touch. She lay awake in her bedroom all Sunday night, counting, figuring, guessing, and in the morning she went to the safe. Not ten million but maybe one. Or even two. She took the long green velvet boxes in which she kept her jewellery to her room, locked the door, and spread everything out on her bed. The emeralds, the new ten-carat ring from Amadeo, a ruby necklace she detested for its garishness, her pearls, the sapphire engagement ring Amadeo had given her ten and a half years before, her mother's diamond bracelet, her grandmother's pearls. She made a careful inventory and quietly folded the list. Then she emptied the contents of all the boxes into one large Gucci scarf and stuffed the heavy bundle into a big old brown leather bag. It would almost pull her shoulder off when she wore it, but she didn't give a damn. To hell with the police and their eternal watching and checking and waiting to see. The one man she knew she could trust was Alfredo Paccioli. Her family and Amadeo's had done business with him for years. He bought and sold jewellery for princes and kings, statesmen and widows, and all the great and near-great of Rome. He had always been her friend.

Isabella dressed silently, pulling on brown slacks and an old cashmere sweater; she reached for her mink jacket but cast it aside. She put on an old suede one, and on her head she wore a scarf. She barely looked like Isabella di San Gregorio. She sat quietly for a moment, thinking, wondering how to get there in spite of the guards. And then she realised that it didn't matter. She didn't have to hide from them. All she had to get was the money. And it was important that no one recognise her once she was inside. She buzzed Enzo in his apartment over the garage and told him that she wanted him at the back door in ten minutes. She wanted to take a little ride.

He was waiting with the car in ten minutes as she had requested, and stealthily she crept from the house. She didn't want Alessandro to see her, didn't want to answer the questions in his eyes. She had told him for the past four days that she was sick and didn't want to give him her germs so he had to keep busy and play with Mamma Teresa, his nurse, in his room or outside. Papa was on a trip; the school had called, and everyone was having a vacation. Thank God, he was only five. But she succeeded in avoiding him once again on her way out and was suddenly grateful for Maria Teresa's busy routine for the child. She couldn't have dealt with him just then, couldn't have faced him without holding him too tight and bursting out in a fierce, frightened cry.

'*Va meglio, signora?*' Enzo gazed at her thoughtfully in the rearview mirror as they pulled away, and she only nodded tersely as her unmarked police escort discreetly pulled away from the kerb.

'*Si.*' She gave him the address of the shop next to Paccioli's, not very far from her own house of couture, and decided that she didn't give a damn if Enzo knew why she was going there. If he was one of the conspirators, then let him know that she was doing her best. The bastards. There was no one left she could trust. Not now. And not ever again. And Bernardo, damn him, how could he have been so right? She fought back tears again as they drove to the address. The ride took less than fifteen minutes, and she made a quick business of stopping briefly in two boutiques and then disappearing quickly inside Paccioli's. Like the House of San Gregorio, it was a discreet facade, in this case marked only by the address. She stepped into the silent beige womb and spoke to a young woman at a large Louis XV desk.

'I want to see Signore Paccioli.' Even in a scarf and no makeup, it was difficult to divest herself of her tone of command. But the young woman was unimpressed.

'I'm terribly sorry, but Mister Paccioli is in a meeting. Clients are here from New York.' She looked up as though expecting Isabella to understand. But she had missed her mark. And the anonymous brown leather bag on Isabella's shoulder was cutting into her skin.

'I don't care. Tell him it's . . . Isabella.'

The woman hesitated, but this time only for a moment. 'Very well.' There was something desperate about the woman, something frighteningly crazy about her eyes as she kept shifting her handbag higher up on her shoulder. For an insane moment the young woman prayed that this

45

oddly dishevelled stranger was not carrying a gun. But in that case there was all the more reason to summon Mr. Paccioli from inside. She walked down a long narrow hall, leaving Isabella alone with two blue-uniformed guards. And she returned in less than a minute, with Alfredo Paccioli walking hurriedly at her side. He was somewhere in his early sixties, almost bald, with a delicate white fringe that matched his moustache and somehow accented his laughing blue eyes.

'Isabella, *cara, come stai*? Shopping for something to show with the collections?'

But she only shook her head. 'May I speak to you for a moment?'

'Of course.' He looked at her more closely then and didn't like what he saw. Something was terribly wrong with her. As though she were very ill, or perhaps a little bit mad. What she did a moment later almost confirmed it as she silently yanked open the brown bag and pulled the silk-wrapped bundle out, spilling its contents on his desk.

'I want to sell it. All of it.' Then had she gone mad? Or was it a fight with Amadeo? Had he been unfaithful? What in God's name was wrong?

'Isabella . . . dearest . . . you can't mean it. But that – that piece has been in your family for years.' He gazed in horror at the emeralds, the diamonds, the rubies, the ring he had sold to Amadeo only months before.

'I have to. Don't ask me why. Please. Alfredo, I need you. Just do it.'

'Are you serious?' Had their business gone suddenly bad?

'Absolutely.' And he could see now that she was neither ill nor insane, but something was very seriously, desperately wrong.

'It may take a little time.' He lovingly fingered the exquisite pieces, thinking of finding each one a home. But it

46

was not a task that he relished. It was like selling family or auctioning off a child. 'Is there truly no other way?'

'None. And I don't have any time. Give me whatever you can for them now. Yourself. And don't discuss this with anyone. No one. It's a matter of . . . it's . . . oh, God, Alfredo, please. You must help me.' Her eyes filled suddenly with tears, and he reached out a hand as his eyes questioned hers.

'I'm almost afraid to ask.' Twice before something like this had happened. Once, a year before. And the second time only a week before. It had been horrible . . . terrible . . . and it hadn't worked.

'Don't ask. I can't answer you. Just help me. Please.'

'All right. All right. How much do you need?' *Ten million dollars. Oh, God.*

'You can't give me what I need. Just give me what you can. In cash.'

He looked startled and then nodded. 'I can give you' – he made a rapid calculation of the cash he had available at the time – 'perhaps two hundred thousand today. And perhaps the same again in a week.'

'Can't you give it all to me today?' She looked desperate again, and for a moment he wondered if she might faint on his desk.

'I can't, Isabella. We just made an enormous purchase in the Far East. All of our main assets are in stones right now. And quite obviously that's not what you want.' He glanced down at the small mountain of diamonds and then back into her eyes with a thought. Suddenly he felt as frightened as she. Her desperation was contagious. 'Can you wait a minute while I make some calls?'

'To whom?' Her eyes were instantly filled with terror, and he saw her hands shake again.

'Trust me. To some colleagues, some friends. Perhaps among us we can come up with some more money. And . . .

47

Isabella . . .' He hesitated, but he thought he had understood. 'It *must* be . . . cash?'

'Yes.'

Then he was right. Now his own hands shook. 'I'll do what I can.' He sat down next to her, picked up the phone, and called five or six friends. Jewellers, furriers, one somewhat shady banker, a professional gambler who had been a customer and become a friend. Among all of them he could come up with another three hundred thousand dollars in cash. He told her and she nodded. That gave her five hundred thousand. Half a million dollars. It was one twentieth of what they wanted. Five percent. His eyes sought hers with a look of sorrow. 'Won't that help?' He found himself praying that it would.

'It will have to. How do I get it?'

'I'll send a courier out immediately. I'll take what I think we need in jewels for the other jewellers.' She watched dispassionately as he took a few pieces. When he took the diamond, she bit her lip to hold back the tears. Nothing mattered – only Amadeo.

'This should do it. I should have the money here in an hour. Can you wait?'

She nodded tersely. 'Send your messenger out the back door.'

'I'm being watched?'

'No. I am. But my car is out front, and they may be watching who leaves here.' He asked no further questions. There was no need.

'Do you want some coffee while you wait?' She only shook her head, and he left her after gently patting her arm. He felt so helpless and he was. She sat in solitary silence for a little over an hour, waiting, thinking, trying not to let her mind drift back to the agonizingly tender moments they had shared. Thinking back to first times and last times, and funny times, to seeing him with tiny

Alessandro in his arms for the first time: to their first collection, which they presented with outrageous courage and delight; to their honeymoon; their first vacation; their first house; and the first time they had made love, and the last time only four days before . . . They tore at her heart in a way she couldn't bear. The moments and voices and faces crowded into her head as she attempted to push them away, as she felt panic rising in her soul. It was an endless hour until at last Alfredo Paccioli returned. The exact amount was in a long brown envelope. Five hundred thousand dollars in cash.

'Thank you, Alfredo. I will be grateful to you all my life.' And Amadeo's. It wasn't ten million. But it was a start. If the police were right, and the kidnappers were indeed amateurs, perhaps even half a million would look good to them. It would have to. It was all she had now that all the accounts were frozen.

'Isabella . . . is there – is there anything I can do?'

Silently she shook her head, opened the door, and strode out, hurrying past the young woman at the desk, who was pleasantly bidding her good day, and then as she heard her, Isabella stopped.

'What did you say?'

'I said, good morning, Mrs. di San Gregorio. I heard Mister Paccioli mention collections and I realised that you were . . . I'm sorry . . . I didn't recognise you at first . . . I '

'You didn't.' Isabella turned on her fiercely. 'You didn't recognise me, because I was never here. Is that clear?'

'Yes . . . yes . . . I'm sorry . . .' Good God, the woman was truly mad. But there was something else about her too. Something . . . the bag . . . it didn't look so heavy now. She swung it over her shoulder as though it were suddenly light. What had she had in there that had been so important and so heavy?

'Did you understand me?' Isabella was still staring at

49

the receptionist, the exhaustion of three sleepless nights making her indeed look crazy. 'Because if you didn't, if you tell anyone, anyone that I was here, you will be out of a job. Permanently. I'll see to it.'

'I understand.' So she was selling her jewellery then. The bitch. The young woman nodded politely as Isabella hurried out the door.

Isabella had Enzo drive her straight home. She sat waiting for hours by the phone. She never moved. She just sat there in her bedroom, behind a locked door. An inquiry about lunch from Louis brought only a terse no. The vigil wore on. They had to call. It was Monday. They wanted the money by the next day. They would have to tell her where to leave it and precisely when.

But by seven that evening they still hadn't called. She had heard Alessandro clattering through the halls and the voice of Mamma Teresa admonishing him to remember that his Mother had the flu. And then all was silent again, until at last there came a fierce banging on the door.

'Let me in.' It was Bernardo.

'Leave me alone.' She didn't want him in the room if they should call. She wouldn't even tell him about the jewellery. He'd probably tell the police. And she'd had enough of that nonsense. She was taking care of it now. She could promise them a million dollars – half tomorrow, the other half by next week.

'Isabella, I have to talk to you. Please.'

'I'm busy.'

'I don't care. Please. I must . . . there's something I – I have to show you.' For a moment she heard his voice crack.

And then she told him, 'Slip it under the door.'

It was the evening paper. Page five. *Isabella di San Gregorio was seen at Paccioli's today* . . . It described what she had worn, how she had looked – and almost every item she had just sold. But how? Who? Alfredo? And then she knew. The girl. The eager little bitch at the desk. Isabella's heart dropped as she unlocked the door.

Bernardo was standing there, crying silently, staring at the floor.

'Why did you do that?'

'I had to.' But suddenly her voice was flat. If it was in the papers, then the kidnappers would know too. And they would know more: that if she was selling her jewellery, her accounts were probably frozen. They would know that she had told the police. 'Oh, no.'

They said nothing more to each other. Bernardo simply walked into the room and silently took his place by the phone.

The call came at nine. It was the same voice, the same man.

'*Capito, signora.* You squealed.'

'I didn't. Really.' But her voice had the frantic ring of untruth. 'But I had to get more money. We couldn't get enough.'

'You'll never get enough. Even if you didn't tell the cops, they'll know now. They'll come snooping around. Someone will tell them if you don't.'

'But no one else knows.'

'Bullshit. How dumb do you think we are? Listen, you want to say good-bye to your old man?'

'No, please . . . wait . . . I have money for you. A million . . .' But he wasn't listening, and Amadeo was already on the phone.

'Isabella . . . darling . . . everything's all right.'

Everything's all right? Was he crazy? But she didn't care if he was. He had never sounded so good to her, and her heart had never turned over, then soared as it did now. He was still there, somewhere; they hadn't hurt him. Maybe everything *would* be all right. As long as Amadeo was still there, somewhere, anywhere, it was all right.

'You've been a very brave girl, darling. How's Alessandro? Does he know?'

'Of course not. And he's fine.'

'Good. Kiss him for me.' She thought she heard his voice tremble then and she shut her eyes tightly. She couldn't cry. Not now. She had to be as brave as he thought she was. Had to be. For him. 'I want you . . . always . . . to know how much I love you,' he was saying. 'How perfect you are. What a good wife. You've never given me a single unhappy day, darling. Not one.' She was openly crying now and fighting back the sobs that clutched at her throat.

'Amadeo, darling, I love you. So much. Please . . . come home.'

'I will, darling. I will. I promise you. And I'm right there with you now. Just be brave for a little while longer.'

'You too, my beloved. You too.' With that the connection was silently severed.

The police found him in the morning near a warehouse in a suburb of Rome, strangled and still very beautiful, and very dead.

Chapter Four

Police cars surrounded the limousine as Enzo guided it slowly into the heart of Rome. She had chosen a church near the House of San Gregorio, not far from the Piazza di Spagna. Santo Stefano. They had gone there when they were first courting and wanted to stop somewhere to rest for a moment after their long walks during lunch. It was ancient and simple and pretty and seemed more appropriate to her than the more elaborate cathedrals of Rome.

Bernardo sat beside her in the car as she stared unseeingly forward, looking only at the back of Enzo's head. Was it he? Was it someone else? Who were the betrayers? It didn't matter now. Amadeo was gone. Taking with him the warmth and the laughter, the love and the dreams. Gone. Forever. She was still in shock.

It had been two days since her visit to Alfredo Paccioli, when she had gone clutching her scarf filled with jewels. Two days. She felt leaden, as though she also had died.

'Isabella . . . bella mia.' Bernardo was gently touching her arm. Silently he took her hand. There was so little he could do. He had wept for an hour when the police called him with the news. And again when Alessandro had flown into his arms.

'They killed my Daddy . . . they . . . they . . .'

The child had sobbed as Isabella stood by, letting him find what solace he could from a man. He would have no man now, no father, no Amadeo. He had looked at his mother with such terror in his dark, unhappy eyes. 'Will they ever take you?' No, she had answered. No, never. As

53

she held him so tightly in her arms. *And they will never take you either*, tesòro. *You are mine.*

It had been more than Bernardo could bear as he watched them and now this. Isabella, frozen and icelike in black coat and hat and stockings and a thick black veil. It only enhanced her beauty, only made her seem more, rather than less. He had brought her back all the jewellery without saying a word. Today she was wearing only her wedding ring and the large anniversary solitaire she had got only a few months before. Was that all? Was it only five days since they had last seen him? Would he truly never return? Bernardo had felt like a five-year-old child himself as he had looked down on the face of Amadeo di San Gregorio, so still and peaceful in death. He looked more than ever like the statues, the paintings, the young graceful boys of long-ago Rome. And now he was gone.

Bernardo helped her quietly from the car and held her arm tightly as they stepped inside. Police and guards at every entrance, and armies of mourners seated inside.

The funeral was brief and unbearably painful. Isabella sat silently next to him, tears rolling relentlessly down her face beneath the black veil. Employees and friends and relatives were sobbing openly. Even the gargoyle was there, with her gold and ebony cane.

It seemed years before they returned to the house. Contrary to tradition, Isabella had let it be known that she would see no one at home. No one. She wanted to be left alone. Who knew which of them had betrayed him? But Bernardo knew now that it was unlikely to be someone of their acquaintance. Even the police had no clue. They assumed, probably correctly, that it had been 'lucky amateurs', greedy for a piece of the San Gregorio wealth. There were no fingerprints, no bits of evidence, no witnesses, there had been no more calls. And there wouldn't be, the police were sure of it. Except from the hundreds, maybe thousands, of cranks who would start their macabre games. The police manned her telephone now, waiting for the onslaught of minor madmen who took pleasure in haunting and taunting and teasing, confessing, and threatening, or breathing obscenities into the phone. They had told Isabella what she could expect. Bernardo cringed at the thought of it; she had been through enough.

'Where's Alessandro?' Bernardo sipped a cup of coffee after the funeral, thinking how unbearably empty the house seemed and ashamed to find himself grateful that if it had to be someone, it had been Amadeo and not the child. Isabella wouldn't have been able to make that choice. But to Bernardo it was clear. As it would have been to Amadeo. He would have gladly sacrificed himself to spare his only child.

'He's in his room with the nurse. Do you want to see him?' Isabella looked at him lifelessly over her cup.

'I can wait. I wanted to talk to you about something anyway.'

'What?' She wasn't easy to talk to these days, and she wouldn't let the doctor give her anything to help. Bernardo guessed accurately that she hadn't really slept in almost a week.

'I think you need to get away.'

'Don't be absurd.' She set her cup down viciously and stared at him. 'I'm fine.'

'You look it.' He stared back at her, and for a moment she gave in to the flicker of a smile. It was the first taste of the old tension between them in a week. It felt comfortable and familiar.

'All right, I'm tired. But I'll be fine.'

'Not if you stay here.'

'You're wrong. This is where I need to be.' *Near his things, his home . . . near . . . him . . .*

55

'Why don't you take a trip to the States?'

'Why don't you mind your own business?' She sat back in her chair with a sigh. 'I'm not going, Bernardo. Don't push me.'

'You heard what the police said. Cranks will be calling, bugging you. Already now the press won't leave you alone. Is this how you want to live? What you want for Alessandro? You can't even send him back to school.'

'Eventually he can go back to school.'

'Then go away until then. A month. A few months. What is there to stay for?'

'Everything.' She looked at him very deliberately as she slowly pulled off her hat and took the veil from her eyes. There was something frightening and determined about the way she looked at him now.

'What does that mean?'

'It means I'm coming back to work on Monday. Part time, but every day. Nine to one, nine to two. Whatever it takes.'

'Are you joking?'

'Not at all.'

'Isabella, you can't mean it.' He was shocked.

'I can and I do. Just who do you think will run the business now – now that . . . he's gone?' She faltered for a moment on the words. But he bridled as soon as she had said them.

'I thought I could do that.' For a moment he sounded hurt and very tough. She looked away and then back at him.

'You could. But I can't do that. I can't sit here and abdicate. I can't give up what Amadeo and I shared, what he built, what we loved, what we made. He's gone now, Bernardo. I owe it to him. And to Alessandro. One day the business will be his. You and I will have to teach him what

56

he needs to know. You and I. Both of us. I can't do that just sitting here. If I did that, all I could do was tell him what it was like twenty years ago 'when your father was alive'. I owe him more than that, and Amadeo, and you and myself. I'm coming back on Monday.'

'I'm not saying you shouldn't come back. I'm just saying it's too soon.' He tried to sound gentle but he was not Amadeo. He couldn't handle her in Amadeo's gentle way, only with fire.

But this time she only shook her head, her eyes filling with tears again. 'It's not, Bernardo . . . it's not too soon at all. It's much . . . much . . . too late.' He put a hand over hers and waited until she caught her breath. 'What would I do here? Wander? Open his closets? Sit in the garden? Wait in my boudoir? For what? For a man . . .' A sob broke from her as she sat very still, her head held very high. '. . . a man . . . whom . . . I loved . . . and who is never again . . . coming . . . home. I have to . . . come back to work. I have to. It is a part of me, and it was a part of him. I will find him there. Every day. In a thousand different ways. In some of the ways that mattered most. I just . . . have to. That's all. Even Alessandro understands. I told him this morning. He understands perfectly.' She looked proud for a moment. He was such a good little boy.

'Then you're making him as crazy as you are.' But Bernardo didn't mean it unkindly, and Isabella only smiled.

'May I make him as crazy as I am, Bernardo. And as lovely as his father was. May I make him just as fine as that.' And with that she stood up, and for the first time in days he saw a real smile and only a glimmer of what had once been the sparkle in her eyes, only days before, only days. 'I need to be alone now. For a while.'

'When will I see you?' He stood up, watching her. Isabella was still there. Somewhere, sleeping, waiting, but she would come alive again. He was sure of it now. There was too much life in her not to.

'You will see me on Monday morning, of course. In my office.'

He only looked at her silently and then he left. He had a lot on his mind.

Chapter Five

Isabella di San Gregorio did indeed appear in the office on Monday morning, and every day after that. She was there from nine to two, inspiring awe, terror, admiration, and respect. She was everything Amadeo had always known she was. She was made of fire and steel, of heart and guts. She wore his hat now as well as her own, and a thousand others. She worked on papers in her room at home at night long after Alessandro went to sleep. She had two interests in her life now, her work and her child. And very little else. She was tense, tired, drawn, but she was doing what she had said she would do. She even sent Alessandro back to school – with a guard, with caution, with care, but with determination. She taught him to be proud, not afraid. She taught him to be brave, not angry. She taught him all that she herself was and still managed to give him something more. Patience, love, laughter, and sometimes they cried together too. Losing Amadeo had cost them both almost everything they had. But now it brought them closer and it made them friends. The only one whose friendship suffered was Bernardo. It was he who took the brunt of her sorrow and anxieties and fatigue. Instead of running more of the business, it seemed to him he ran less. He worked harder, longer, more, and yet she was trying to be everything, the root, the core, the heart and the soul of the House of San Gregorio. It left him drudgery. And bitterness. And anger. Which showed in every meeting between them now. The wars were constant, and Amadeo was no longer there to temper them. She was trying to be Amadeo as well as herself, and she was not sharing with him as she had with

59

Amadeo. She was still in command. It created more tension than ever between them. But at least the business hadn't suffered from the blow of Amadeo's passing. After a month, the figures were stable; after two months they were better than they had been the year before. Everything was better, except the relationship between Bernardo and Isabella, and the way Isabella looked. The phone rang constantly day and night, at home and in the office. The cranks had arrived, as promised. Threats, arguments, confessions, harangues, sympathy and accusations, obscenities and propositions. She no longer ever answered the phone. Three men covered it twenty-four hours a day at the villa, and another three covered the phone at the office. But still no clue had turned up to identify the kidnappers, and it was clear now that they would never be found. Isabella understood that. She had to. She also knew that eventually they would leave her alone. The cranks, the maniacs, the fools. All of them. One day. She could wait. But Bernardo disagreed.

'You're crazy. You can't go on living like this. You've already lost twenty pounds. You're practically scrawny.' He didn't mean it of course; she was always beautiful to him – but still she looked ill.

'That has nothing to do with the phone calls. It has to do with what I eat, or don't.' She tried to smile at him from across her desk, but she was too tired to argue anymore. They'd been at it all morning.

'You're jeopardising the child.'

'For chrissake, Bernardo, I'm not!' Her eyes raged at him now. 'We have seven guards on the house. One with Enzo in the car. Another at school. Don't be a horse's ass.'

'Wait, just wait, you bloody fool. Did I tell you that day, did I, about the way you two lived? Was I wrong?'

It was a bitter blow.

'Get out of my office,' Isabella shouted.

'Get out of my life!'

'*Va cagare*!' He slammed the door as he left. For a moment she was too stunned to go after him to apologise and she felt too tired even to try. She was so goddamn tired of fighting with Bernardo. She tried to remember if it had always been like that. Hadn't it been fun before too? Hadn't they laughed together at times? Or had they only laughed when Amadeo was there to coax them away from their battles? She couldn't remember anymore. She couldn't remember anything except the mountains of papers that lay on her desk – except at night. Then she remembered. Too much. She remembered Amadeo's soft sleeping sounds in the bed at night and his hands on the warm flesh of her thighs. She remembered the way he yawned and stretched when he awoke, the look in his eyes as he smiled at her over the morning paper, the way he smelled just after he had shaved and bathed, the way his laughter rang out in the hall when he chased Alessandro, the way . . . She lay with the memories every night. She took work home with her now, hoping to keep the visions at bay, hoping to lose herself in fabric orders and collection details, statistics and figures and investments. The nights were too long after Alessandro went to bed.

She shut her eyes very tightly and sighed as she sat in her office, trying to will herself back to work, but there was a soft knock at her door. Unwillingly she jumped, startled. It was the side door to Amadeo's office, the door he had always used. For a moment she felt herself tremble. She still had that mad feeling that he was going to come back. That it was all a bad dream, a terrible lie, that one of these evenings the Ferrari would slide down the gravel driveway, the door would slam, and he would call out to her, 'Isabellezza! I'm home!'

'Yes.' She stared at the door as the knock came again.

'May I?' It was only Bernardo, still looking strained.

'Of course. What are you doing in there?' He had been in Amadeo's office. She didn't want him in there. She didn't want anyone there. She used it to find refuge sometimes, for a moment, at lunch, or at the end of a day. But even she knew that she couldn't keep Bernardo out. He had a right to access to Amadeo's papers, to the books he kept on the wall behind his desk.

'I was looking for some files. Why?'

'Nothing.' The look of pain in her eyes was unmistakable. For a moment Bernardo ached for her again. No matter how impossible she was at times, no matter how they differed in their aspirations for the business, he still understood the magnitude of her loss.

'Does it bother you so much when I go in there?' His voice was different now than it had been a little while before when he had shouted and slammed the door.

She nodded, looking away for a moment and then back at him. 'Stupid, isn't it? I know you need to get things from his office sometimes. So do I.'

'You can't turn it into a shrine, Isabella.' His voice was soft, but his eyes firm. She was already doing that to the business. He wondered how long it would go on.

'I know.'

He stood uneasily in the doorway, not sure this was the time. But when? When could he ask her? When could he tell her what he thought? 'Can we talk for a minute, or are you very busy?'

'I have some time.' Her tone wasn't very inviting. She forced herself to gentle her voice. Maybe he wanted to apologise for what he had just said as he slammed out of her office a little while before. 'Is there something special?'

'I think so.' He sighed softly and sat down. 'There's something I haven't wanted to bother you with, but I think that maybe it's time.'

'Oh, Christ. Now what?' Who was quitting, what had

62

been cancelled, and what wasn't going to arrive? 'That goddamn soap again?' She'd heard enough, and every time they had to discuss it, it reminded her again of the day when . . . when Amadeo . . . that last morning . . . She averted her eyes.

'Don't look like that. It's nothing unpleasant. In fact' – he tried to convince her by smiling – 'it could be very nice.'

'I'm not sure I could stand the shock of something "very nice".' She sat back in her chair, fighting exhaustion and a pain in the small of her back. Nerves, strain, it had been there since . . . 'All right, out with it. Tell me.'

'*Ècco, signora.*' And suddenly he regretted not taking her to lunch. Maybe that would have been better, a few hours away, a good bottle of wine. But who could get her to go anywhere anymore? And moving three feet out of the building meant taking with them her army of guards. No it was better here. 'We've had a call from the States.'

'Someone has ordered ten thousand pieces, we're dressing the First Lady, and I just won an internationally coveted award. Right?'

'Well . . .' For a moment they both smiled. Thank God, she was mellower than she had been earlier that morning. He wasn't sure why, maybe because she needed him so much, or maybe she was just suddenly too tired to fight. 'It wasn't quite that kind of call. It was a call from Farnham-Barnes.'

'The omnivorous department store monster? What the hell do they want now?' In the past ten years F-B, as it was called, had been carefully devouring every major top-notch department store in the States. It was now a powerful entity to be reckoned with, and an account coveted by everyone in the trade. 'Were they happy or not with their last order? No, never mind. I know the answer to that, they want more. Well, tell them they can't have

63

more. You already know that.' Because of the number of stores in their chain, Isabella was careful to keep the reins well in hand. They could only have so much of her ready-to-wear line and a miniscule quantity of the designer line. She didn't want women in Des Moines, Boston, and Miami all wearing hundreds of the same dress. Even in ready-to-wear Isabella was careful and kept an iron control. 'Is that it?' She glared at Bernardo, already bridling, and he felt his upper lip grow stiff.

'Not exactly. They had something else on their minds. The parent company, something called IHI, International Holdings and Industries, which happens to own Farrington Mills, Inter Am Airlines, and Harcourt Foods, has been making discreet inquiries of us since Amadeo's ... for the past two months.'

'What kind of inquiries?' Her eyes were black slate. Cold and hard and flat.

But there was no point beating around the bush any longer. 'They want to know if you'd be interested in selling out.'

'Are you crazy?'

'Not at all. For them it would be a brilliant addition to what they've done with F-B. They've acquired almost every major department store worth having in the States, yet they've maintained each one's identity. It's a chain without being a chain. Each store has remained every bit as exclusive as it was before, yet it benefits from being part of a much larger organisation, more extensive funding to draw on, greater resources. Business-wise, the system is brilliant.'

'Then congratulate them for me. And tell them to go screw. What do they think? That San Gregorio is some little Italian department store to add to their chain? Don't be absurd, Bernardo. What they're doing has nothing to do with us.'

'On the contrary. It could have everything to do with us. It gives us an international feeding system for all other lines, production facilities, mass marketing if we want it, for the colognes, the soap. It's a top-ranking operation and would fit in perfectly for all our main lines.'

'You're out of your mind.' She looked at him and laughed nervously. 'Are you actually suggesting that I sell to them? Is that what this is all about?'

He hesitated for only a fraction of a second and then nodded, fearing the worst. It was quick to come. 'Are you mad?' She was shrieking at him and rapidly got to her feet. 'Is that what that bullshit was about this morning? About how tired I look? How thin? What is it, Bernardo? Are they offering you an enormous fee if you can talk me into it? Greed, everyone is motivated by greed, like the ... those . . .' She choked on the words, thinking of Amadeo's kidnappers, and turned away quickly to hide a sudden dew of tears. 'I don't want to discuss this.' She stood with her back to him, looking out of the window, unconsciously searching for Amadeo's car. It had already been sold.

Behind her Bernardo's voice was surprisingly quiet. 'No one is paying me a fee, Isabella. Except you. I know it's too soon for you to think about this. But it makes sense. It is the next obvious step for the business. Now.'

'What does that mean?' She wheeled to face him, and he was pained to see the tears still in her eyes. 'Do you think Amadeo would have done this? Sold out to some commercial monster in America? To a corporation? An F-B and an IHI, and a God-knows-what-else. This is San Gregorio, Bernardo. San Gregorio. A family. A dynasty.'

'It is an empire with an empty throne. How long do you really think you can manage this? You'll die of exhaustion before Alessandro comes of age. And not even that. You run the same risk that Amadeo did and so does Alessandro.

You know what's happening in Italy now. What about you? What if something happens to you? How constantly can you keep yourself guarded, every time you go in or out, or stand up or sit down.'

'For as long as I have to. It will die down. You actually think selling out is the answer? How can you even say that after what you've put into it, after what you've built with us, after . . .' Again the tears filled her eyes.

'I'm not betraying you, Isabella.' He fought for control. 'I'm trying to help you. There's no other answer for you except to sell out. They're talking about enormous sums of money. Alessandro would be an immensely rich man.' But he knew as he said it that that wasn't the key.

'Alessandro will be what his father was. The head of the House of San Gregorio. Here. In Rome.'

'If he's still alive.' The words were spoken softly, with a film of anger.

'Stop it! Stop!' She stared at him, her hands trembling, her face suddenly contorted into a hideous frown. 'Stop saying that! Nothing like that will ever happen again. And I won't sell out. Ever. Tell those people no! That's all, that's final. I don't want to hear the offer. I don't want you to discuss anything with them. In fact I forbid you to talk to them!'

Christ, women! 'Don't be a fool.' Bernardo shouted, 'We do business with them. And in spite of your asinine restrictions IHI is still one of our biggest accounts.'

'Cancel it.'

'I won't.'

'I don't give a damn what you do, damn you. Just leave me alone!'

This time it was Isabella who slammed out of the room and took refuge in Amadeo's office next door. Bernardo sat in hers for only a moment, then retreated to his own quarters down the hall. She was a fool. He knew she'd never agree to it, but this sale was her best bet. Something was happening to her. Once, the business had added joy and zest and something wonderful and powerful to her life. Now he could see it destroying her. Every day in these offices made her more lonely, more bitter. Every day surrounded by guards made her more frightened, no matter how much she denied it. Every day dreaming of Amadeo broke off another piece of her soul. But she had the reins now. Isabella di San Gregorio was in control.

The next morning Bernardo called the president of IHI and told him Isabella had said no. After he did and thought mournfully of the opportunity Isabella had turned down, his secretary buzzed him on the intercom.

'Yes?'

'There's someone here to see you.'

'Now what?'

'It's about a bicycle. He said you told him to deliver it here.' Bernardo smiled tiredly to himself and let out another sigh. The bicycle. It was about all he was ready to handle after a difficult start to his day.

'I'll be right out.'

It was red, with a blue-and-white seat, and red, white, and blue streamers flying from the handlebars, a bell, a speedometer, and a tiny licence plate with Alessandro's name. It was a beautiful little bicycle, and he knew it would delight the child, who had been dying for a 'real bike' since the summer. Bernardo knew that Amadeo had planned to give him one for Christmas. He had ordered this one, a tiny silver astronaut suit, and half a dozen games. This was going to be a difficult Christmas, and with a glance at his calendar as he stood up, he realised that it was only two weeks away.

Chapter Six

'Mamma, Mamma . . . it's Bernardo!' Alessandro's nose was pressed to the glass; the Christmas tree sparkled behind him. Isabella put her arms around him and looked outside. She was smiling. She and Bernardo had set aside the wars a few days before. She needed him this year, desperately, and so did the child. She and Amadeo had both lost their parents over the last decade, and as only children they had nothing to offer Alessandro in the way of family, except themselves and their friend. As always Bernardo had come through. 'Oh, look . . . look! It's tremendous! He has a package . . . and look! More!' Bernardo did a hilarious pantomime, staggering under the weight of his bundles, all of them shoved into a huge canvas sack. He was wearing a Father Christmas hat with one of his dark suits.

Isabella was laughing too as the guard opened the door. '*Ciao, Nardo, come va?*' He kissed her lightly on the cheek and turned his attention instantly to the little boy. It had been a rough couple of weeks in the office. The IHI matter was definitely closed. Isabella had sent them a brutally succinct letter, and Bernardo had been livid to his very core. Other problems had cropped up; all finally had been handled and resolved. It had been a wearying time for both of them. But somehow, with the depressing threat of Christmas, they had both managed to put their differences aside. She handed him a glass of brandy as they all sat down next to the fire.

'When can I open them? Now? . . . Now?' Alessandro was hopping up and down like a little red elf in sleepers as

Mamma Teresa hovered somewhere near the door. The servants were all celebrating in the kitchen, with wine and the presents Isabella had given them the night before. The only members of the household not included in the celebration were the guards. They were treated as invisibles, and the safety of the entire household depended on their remaining on duty at all the entrances to the villa and just outside. The phone men were posted as usual in Amadeo's old study, and the crank calls raged on, doubled now, for some reason, during the holidays. As though what they had already been through hadn't been enough. There had to be more. And Bernardo knew it was taking its toll on her. She always knew about the calls, as though she sensed them. She trusted no one now. Something tender and giving that had been so much a part of her was slowly dying inside.

'When can I open them? When?' Alessandro tugged at Bernardo's sleeve. He pretended not to hear.

'Open what? That's just my laundry over there in that bag.'

'No, it's not . . . no, it's not! Mamma . . . please . . .'

'I don't think he'll make it till midnight, let alone Christmas Day!' Even Isabella was smiling as her eyes gently caressed the child. 'What about Mamma Teresa, darling? Why don't you give her her present first?'

'Oh, Mamma!'

'Come on.' She pushed a large package into his arms and he scampered off to deliver a handsome pink satin robe to her, the finest from Isabella's American line. From Isabella there had already been a handbag and a small elegant watch. This was a year to be good to everyone, all of those who had shown themselves so devoted to her and the child. At least she no longer suspected the members of her household. She believed, at last, that the betrayers had been people from outside. She had given Enzo a new coat, a warm, black cashmere to wear over his uniform when he chauffeured her around town, and an excellent new radio for his room. He could even get Paris and London on it, he had told her with pride that day. There had been presents for the entire household, and equally handsome, thoughtful ones for everyone at the office. But for Alessandro there had been the most special gift of all. He had not seen it yet, but Enzo already had it mounted and everything prepared.

He had just scampered back into the room. 'She says it's beautiful and she'll wear it all her life and think of me.' Alessandro looked happy with the effect the large pink bathrobe had had. 'Now me.'

Isabella and Bernardo laughed as they looked at him, with eyes so bright and opened so wide. For a moment it was as though nothing ugly had ever happened. For an instant the pain of the last months was not.

'All right, Master Alessandro. Go to it!' Bernardo waved grandiosely toward the large canvas bag, and the boy dived towards it and then into it with loud squeals of glee. Paper and ribbons instantly started flying, and in a moment he was wearing the silver astronaut suit, the feet of his red sleepers peeking through. He was laughing and giggling and slid rapidly across the highly polished wood floor to give Bernardo a kiss, before diving back for more. The games, new crayons, a large cuddly brown bear, and then the bicycle at last, pushed way to the back of the large canvas sack.

'Oh . . . oh . . . it's beautiful . . . Is it . . . is it a Rolls-Royce?' They both laughed as they watched him, already astride the new bike.

'Of course it's a Rolls. Would I give you anything less?' He was already weaving across the living room, aimed first at a Louis XV table, then at the wall, as the two people who loved him laughed till they cried. And then they all saw Enzo, smiling hesitantly from the door. His eyes questioned Isabella, and she nodded with a smile. She whispered something to Bernardo, and he raised his eyebrows and then laughed.

'I think I may have been outdone.'

'Not at all. He'll probably come to breakfast on the bicycle tomorrow morning. But this . . . I just wanted to give him something to make him less unhappy about being confined at home. He can't . . .' she hesitated painfully for a moment, '. . . he can't go to the playground anymore.' Bernardo nodded silently, put down his brandy, and rose. But the momentary sadness in Isabella's eyes was gone again, as she turned smilingly to the child. 'Go get Mamma Teresa and your coat.'

'Are we going out?' He looked intrigued.

'Just for a minute.'

'Can't I wear this?' He looked down happily at his astronaut suit, and Bernardo took a gentle swing at his behind.

'Go on, you can wear your coat over it.'

'Okay.' He said the American word with his own Roman accent and disappeared at full speed as Bernardo winced.

'I may have to replace the mirrors in your hall.'

'Not to mention the dining room table, all the cabinets between here and his room, and possibly the glass doors.' They both listened smilingly as the bicycle bell rang out from the long hall. 'It was just the right gift.' She also knew that it had been what Amadeo planned for him, and for a moment no one spoke. She looked at him searchingly then and let out a small sigh. 'I'm glad you could be here with Alessandro this year, Nardo . . . and with me too.'

Gently he touched her hand as the fire in the hearth crackled and blazed. 'I wouldn't have been anywhere else.' And then he smiled at her. 'Despite the ulcers you give me at work.' But this was different. And now suddenly there was a different kind of electricity in the air.

'I'm sorry, I – I feel so much on my shoulders now. I keep thinking you'll understand.' She looked up at him, the beautifully etched face so pale and so perfectly set around the dark eyes.

'I do understand. I could help more, you know, if you'd let me.'

'I'm not sure I can. I have this insane urge to – to do it all myself. It's difficult to explain. It's all I have left, except Alessandro.'

'One day there will be more.' One day . . . but she only shook her head.

'Never again. There is no one like him. He was a very special man.' Tears rolled into her eyes again as she pulled her hand away and looked silently into the fire. And Bernardo looked away and sipped at his brandy again as he heard the bicycle bell chime and Alessandro come careering down the hall with Mamma Teresa in tow 'Ready?' Isabella's eyes were a little too shiny, but nothing in the face she turned to her child showed how great was her pain.

'*Si.*' The little face looked out impishly from the large plastic astronaut hat.

'*Allora, andiamo.*' Isabella stood up and led the way to the double doors leading into the garden. A guard was unobtrusively standing off to the side, and they all saw now that the garden was brilliantly lit. She looked down at the child, and she heard him catch his breath.

'Mamma! . . .!' It was a small but beautiful carousel, just the right size for a five-year-old child. It had cost her a fortune, but it was worth every bit of it when she saw the light in his eyes. Four horses danced gaily beneath a carved wooden tent painted red and white; there were

72

bells and clowns and decorations. Bernardo thought he had never seen the boy's eyes so wide. Enzo helped him carefully into the saddle of a blue-painted horse with green ribbons attached to a golden halter with little silver bells. A switch was flicked on, and the carousel began to turn. Alessandro squealed with excitement and delight. The night was suddenly filled with carnival music as the servants came to the windows, and everywhere his audience smiled.

'*Buon Natale!*' Isabella called out to him and then ran to jump into the saddle of the next horse, a yellow one with a little red saddle edged in gold. They laughed at each other as the carousel spun slowly around. Bernardo watched them, feeling something very tender tear at his heart. Mamma Teresa turned away, wiping a tear from her eye, and Enzo and the guard shared a smile.

Alessandro rode round and round for almost half an hour, and them at last Isabella urged him back inside.

'It will still be there in the morning.'

'But I want to ride it tonight.'

'If you stay out here all night, Santa Claus won't come.'

Santa Claus? Bernardo smiled to himself. What didn't the child have? The smile faded. A father. That's what Alessandro didn't have. He helped the child down from the carousel and held his hand tightly as they walked back inside. He disappeared quickly to the kitchen as Bernardo and Isabella regained their seats by the fire.

'What a marvellous thing, Isabella.' The echo of the carnival chimes still rang in his head. And finally she was smiling as she hadn't in months.

'I always wanted one of my very own when I was a child. It's perfect, isn't it?' For a moment her eyes were almost as bright as the fire. For an instant he wanted to say 'So are you.' She was a remarkable woman. He hated her and loved her, and she was his dearest friend.

73

'Do you suppose he'll let us ride it with him if we're very, very nice?' She laughed with him and poured herself a small glass of red wine. And then as though she had forgotten something, she jumped to her feet and ran to the tree.

'I almost forgot.' She picked up two small boxes wrapped in gold and returned to the fire. 'For you.'

'If it's not a carousel of my very own, I don't want it.' And again they both laughed. But the laughter dimmed very quickly as he discovered what was inside. The first was a tiny immensely intricate calculator in its own silver case; it looked like a very elegant cigarette case and could be worn concealed in his vest.

'I had it sent from the States. I don't understand it. But you will.'

'Isabella, you're crazy!'

'Don't be silly. I should have got you a hot-water bottle for your ulcer, but I thought this might be more fun.' She kissed him fondly on the cheek and handed him the next box. But this time she turned away, staring into the fire. And when he had opened it, he fell silent as well. There was very little he could say. It was the pocket watch he knew Amadeo had treasured and had almost never worn because it was so sacred to him. It had belonged to his father, and on its back initials of three generations of San Gregorios were elaborately engraved. Beneath them, he suddenly realised, were his own.

'I don't know what to say.'

'*Niènte, caro.* There is nothing to say.'

'Alessandro should have this.' But she only shook her head.

'No, Nardo. You should.' And for an endless moment her eyes held his. She wanted him to know that no matter how great the friction between them at work, he was

74

precious to her, and he mattered. A great deal. He and Alessandro were all she had left now. And Bernardo would always be special to her. He was her friend. As he had been Amadeo's friend too. The watch was to remind him of that, that he was something more than simply the director of San Gregorio or the man she yelled at every day, twenty-seven times before noon. Away from the office he was someone important to her, a kind of family. He was a part of her other life. And the look in her eyes told him all that now as he watched her. His eyes seemed to hold hers for a very long time as though he were wondering about something, as though he were trying to resist a tidal wave over which he had no control.

'Isabella . . .' He sounded suddenly oddly formal, and she waited, knowing he was deeply moved by the gift. 'I – I have something to say to you. I have for a long time. It may be the wrong time. It probably is . . . I'm not sure. But I have to tell you. I must be honest with you now. It's . . . very important . . . to me.' He hesitated lengthily between words as though what he was saying was very difficult for him, and the look in his eyes told her it was.

'Is something wrong?' Her eyes suddenly filled with compassion. He looked agonised, poor man, and she had been so hard lately. What in God's name was he about to say? She sat very still and waited. 'Nardo . . . you look frightened, *caro*. You needn't. Whatever it is, you can say it to me. God knows we've been outspoken enough for all these years.' She tried to make him smile and he wouldn't, and for the first time in all the years he had known her, he thought her insensitive. My God, how could she not know? But it wasn't insensitivity, it was blindness. He knew it as he watched her, and then he nodded and put down his glass.

'I am frightened. What I have to tell you used to frighten

me a great deal. And what worries me now is that is might frighten you. And I don't want it to. That's the last thing I want.' She sat very still, watching him, waiting.

'Nardo . . .' She started to speak, holding out a long graceful white hand. He took it and held it fast in his own. His eyes never left hers.

'I will tell you very simply, Bellezza. There's no other way. I love you.' And then softly, 'I have for years.'

She seemed almost to jump at his words, as though a current had suddenly gone through her and shocked her entire body. 'What?'

'I love you.' He seemed less frightened this time and more like the Bernardo she knew.

'But Nardo . . . all these years?'

'All these years.' He said it proudly now. He felt better. At last it was out.

'How could you?'

'Very easily. You're a pain in the ass a lot of the time, but strangely enough that doesn't make you hard to love.' He was smiling and she laughed suddenly; it seemed to break some of the tension in the room.

'But why?' She stood up now and walked pensively toward the fire.

'Why did I love you or why didn't I tell you?'

'All of it. And why now? Why now, Nardo . . . why must you tell me now?' There were suddenly tears in her voice and her eyes as she leaned against the mantelpiece, staring into the fire. He walked softly toward her, stood next to her, and turned her face gently toward his so he could look into her eyes.

'I didn't tell you for all these years because I loved both of you. I loved Amadeo too, you know. He was a very special man. I would never have done anything to hurt him or you. I put away my feelings, I sublimated them. I put what I felt into the business, and maybe' – he smiled

76

– 'even into fighting with you. But now . . . everything has changed. Amadeo is gone. And day after day after week I watch you, lonely, destroying yourself, pushing yourself, alone, always alone. I can't bear it anymore. I'm there for you. I have been for all these years. It's time you knew that. It's time you turned to me, Isabella. And . . .' he hesitated for a long moment, and then he stood very still and said it, '. . . and it's time I got mine too. Time I was able to tell you that I love you, to feel you in my arms, to be Alessandro's stepfather, if you let me, and not just his friend. Maybe I'm mad to tell you all this, but . . . I – I have to . . . I've loved you for too long.' His voice was hoarse with the pent-up passion of years, and as she watched him tears wended their way slowly down her face, rolling mercilessly down her cheeks and on to her dress. He watched her and slowly let his hand go to her face and brush away the tears. It was the first time he had touched her that way, and he felt unbridled passion tear through his loins. Almost without thinking, he pulled her toward him and crushed his mouth against hers. She didn't fight him, and for an instant he thought he felt her kiss him back. She was hungry and lonely and sad and afraid, but what was happening was too much for her, and suddenly she pushed him firmly away. They were both breathless, and Isabella was wild eyed as she looked at her old friend.

'No, Nardo! . . . No!' She was as much fighting against what he had just told her as against his kiss.

But suddenly he looked even more frightened than she did, and he shook his head. 'I'm sorry. Not for what I've said. But for – for pushing you too quickly. . . . I . . . my God, I'm so sorry. It *is* too soon. I was wrong.'

But as she watched him she felt achingly sorry for him. It was obvious that he had suffered for years. And during all of the time she had never known and she was certain that Amadeo had been as ignorant as she. But how could she

77

have been so stupid? How could she have not seen? She looked at him with compassion and tenderness and held out both hands. 'Don't be sorry, Nardo, it's all right.' But as a bright light of hope came into his eyes, she quickly shook her head. 'No, I don't mean it like that. I – I just don't know. It's too soon. But you weren't wrong; if that's what you feel, you should tell me. You should have told me a long time ago.'

'And then what?' For a moment he sounded bitter and jealous of his old friend.

'I don't know. But I must have seemed very stupid and cruel over the years.' She looked at him warmly, and he smiled.

'No: Just very blind. But perhaps it was better that way. Had I told you, it would have complicated things. It may do that now.'

'It doesn't have to.'

'But it might. Do you want me to leave San Gregorio, Isabella?' He said it honestly, and his voice sounded very tired. It had been a difficult evening for him.

But she looked at him now with fire in her eyes. 'Are you crazy? Why? Because you kissed me? Because you told me you loved me? For that you would leave? Don't do that to me, Nardo. I need you, in too many ways. I don't know what I feel right now. I'm still numb. I still want Amadeo night and day . . . about half of the time I don't understand that he's never coming home. I still expect him to . . . I still hear him and see him and smell him . . . There's no room for anyone else in my life, except Alessandro. I can't make you any promises now. I can barely hear what you're saying. I hear it, but I don't really understand it. Not really. Maybe one day I will. But until then all I can do is love you as I always have, as a brother, as a friend. If that's a reason for you to leave San Gregorio, then do it, but I will

78

never understand. We can go on as we always have; there is no reason not to.'

'But not forever, *cara*. Do you understand that?'

She looked pained as their eyes met. 'What do you mean?'

'Just what I said, that I can't go on like this forever. I had to tell you because I can't live with the secret of my feelings any longer, and there's no reason to. Amadeo is gone, Isabella, whether you recognise it or not. He's gone, and I love you. Those are two facts. But to go on forever, if you don't love me in quite that way, to go on working for you, because in truth I do work *for* you and not *with* you, especially now, to go on playing second fiddle forever, Isabella . . . I can't. One day I want to share your life with you, not exist on the fringe of it. I want to give you what there is of my life. I want to make you better and happier and stronger. I want to hear you laugh again. I want to share the victory of our collections and fabulous deals. I want to stand beside you as Alessandro grows up.'

'You will anyway.'

'Yes.' He nodded simply. 'I will. As your husband or as your friend. But not as your employee.'

'I see. Then what you're saying is that either I marry you or you quit?'

'Eventually. But it could take a very long time . . . if . . . I thought there were hope.' And then after a long pause, 'Is there?'

But she was equally long to answer. 'I don't know. I have always loved you. But not in that way. I had Amadeo.'

'I understand. I always did.' They sat in silence for a long time, watching the fire, each lost in thought, and gently once again he took her hand. He opened it, looked

79

into the delicate, finely lined palm, and kissed it. She did not withdraw her hand, but with sad eyes she only watched him. He was special to her, and she loved him, but he wasn't Amadeo. He never would be . . . never . . . and as they sat there they both knew. He looked at her long and hard as he took his hand from hers. 'I was serious before. Would you like me to quit?'

'Because of tonight?' She sounded tired and sad. It hadn't been a betrayal but it had been a loss. In a way she felt that she had just lost him as her friend. He wanted to be her lover. And there was no opening for the job.

'Yes. Because of tonight. If I've made it impossible for you to exist with me at the office now, I'll go. Immediately if you like.'

'I don't like. That would be even more impossible, Nardo. I'd go under in a week.'

'You'd surprise yourself. You wouldn't. But is it what you'd prefer?'

She shook her head honestly. 'No. But I don't know what to say to you about all this.'

'Then say nothing. And one day, if the time is ever right, a long time from now, I'll say it again. But please don't torment yourself or feel that this is hanging over your head. I won't leap out of doorways and take you in my arms. We've been friends for a long time. I don't want to lose that either.' Suddenly she felt relieved. Perhaps she hadn't lost everything after all.

'I'm glad, Nardo. I can't deal with an either-or situation at this point. I'm not ready. Maybe I never will be.'

'Yes, you will. But maybe never for me. I understand that too.'

She looked at him with a tender smile and leaned slowly toward him to kiss his cheek. 'And when did you get so smart, Mister Franco?'

'I always was; you just never noticed.'

'Is that so?' He was smiling and she was laughing, the whole atmosphere of the room had changed again.

'Yes, that's so. I happen to be the genius around the office these days, or hadn't you noticed?'

'Not at all. And every morning when I look in the mirror and say, "Mirror, mirror on the wall, who's the genius of them all . . . ?" ' But they were both laughing now and suddenly their faces were closer again and he could feel her soft breath on his cheek, and all he wanted to do was kiss her again, and he could see her mouth waiting for his, but this time he didn't do it, the moment passed, and in embarrassment Isabella laughed oddly, stood up, and walked away. No, it was not going to be easy at the office. They both knew that now.

'Look what Laura baked for Santa!' On his soft sleeper-clad feet, he had approached unheard. But they looked up now to see Alessandro carrying two plates covered with gingerbread that he deposited carefully on a little stool he placed next to the fire. He looked at them soberly and then picked up one large warm piece of the gingerbread, which he rapidly ate. And then he disappeared again, having broken the painful spell.

'Isabella . . .' He looked at her and smiled. 'Don't worry.' She only patted his arm, and they exchanged a smile as Alessandro returned, uneasily carrying two mugs of milk.

'Are you having a party or feeding Santa?' Bernardo grinned at him and sat down again.

'No. Nothing's for me.'

'All of this is for Santa?' Bernardo watched him with a broad grin, but the boy's face grew slowly serious, and he shook his head. 'Is it for me?' The head shook soberly again.

'It's for Papa. In case . . . the angels let him come home
. . . just for tonight.' He looked again at the two places he
had set near the fireplace and then kissed his mother and
Bernardo good night. And five minutes later Bernardo left
and Isabella went quietly to her room. It had been a very
long night.

Chapter Seven

'How's the carousel holding up?' Bernardo stretched his legs in front of him as he and Isabella ended a private conference at the end of a long day. It was three weeks after Christmas, and they had been doing nothing but work. But at last things seemed to be settling into a routine again. It had even been almost ten days since they'd had a good fight. And he hadn't mentioned his Christmas 'confession' again. Isabella was relieved.

'I think he likes it almost as much as your bike.'

'Has he broken any of the furniture with it yet?'

'No, but he's certainly trying. Yesterday he set himself a race course in the dining room and only knocked over five chairs.' They laughed for a moment, and Isabella stood up and stretched. She was relieved that the holidays were over and she was pleased with the work they had done. With some effort they had both returned to their old relationship, and even Bernardo could see that she was in a peaceful mood. And then he saw her stiffen as she heard Amadeo's phone. 'Why are they ringing that office?'

'Maybe they couldn't get through to yours.' He tried to underplay it, although for a moment it had startled him too. But they both knew that the men who cleared her phone calls sometimes tied up all the lines. 'Do you want me to get it?'

'No. It's all right.' She walked quickly into Amadeo's office and was gone for only two minutes when Bernardo heard a scream. He ran in to find her white-faced and hysterical, with both hands to her mouth, staring at the phone.

'What is it?' But she didn't answer, and when she tried, all that came from her was a croak and then another scream. 'Isabella, tell me!' He was holding her by both shoulders and shaking her desperately as he searched her eyes. 'What did they say? Was it something to do with Amadeo? Was it the same man? Isabella . . .' He was seriously considering slapping her as the guard who haunted her outer office rushed inside. 'Isabella!'

'Alessandro! . . . They . . . said . . . they . . . have him! . . .' She fell, sobbing, into Bernardo's arms as the guard ran frantically for the phone, dialling her home number, but he couldn't get through.

'Call the police!' Bernardo shouted over his shoulder as he grabbed her coat and her handbag and rushed her through her own office and out the door. 'We're going to the house.' And then, stopping for a moment in the doorway, he looked hard at Isabella and held her by both arms. 'It's probably only cranks again. You know that, don't you? He's probably all right.' But all she could do was stare at him and shake her head frantically from side to side.

'Was it the same voice, the same man?' he asked.

She shook her head again. Bernardo motioned to the guard to follow him, and the three of them ran down all three flights of stairs and outside. They collected another guard on the way. Isabella's car was already waiting for her as it did at the end of every day. Enzo stared at them in confusion as the four of them hurtled into the car, one of the guards shoving Enzo aside as he slid over, taking command of the wheel.

'*Ma, che* . . .' Enzo began, but one look at Isabella told him what he didn't want to know. '*Cosa c'e*? What is it? *Il bambino*?'

No one answered him. Isabella continued to clutch

Bernardo, and they roared toward the villa on Via Appia Antica.

The driver barely waited for the electric gates to slide open. One of the guards was already out of the car before they came to a stop. He ran into the house, followed an instant later by Isabella, Bernardo, Enzo, and the last guard, all of them pounding frantically through the house. The first person Isabella saw was Luisa.

'Alessandro? Where is he?' She could speak now and she grabbed the frightened servant roughly with both hands.

'I . . . signora . . . he . . .'

'Tell me!'

The elderly cook began to cry, confused. 'I don't know. Mamma Teresa took him out an hour ago, I thought . . . What is wrong?' Then seeing Isabella hysterical before her, she knew. 'Oh, God, no. Oh, God! . . .' The air was filled with her long sorrowful scream. The sound cut into Isabella like a blade. All she could think to do was to stop it, cut it off. Unthinking, she reached back and slapped Luisa before Enzo could take the cook away. A moment later Bernardo's arm was around her waist and he was half steering, half dragging Isabella across the hall to her room. Just as they reached the door there was a commotion at the other end of the house. The sound of feet. The guards thundering through the house. And then, like music, the voice of Alessandro, and that of Mamma Teresa, as usual, unruffled, as she came in with the child. Isabella stared at Bernardo, wild-eyed, and ran into the hall.

'Mamma!' Alessandro began, then stopped. She hadn't looked like that since they had told him four months before that she had the flu, and that had been when . . . Looking at her, frightened, reminded, he ran toward her and began to cry.

Clutching him warmly against her, her voice wracked

by sobs, she looked at Mamma Teresa. 'Where were you?'

'We went for a ride.' The elderly nurse was beginning to understand what must have happened as she looked at Isabella and the phalanx of guards. 'I thought a change would do the boy good.'

'Nothing happened?' Mamma Teresa shook her head as Isabella looked back at Bernardo. 'Then it was only . . . another one of those calls,' she said. But she had believed them. It had been so like those others, those horrible threatening voices. And how had they got through? She felt herself swaying and dimly aware of someone removing the child from her arms.

Five minutes later she came to in her room with Bernardo and one of the maids standing over her, staring anxiously as she returned from unconsciousness.

'*Grazie*.' Bernardo nodded dismissal to the maid, handed Isabella a glass of water, and sat down at the edge of the bed. He looked almost as pale as Isabella. She sipped the water silently from a glass held in a trembling hand.

'Do you want me to call the doctor?'

She shook her head, and they sat for a moment, shaken, silent, stunned by what they had thought.

'How did they get through?' Isabella said finally.

'One of the guards says there is something wrong with the lines today. The intercept system on the phones at the office must have gone out for a few minutes. Or maybe they just missed the call. It could have rung in Amadeo's office for any reason. Even a crossed wire.'

'But why would they do that to me? Oh, God, Bernardo . . .' She closed her eyes and leaned her head back on the pillows for a moment. 'And poor Luisa.'

'Never mind Luisa.'

'I'll go to see her in a few minutes. I just thought – '

'So did I. I thought this was for real, Isabella. And what

86

if one day it is? What if someone takes him too?' He stared at her mercilessly as she closed her eyes and shook her head.

'Don't say that.'

'What will you do? Add another dozen guards to the retinue? Build a fortress just for you and the boy? Have a heart attack the next time you get a crank call?'

'I'm not old enough to have a heart attack.' She looked at him bleakly with an attempt at a smile, but Bernardo did not return it.

'You can't live like this any longer. And don't make me speeches about what you're doing for Amadeo, about taking his place. If he knew what you were doing, how you were living, locked in, here, in the office, keeping the child locked up. If he knew the risks you're taking with that boy just by continuing to live in Rome, he would kill you, Isabella. You know it yourself. Don't you dare ever try to justify this by telling me that you're doing it all for him. Amadeo would never forgive you. And maybe one day neither will Alessandro. You are giving him a childhood of terror, not to mention what you're doing to yourself. How dare you! How dare you!' Bernardo's voice had risen steadily as he spoke. He stalked around the room turning to glare at her, waving his hands. He ran one hand through his hair and then sat down again, regretting his own outburst, prepared for Isabella's wrath. But as he looked at her he was stunned to realise that this time Isabella hadn't told him to go to hell. She hadn't invoked the sacred name of Amadeo, hadn't told him that she knew she was right.

'What do you think I should do? Run away? Leave Rome? Hide for the rest of my life?' she said. But there was no sarcasm this time. Only the shadow of the terror she had just felt again.

'You don't need to hide for the rest of your life. But maybe you have to do something like that for a while.'

'And then what? Bernardo, how can I?' She sounded like a frightened, tired, little girl. Gently Bernardo reached for her hand.

'You have to, Isabella. You have no choice. They'll drive you mad if you stay here. Go away. For six months, a year. We'll work it out. We can communicate. You can give me orders, instructions, ulcers, anything, but don't stay here. For God's sake, don't stay here. I couldn't bear it if . . .' He shocked them both by dropping his head into his hands. He was crying. '. . . if something happened to Alessandro or to you.' He looked up at her then, the tears still flowing from his blue eyes. 'You're like my sister. Amadeo was my best friend. For God's sake. Go away.'

'Where?'

'You could go to Paris.'

'There's nothing there for me anymore. Everyone's gone My grandfather, my parents. And if these people can do this to me here, they'll do it to me just as easily in France. Why can't I just find a secluded place in the country here, maybe not that far from Rome? If no one knows where I am, it would be the same thing.'

But Bernardo looked at her angrily now. 'Don't start playing games. Get out, dammit! Now! Go somewhere. Anywhere. Not ten minutes out of Rome, not in Milano, in Florence. Get the hell out!'

'What are you suggesting? New York?' She had said it sarcastically, but the moment she had said it, she knew, and so did he. She paused for a long moment, thinking, as he watched her, hoping, praying. Silently she nodded yes. She looked at him soberly, thinking it all out, and then slowly she got up from the bed and walked to the phone.

'What are you doing?'

The look in her eyes said that she wasn't beaten, that she

hadn't given up. That there was still hope. She wouldn't stay away for a year. She wouldn't let them drive her away from her home, from her work, from where she belonged. But she would go. For a while. If it could be arranged. There was fire in her eyes again as she picked up the phone

Chapter Eight

A long lanky blonde, with her hair falling over one eye, sat in a tiny bright yellow room pounding away at a typewriter. At her feet a small brown cocker spaniel slept, and spread around the room were books, plants, and mountains of papers. Seven or eight coffee cups lay empty and overturned, having been checked out by the dog, and tacked over the window was a poster of San Francisco. She called it her view. It was clearly the den of a writer. And the framed covers of her last five books hung crookedly on the far wall, scattered among equally askew photographs of a yacht moored in Monte Carlo, two children on a beach in Honolulu, a president, a prince, and a baby. All of it related somehow to publishing, lovers, or friends, except for the baby, which was hers. The date on the photograph went back five years.

The spaniel stirred lazily in the winter heat of the New York apartment, and the woman at the typewriter stretched her bare feet and reached down absentmindedly to stroke the dog.

'Hang in, Ashley. I'm almost through.' She grabbed a black pen and made a few hasty corrections with a long slender hand, bare of rings. The voice in which she had spoken to the dog was decidedly southern. Savannah. It was a voice reminiscent of plantations and parties, elegant drawing rooms of the Deep South. It was the voice of gentility. A lady. 'Goddamn!' She grabbed at the pen again, crossed out half a page and scrambled frantically on the floor for two pages she hadn't seen in an hour. They were there somewhere. Reworked, taped, patched. And, of course, essential. She was rewriting a book.

At thirty she still had the same shape she'd had when she'd come to New York at nineteen to model, despite her family's violent protests. She'd hung in for a year, hating it, but admitting it to no one, except her beloved room-mate from Rome, who had come to the States for a year to study American design. Like Natasha, Isabella had come to New York for a year. But Natasha had taken a year off from college to try and make it on her own. It was not what her parents had had in mind for her. Rich in artistic southern ancestry and poor in cold cash, they wanted her to finish school and marry a nice southern boy, which was not what Natasha had in mind.

At nineteen all she had wanted was to get out of the South, get to New York, make money, and be free. And she had. She'd made money as a model and then as a free-lance writer. She'd even been free, for a while. Until she met and married John Walker, theatre critic. A year later they had had a child and a year after that, they'd had a divorce. All she had left was a great body, a sensational face, a talent for writing, and a fifteen-month-old child. And five years later she had written five novels and two movies, and in the literary world she was a star.

She had moved to a large comfortable co-op on Park Avenue, put her son in a private school, hired a housekeeper, invested her money and Natasha Walker was having a ball. Having acquired success to add to her beauty, Natasha had it all.

'Mrs. Walker?' There was a soft knock on her door.

'Not now, Hattie, I'm working.' Natasha pushed the long blonde hair out of her eyes and began to sift through the pile of papers again.

'Are you sure? There's a phone call. I think it's important.'

'Take my word for it. It's not.'

'But they said it's from Rome.'

The door was opened before Hattie could add another word to her exhortation. There was no longer any need. Natasha marched across the kitchen, her bare feet long and slender on the bright yellow floor, her tight jeans showing her hip bones, the man's shirt she wore tied just beneath her small breasts.

'Why didn't you tell me it was Rome?' She looked reproachfully at the black woman with the soft, curly grey hair and then flashed her a quick smile. 'Don't worry about it. I know what a pain in the ass I am when I'm working. Just don't go in there. No clean coffee cups, no plant watering, nothing. I need the mess.' Hattie made a mock-frown at the familiar refrain and disappeared down a bright, sunny hall to the bedrooms as Natasha grabbed the phone. 'Yes?'

'Signora Natasha Walker?'

'Yes.'

'We have a communication to you from Roma. One instant, if you please.' Natasha sat very still and waited. She hadn't spoken to Isabella since she'd first heard the news. She had wanted to fly to Rome for the funeral. But Isabella hadn't wanted her to. She had asked her to wait. She had written, and waited, but for the first time in the eleven years of their friendship, there had been no answers, no news. It had been four months since Amadeo had been murdered, and she had never felt as cut off from Isabella since the day she had left the apartment they'd shared for a year and gone back to Rome. She hadn't written during those first few months either, but that was because she'd been so busy with her designing, and then so much in love. So much in love – Natasha could still remember the excitement in Isabella's letters when she had written to tell her: '. . . and he's marvellous . . . and I love him . . . so handsome . . . so tall and blond and I'll work for him at San Gregorio, doing real couture . . .' The joy and the excitement had gone on for years. It had been a permanent honeymoon with those two. And then suddenly he was dead. Natasha had sat in shock and horrified silence when she'd heard the story on the six o'clock news.

'Signora Walker?'

'Yes, yes, I'm here.'

'We have your party.'

'Natasha?' Isabella's voice was strangely subdued.

'Why the hell haven't you answered my letters?'

'I . . . don't know, Natasha . . . I didn't know what to say.'

Natasha frowned and then nodded. 'I've been worried about you. Are you all right?' The concern in her voice travelled five thousand miles to greet Isabella, who brushed the tears from her eyes and almost smiled.

'I suppose so. I need a favour.' It was always like that with them. They could pick up where they had left off, not speak to each other for six months, then instantly be sisters again when they met or spoke. It was one of those rare friendships that could always be put down without cooling off.

'Name it,' Natasha said.

Isabella briefly explained what had happened with Alessandro that day – or what hadn't, but could have. 'I can't bear it anymore. Not like this,' she said. 'I can't take a chance with him.'

Thinking of her own child, Natasha felt a tremor just listening to the story. 'No one could. Do you want to send him to me?' Their sons were within four months of the same age, and Natasha was not one to be undone by an additional child. 'Jason would love it,' she added. 'He keeps bitching me about not having a brother. Besides, they're two of a kind.' A year before, when they'd all met to

93

go skiing in Saint Moritz, the two boys had amused themselves by cutting off each other's hair. 'I'm serious, Isabella. I think you should get him out of Rome.'

'I agree.' There was a fraction of a pause. 'How would you feel about having a room-mate again?' She waited, not knowing what Natasha would say, but her answer was instant. It took the form of a long, delighted, southern little-girl squeal. Isabella suddenly found herself laughing.

'I'd love it. Are you serious?'

'Very. Bernardo and I have come to the conclusion that there's no other way. Just for a while. Not permanently of course. And, Natasha' – she paused, wondering how to explain that she was not just getting away – 'it may be awkward. I'll have to stay hidden. I won't want anyone to know where I am.'

'That's going to be a bitch. You won't be able to set foot out of the apartment.'

'Do you really think people there would know my face?'

'Are you serious? Not the construction workers going to work on the subway maybe, but just about everyone else. Besides, if you do a disappearing act in Rome, it'll be in the papers all over the world.'

'Then I'll just have to stay hidden.'

'Can you live with that?' Natasha had her doubts.

'I have no choice. For the moment anyway. This is what I have to do.'

Natasha had always admired her sense of duty, her courage, her style.

'But you're sure you can stand living with me? I could stay somewhere else,' Isabella said.

'The hell you will. If you stay anywhere else, I'll never speak to you again! How soon are you coming?'

'I don't know. I've only just made the decision. It will take time to work it out at the office. I'm going to have to continue to run San Gregorio from wherever I am.

Natasha let out a long slow whistle in answer. 'How the hell are you going to manage that?'

'We'll just have to work it out. Poor Bernardo, as usual, will wind up with the brunt of the work. But I can talk to him by phone every day if I have to, and we have a New York office for our representative there. I can call in without telling them I'm in New York. I think it can be done.'

'If it can, then you'll do it. And if it can't, you'll do it anyway.'

'I wish I felt as sure. I hate leaving the business here. Oh, Natasha . . .' She let out a long, unhappy sigh. 'It's been such an awful time. I don't even feel like me anymore.'

Natasha didn't say it, but Isabella didn't sound like herself either. The past four months had obviously taken a hell of a toll.

'I feel like a machine,' Isabella went on. 'I just manage to get through the days, killing myself in the office and playing with Alessandro when I can. But I keep . . . I keep thinking . . .' Natasha could hear her friend's voice crack at the other end of the line. 'I keep thinking he'll come home again. That he's not really gone.'

'I think that's what happens when somebody we love disappears suddenly like that. You don't have time to absorb it, to understand.'

'I don't understand anything anymore.'

'You don't have to.' Natasha's voice was gentle. 'Just come home.' There were tears in her own eyes now as she thought of her friend. 'You should have let me come to Rome four months ago. I'd have brought you back then.'

'I wouldn't have gone.'

'Yes, you would. I'm six inches taller than you are, remember?'

Suddenly Isabella laughed. It would be lovely to see

95

Natasha again. And maybe it would even be fun to go to New York. Fun! What an insane thing to think about after all that had happened in the past four months.

'Seriously, how soon do you think you can make it?' Natasha was already making rapid calculations and had started to scribble notes. 'Do you want to send Alessandro on ahead? Or do you want me to come and get him now?'

For a moment Isabella considered it but she said, 'No. I'll bring him with me. I'm not going to let him out of my sight.' As she listened Natasha began to wonder what kind of effect all this was having on the boy, but it was not the moment to ask and Isabella had already gone on. 'Remember, don't say anything to anyone about this. And Natasha . . . thank you.'

'Go to hell, spaghetti face.'

Spaghetti face – Natasha's pet name for her, one Isabella hadn't heard in years. As she said good-bye she realised that for the first time in months she was laughing. She hung up the phone and looked up to see Bernardo, his face a study in anxiety and strain. She had forgotten he was there.

'I'm going.'

'How soon?'

'As soon as we can work it out at the office. What do you think? A few weeks?' She looked at him, her mind suddenly beginning to whirl. Was it even possible? Could it be done? Could she run the business from her hiding place with Natasha in New York?

But Bernardo was nodding. 'Yes. We'll get you out of here in the next few weeks.' And with that he took a pad of paper from the desk in her bedroom, and they began to map out a plan.

Chapter Nine

For the next three weeks, the phone calls flew between New York and Rome. Did Isabella want one phone line or two? Would Alessandro go to school? Was she bringing guards?

Isabella laughed and threw up her hands. Amadeo had once declared that Natasha could build a bridge, run a country, or win a war without so much as smudging her manicure. Now Isabella decided he had been right.

Two phones, Isabella decreed. She would decide later whether or not to send Alessandro to school. And no, there was no need for bodyguards. Park Avenue co-ops were veritable fortresses of security these days, and Natasha's was one of the most well guarded in New York.

Isabella's plans for departure were equally well guarded. No general had ever mapped a campaign as thoroughly or as secretly as she and Bernardo had planned for the escape of the San Gregorios. No one, not even the highest echelon of San Gregorio, knew her destination; most did not even know she was leaving at all. It had to be that way. Everything had to be a secret. For her sake and the sake of the child.

She would simply disappear. Rumour would whisper that she was hiding in the penthouse above her offices. Just Isabella, alone with the child. Meals were to be sent up, empty plates returned; laundry would come and go. There was in fact to be a tenant in that apartment; Livia, Amadeo's trusted secretary, had volunteered to closet herself there, making the appropriate noises, walking around on the creaky parquet floor. Everyone would know that someone was living there in hiding. How could anyone suspect that Isabella herself was in New York? It would work. At least for a while.

'Is everything ready?' Isabella looked up at Bernardo. He was slipping another stack of file folders into a large leather bag.

He nodded silently, and Isabella realised how drawn and tired he looked.

'I think I've got copies of every file we have,' she said. 'What about the exports to Sweden? Do you want me to sign some of that stuff now, before I go?'

She continued packing as Bernardo retreated to his office for the papers. Another leather briefcase. More files, more swatches, some of Amadeo's figures, financial sheets from their rep in the States. She had enough work to keep her busy for six months. There would be more, a constant flow of documents, files, reports, information. What could not be done by telephone, Bernardo would forward through Natasha's literary agent, addressed only to Mrs Walker. Isabella focused on the plan, the work to be done. To think why she was packing, to admit she was leaving, was more than she could bear.

Bernardo was back in a moment with the papers. Isabella uncapped the gold Tiffany pen that had been Amadeo's and signed her name.

'You know, I don't suppose this is the time or the place for it, but I still wish you'd consider that idea,' Bernardo said.

'What idea?' Isabella looked at him stupidly. She could hardly think anymore. She had too much on her mind.

'The IHI–F-B takeover. Maybe eventually in New York you could meet with them.'

'No, Bernardo. And I'm telling you that for the last time.' She didn't want even to argue about it anymore.

And now she didn't have the time. 'I thought you promised me you wouldn't bring that up again.'

'All right. All right.' In a way she was right. They had too much else to tackle right now. Later. They could always discuss it later when she had tired of trying to run the business from five thousand miles away. The thought stopped him. Who would have believed six months ago that Amadeo would be dead, Isabella in hiding, and he, Bernardo, alone? He felt a wave of desolation wash over him as he watched her lock the last case. He was remembering the summer they had all gone to Rapallo. Amadeo had counted Isabella's seventeen bags – table linens, sheets, bathing suits . . . hat boxes, one suitcase just for shoes. But this was not going to Rapallo. This was a whole other life – a life begun with two briefcases, one bag for Isabella's clothes, and another for Alessandro's.

'Alessandro will be heartbroken we're not taking his bike,' Isabella said suddenly, interrupting his thoughts.

'I'll send him one in New York. A better one.' God, how he was going to miss the child. And Isabella too. It would be strange not having her near. No shouting matches, no onyx eyes burning into his. His ulcer relied on her, and so did he.

'We'll be back very shortly, Nardo. I don't think I'll be able to stand this for very long.'

She stood up again, looking around her office, wondering what she'd forgotten, opening her file cabinet for a last time as Bernardo watched her, silent. She glanced over her shoulder at him with a tired half-smile. 'Listen, why don't you go home and get some sleep? It's going to be a long night.'

'Yeah, I suppose. I . . . Isabella . . .' There was an odd catch in his voice as slowly she turned around. 'I'm going to miss you. And the boy.' The look in his eyes was the first hint of his real feelings since Christmas.

'We'll miss you too.' Her voice was muffled as she held out her arms, and they hugged in the familiar room. How soon would she see it again? Or him? 'But we'll be back. Soon too! You'll see.'

'*Ecco*.' There were tears in his eyes, which he blinked back as she stepped aside. It was one thing to hide his feelings and quite another not to be near her at all. He already ached at the loss of her, but it was the only way. For her sake and the boy's.

'Now go home and get some sleep.'

'Is that an order?'

'Of course.' She grinned lopsidedly at him and slid into a chair. 'What a hell of a time of year to go to the Riviera.' She tried to look bored and nonchalant as he laughed from the door. That was the plan they had. He would drive her across the border into France, across the Riviera to Nice, where she would take a morning flight to London, and from there the change of guards and on to New York. Most likely she and Alessandro would be in transit for almost twenty-four hours.

'Is there anything I should bring tonight for Alessandro? Some cookies? A game?'

'Cookies are always a great idea, but maybe a blanket and a small pillow. And some milk.'

'Anything else? For you?'

'Just be there, Nardo. And pray we'll all be safe.' He nodded soberly, pulled the door open, and was gone. He prayed not only that she would leave safely, but that she would return safely, and soon as well. And that she would return to him.

Chapter Ten

'Mamma, can you tell me a story?'

Isabella perched on the edge of Alessandro's bed. A story . . . a story . . . she could barely think tonight, let alone weave elaborate tales.

'Please?'

'All right, let's see.' Her brow puckered into a frown as she looked at him, her long elegant fingers clasping his tiny white hand. 'Once upon a time there was a little boy. He lived with his mother, and – '

'Didn't he have a daddy?'

'Not anymore.'

Alessandro nodded, understanding, and settled into his bed. She told him of the place where the boy lived with his mother and all the friends that they had, people who loved them, and a few who did not.

'What did they do?' He was beginning to like the story; it had a believable ring.

'About what?' It was easy to distract her, she had a thousand things on her mind.

'What did they do about the people who didn't like them?'

'They ignored them. And you know what else they did?' She lowered her voice conspiratorially. 'They ran away.'

'They did? That's terrible!' Alessandro looked shocked. 'Papa always said it was wrong to run away. Except when you absolutely have to, like from a lion or a very bad dog.'

She wanted to tell him that some people were like dogs but she wasn't quite sure what to say. She looked down at him pensively; his hand was still in hers.

'What if running away made them safer? If it kept them from being bothered by lions and bad dogs? And what if they went to a wonderful place where they could be happy again? Wouldn't that be all right?' She found as she looked at him she had a great deal to say.

'I guess so. But is there a place like that? Where everyone is safe?'

'Maybe. But you're safe anyway, my darling. You know that. I won't ever let anything happen to you.'

He looked up at her worriedly. 'But what about you?' He still had nightmares about it. If they had got his Papa, couldn't they also take his Mamma? It was useless to tell him over and over again they could not. If not, why would they have a houseful of bodyguards? Alessandro was nobody's fool.

'Nothing will happen to me either. I promise you.'

'Mamma . . .'

'What?'

'Why don't we run away?'

'If we did, wouldn't it make you sad? There'd be no Mamma Teresa, no Enzo, no Luisa . . .' *No carousel, no bicycle, no Rome. No reminders of Amadeo . . .*

'But you'd be there!' He looked enchanted.

'Would that be enough?' She was amused.

'Sure!'

His gentle smile gave her the courage to continue the story, the tale of the little boy and his mother who found a new home in a new land, where they were magically safe and they had new friends.

'Did they stay there forever?'

She looked at him for a long moment. 'I'm not sure, I think they went home again. Eventually.'

'Why?' It seemed a ridiculous idea to him.

'Maybe because home is always home, no matter how difficult it is.'

'I think that's stupid.'

'Wouldn't you want to come home if you went away?' She looked at him in astonishment, surprised by what he had said.

'Not if bad things had happened there.'

'Like here?'

He nodded silently. 'They killed my Papa here. They're bad people.'

'Everyone didn't do it, Alessandro. Just one or two very bad men.'

'Then how come no one found them, to punish them, or hurt them, or spank them?' He looked at her woefully, and she pulled him gently into her arms.

'Maybe they will.'

'I don't care. I want to run away. With you.' He snuggled closer to her, and she felt the warmth of him in her arms. It was the only warmth she felt these days now that Amadeo was gone.

'Maybe one day – we'll run away to Africa together, and live in a tree.'

'Ooooohhh, I'd like that! Can we? Can we please?'

'No, of course not. Besides, you couldn't sleep in your nice cosy bed in a tree. Could you?'

'I guess not.' He gazed at her softly for a long moment, then smiled and patted her hand. 'It was a good story.'

'Thank you. By the way, did I tell you today how much I love you?' She was leaning toward him and whispering in his ear.

'I love you too.'

'Good. Go to sleep now, darling. I'll see you soon.'

Very soon. In seven hours. She tucked him tightly and closed the door softly as she walked into the long mirrored hall.

The evening was an agony of waiting. She sat in the living room, going over some papers and watching the

Fabergé clock crawl slowly toward eight. At eight o'clock dinner was served in the dining room, and she ate as always, quickly and alone. By twenty to nine she was back in her room again, staring out the window, at herself in the mirror, at the phone. She could do nothing until all was quiet. She didn't even dare go back to the hall. She sat there alone for three hours, thinking, waiting, looking outside. From her bedroom window she could see the carousel in the garden, the kitchen windows, the dining room, and the little study Amadeo had used to do paperwork at home. By midnight every window in the house had been darkened, except her own. She crept out stealthily to a locked closet at the end of the long hall, opened the door quickly, glanced inside and pulled out two large Gucci bags. There were a soft chocolate leather with the classic green and red stripe. She looked at them, wondering. How could you pack a whole lifetime into two bags?

Back in her room she locked the door, pulled the shades, and opened her closet, looking things over without making a sound. And then quickly she pulled trousers from the hangers, cashmere sweaters from the specially made silk-lined plastic bags. Handbags, stockings, underwear, shoes. It was easier now. Everything she wore these days was still black. It took her exactly half an hour to pack three skirts, seven sweaters, six black wool dresses, and one suit. Black loafers, five pairs of high heels, one pair of black suede-and-satin evening shoes. Evening shoes? She glanced into the closet again and carefully extracted one perfectly simple. long black satin dress. She was finished in less than an hour. She went to the safe. Everything was back in its box again as it had been since Bernardo brought it all back from Paccioli, having returned Alfredo's five hundred thousand dollars. The money she had never been able to deliver to the kidnappers. The jewellery she no longer wore. But she didn't dare leave it here. What if someone broke in? If someone stole it. If! She felt like a refugee fleeing her country during a war as she emptied the green velvet boxes into satin jewellery cases and stowed them in the secret compartment of a large black alligator Hermès handbag. She would wear that over her arm on the trip. At last she swung her suitcase to the floor and slipped from the room, locking it behind her. She carried an empty suitcase down the hall to Alessandro's room, locking his door from the inside. The child was asleep, snuggled deep in his covers, one hand clutching a teddy bear, the other hanging out of the bed. She smiled at him briefly and began to empty his dresser. Warm clothes, a snowsuit, mittens and woollen caps, play clothes to wear in the apartment, and games and a few of his favourite toys. She looked around, wondering what would be most precious as she made the choice. By one thirty she was ready, the suitcases next to her, the room dim in the soft light. Bernardo would be bringing the two suitcases she had packed in the office. She was ready.

The clock on her bedtable ticked relentlessly. She had decided to wake Alessandro at one forty-five. She knew that somewhere, outside, the two guards were waiting, prepared to travel, though they had no idea where. They had been carefully screened by Bernardo and had been told to concoct a story explaining their whereabouts for the day. They would be back in Rome by the next night after depositing Isabella and Alessandro in London, where they would catch their afternoon flight.

Isabella sat breathlessly, feeling her heart pound in her chest. What was she doing? Was she right to leave? Could she really leave everything in Bernardo's hands? And why was she leaving her home?

Soundlessly she opened the door again and stepped softly outside. The house was totally silent as she drifted slowly down the hall. She still had ten minutes before she went to wake Alessandro   ten minutes to say goodbye. She found herself in the living room, glancing around in the moonlight, touching a table, staring at the empty couch. Here there had been countless parties with Amadeo, happy evenings, better days. She remembered the fuss she had made choosing the fabrics, the pieces they had bought in Paris, the clock they had lovingly brought back from New York. She wandered on then, past the dining room, to a smaller living room they had rarely used. Finally, silently, she stood in the doorway of the tiny study Amadeo had loved so much. Usually it was flooded with sunshine and daylight, filled with treasures and books and trophies and bright-flowering plants. She had made it a haven for him, and they had retreated there often, talking about business or laughing at Alessandro from the French doors that led out to the garden. It was here that they had watched him take his first steps, here that Amadeo had so often told her he loved her, here that he had now and then made love to her on the comfortable brown leather sofa and once or twice on the thickly carpeted floor. Here they had drawn the shades and the curtains, hidden and plotted and cavorted and lived – here in the room that was now so empty as she stared into it, barely daring to enter it, one hand resting on the door.

'Ciao, Amadeo, I'll be back.' It was a promise to herself, and to him, to the house, and to Rome. She crossed the carpet and stopped when she reached the desk. There was still a photograph of her there, in a silver frame that had been a gift from Bernardo. As she looked at it in the darkness she remembered the little golden Fabergé egg. She had given it to him for their anniversary, just before Alessandro was born. She fingered it gently, touched the leather on the desk, and then slowly turned. 'Ciao

Amadeo.' As she closed the door quietly behind her she whispered, 'Good-bye.'

She stood for a moment in the hallway, then walked quickly to Alessandro's room, praying he would wake easily and not cry. Briefly Isabella felt a pang. It seemed an act of cruelty to take the child without even letting Mamma Teresa say good-bye. She had cared for him lovingly, sometimes even fiercely, for all of his five years. She prayed that the woman would bear the shock of his disappearance courageously and somehow understand when she read Isabella's letter the next day.

She opened the door softly bent over him, holding him close to her, feeling his soft, purring breath on her neck.

'Alessandro, *tesòro*. It's Mamma. Darling, wake up.'

He stirred gently and shifted on to his side. She touched his face with a soft finger and kissed him on both eyes.

'Alessandro . . .'

He opened his eyes to look at her then and smiled sleepily. 'I love you.'

'I love you too. Come on, darling, wake up.'

'Isn't it night time still?' He looked at her strangely, glancing at the darkness outside.

'Yes. But we're going on an adventure. It's a secret. Just you and I.'

He stared at her with interest, eyes widening. 'Can I take my bear?'

She nodded, smiling, hoping he couldn't hear the rapid trip-hammer of her heart. 'I packed some of your toys and your games in a suitcase. Come on, sweetheart. Get up.' He sat up sleepily, rubbing his eyes, and she swung him up into her arms. 'I'll carry you.' She walked softly to the doorway, locked the door behind them, and hurried to her room, whispering to him that they mustn't talk, then sat him on her bed, removing his sleepers and dressing him in warm clothes.

'Where are we going?' He held out a foot as she put on his sock.

'It's a surprise.'

'To Africa?' He looked delighted. On with the other sock. A blue T-shirt, blue corduroy overalls. A red sweater. His shoes. 'To Africa, Mamma?'

'No, silly. Some place better than that.'

'I'm hungry. I want a glass of milk.'

'Uncle Bernardo will have milk and cookies for you in the car.'

'Is he coming too?' Alessandro looked intrigued.

'Only part of the way. The only people going all the way on our adventure are you and I.'

'Not Mamma Teresa?' He pulled away from her, and Isabella stopped. She looked him in the eye and slowly shook her head.

'No, darling, she can't come with us. We can't even say good-bye.'

'Won't she be very sad at us and hate us when we come back?'

'No. She'll understand.' At least she hoped so.

'Okay.' He sat down on the bed again, picking up his teddy bear with one hand. 'I like going places better with you anyway.' They were whispering, and Isabella smiled.

'I like going places with you too. Now are we ready?' She looked around. Everything was put away or packed. Only his sleepers lay forlornly on her bed. On her desk was a note explaining to Mamma Teresa and the housekeeper that Mr Franco had decided it would be wiser for her and the child to go out of town. They could contact Mr. Franco immediately with any problems in the house. They were not to report her disappearance or speak to the press. 'Oh, we almost forgot something.' She smiled at him as he stifled a yawn. 'Got your teddy bear?' He picked up the bear as she helped him into his coat. 'All ready?' He nodded again and took a firm grip of her hand. Suddenly, at the door, she stiffened. She could hear the grinding of the electric gates, a slow churning of gravel, and then the hushed voices of Bernardo and the two men. A moment later there was a soft knock.

'Isabella, it's me.' It was Bernardo. Alessandro let out a giggle.

'This is fun.'

She opened the door to him and saw one of the guards at his side. 'Are you ready?'

She nodded, looking at him, her eyes very wide.

'I'll carry Alessandro. Giovanni will take the bags. This is it?'

'That's everything.'

'Fine.' They were speaking in whispers. She turned off the light. The headlights of the Fiat cast a shadowed glow in the hall. Silently he picked up Alessandro as the other man took the bags. Isabella was last. She closed the door. It was over. Her good-byes had been said. She was leaving her home.

Bernardo took the wheel with one of the guards next to him. The other sat next to Isabella and Alessandro in the back seat. She glanced over her shoulder once as they pulled away. The house looked as it always had. But it was only a house now. An empty house.

Chapter Eleven

'*Va bène?*' Isabella glanced over at Bernardo. They had been driving for hours, racing through the night. 'Aren't you tired?'

He shook his head. He was too nervous to think of his own weariness. The sun would be up in an hour, and he wanted to cross the border before daybreak. For the first time he regretted taking his Fiat and longed for Amadeo's Ferrari. As it was, he had been going ninety-five miles an hour, but he could have used some extra speed now. In normal hours the customs men might connect the name on her passport with her face and call the newspapers.

'How much longer?' Isabella said.

'Another hour. Maybe two.' The guard said nothing. Alessandro was sound asleep on her lap. Bernardo had passed him some milk and the cookies; he had munched them happily, had two sips of milk, and passed out.

It was almost sun-up when Bernardo finally ground to a halt. Two customs booths sat stolidly on either side of the border. One Italian, the other French. They inched to the gate on the Italian side and honked.

'*Buon giorno.*' Bernardo looked pleasantly at the uniformed guard and handed him five passports. The man in uniform stared disinterestedly at the car. He held the passports in his hand and then motioned to Bernardo to open the trunk. He hopped out of the car, unlocked it, revealing Isabella's four bags, two filled with papers, the other two with clothes.

'Just your belongings?' Bernardo nodded. 'You're going to France?'

'Yes.'

'For how long?'

'A couple of days.'

The official nodded, still holding the passports in one hand he began to open the first one, which belonged to one of the guards, as Bernardo prayed fervently that he wasn't a man who was abreast of the news. The name of San Gregorio was more familiar now than it had ever been. But they were both startled by a sudden honking as two trucks pulled up right behind the car. The customs man made an impatient gesture, and the first truck driver used an arm and a fist to express something crude. With that the officer slapped shut the passport, shoved them all at Bernardo, and waved them back into his car. '*Ècco*. Have a good trip.' He marched off toward the truck driver with a look of repressed fury. Gratefully Bernardo started the car.

'What happened? What did he say?' Isabella was looking at him anxiously from the back seat. He smiled. 'He said have a good trip.'

'Did he say anything about my passport?'

'Nope. That jerk behind us did us a big favour. I'm so happy, I'd give him a kiss.' The two guards smiled in spite of themselves as they rolled quietly across the border and once again stopped. 'He made a rude gesture at the customs guy, and he lost interest in us,' Bernardo explained.

'Now what?' Isabella looked nervously at the man walking towards them in dark blue.

'The French customs man stamps our passports, and we're off.' Bernardo rolled down the window and once again smiled.

'Bonjour, messieurs, madame.' He smiled benignly at them, glanced appreciatively at Isabella and briefly at the child. Isabella found herself staring at the red trim on his uniform and wishing herself miles away. 'A holiday? Or business?'

'A little of both.' There was no other way to explain the two suitcases crammed with papers, in case they were inspected. 'My sister, our cousins, and my nephew. Family business.'

'I see.'

He took the passports from Bernardo. Isabella held Alessandro very tight.

'You will be staying long in France?'

'Only a few days.' It didn't matter what he told him; they would all be returning by different ways – and Isabella and Alessandro not at all.

'Anything in the trunk? Food? Plants? Seeds? Potatoes?'

Oh, Christ. 'No, only our luggage.' Bernardo made to step out but the guard waved his hand.

'Not necessary. *Merci.*' He went to the window, picked up his stamp, flicked through the passports, and endorsed their entry, without even looking at the names. '*Bon voyage.*' He waved them on as the gate opened, and Isabella smiled at Bernardo with tears in her eyes.

'How's your ulcer?'

'Alive and kicking.'

'So is mine.' They both laughed then as Bernardo stepped hard on the accelerator.

They were in Nice by mid-morning, and Alessandro had just begun to stir. His mother, like the others, had not slept all night

'Is this Africa? Are we here yet?' He sat up with a broad sleepy smile.

'We're here, darling. But this isn't Africa. It's France.'

'Is that where we're going?' He looked disappointed. He'd been to France before, several times.

'Want some more cookies?' Bernardo glanced at him as they sped on.

'I'm not hungry.'

'Neither am I.' Isabella was quick to second his sentiments, but ten miles from the airport Bernardo stopped at a small stand. He bought them fruit and then stopped and bought four cups of coffee and a container of milk.

'Breakfast, everyone!'

The coffee did wonders for all of them. Isabella combed her hair and freshened her make-up. Only the men looked as though they'd spent the night driving, with tired eyes and dark beards.

'Now where are we going?' Alessandro was wearing a white moustache of milk, which he wiped with the teddy bear's arm.

'To the airport. I'm going to put you and your Mummy on a plane.'

'Oh, goodie!' Alessandro clapped his hands with glee as Isabella watched him. It was extraordinary, not a murmur, not a regret, not a tremor or a good-bye. He had accepted their departure and their 'adventure' like something they'd been planning for weeks. Even Bernardo was a little startled. And still more so as they said good-bye at the airport.

'Take good care of your Mamma! I'll talk to you soon on the phone.' He looked at the child tenderly, praying that he wouldn't cry. But Alessandro looked him over disapprovingly.

'They don't have phones in Africa, silly.'

'Is that where you and your Mamma are going?'

'We are.'

Bernardo ruffled the boy's hair gently and watched nervously as passengers hurried toward the plane. 'Ciao,

Isabella. Please . . . take care.'

'I will. You too. I'll talk to you as soon as we get there.'

He nodded and then took her gently into his arms. '*Addio*.' He held her longer than he should have, feeling a lump in his throat.

But she only held him tightly and looked at him soberly at last. 'Until soon, Bernardo.' She held him fiercely again for one last moment, and then with the guards walking on either side of her and the child in her arms, the long swirl of mink coat disappeared. He hadn't wanted her to wear that. Just something simple and black, one of her wool coats, but she had insisted that she might need it in New York. Isabellezza. He felt something terrible tremble within him. What if he had lost her forever? But he didn't let himself think of it further as he slowly wiped a tear away and walked out of the airport whispering, 'Good-bye.' She still had a long journey ahead of her, and he wanted to be back in Rome by that night.

Chapter Twelve

The new bodyguards were waiting as Isabella stepped into the lounge at Heathrow Airport, holding Alessandro in her arms. She felt her heart leap as she watched them move toward her. They were tall, dark, and had the wholesome look of American football players.

'Mrs. Walker?' They were referring to Natasha and the password she and Natasha had agreed on.

'Yes.' She stared at them for a moment, not knowing what to say, but the taller of them handed her a letter, written in Natasha's hand. She opened it hastily, read what it said, and put it down:

You're almost home, spaghetti face. Kiss your little clown for me and relax.

Love, N.

'Thank you. What do we do now?' They pulled out their tickets and handed hers to her. They had been instructed not to say anything in front of Isabella's men. She opened the envelope and glanced at the time. She'd have to dismiss her two men now. She turned to them, spoke to them quickly in Italian, and they rose and shook her hand. They wished her good luck, hoped she would return quickly, and then they surprised her by stooping quickly to kiss Alessandro. Tears sprang to her eyes again as they left her. She had just lost the last reminder of home. They had been in and out of the house for so many months now, it was odd to think that now they would be gone. Like Alessandro, she was getting tired. It had been a long, draining night, and a nervous morning, wondering if she would find and recognise Natasha's men and what would happen if somehow she did not.

'We'd better go now.' The first man took her arm, and she found herself being propelled toward the gate, with Alessandro still in her arms.

As they boarded the plane she found herself waiting for something ghastly to happen – a bomb scare, an explosion, someone trying to grab Alessandro . . . anything. It was like living in a nightmare; she had never felt so far from home. But the plane took off uneventfully, and at last they were in the air.

'Where are we going, Mamma?' Alessandro looked at her tiredly now, the wide brown eyes a little confused.

'To Aunt Natasha, darling. In New York.' She kissed him gently on the forehead, and with one hand in hers they both fell asleep.

She woke four hours later, when Alessandro climbed out of her arms. She gave a quick start, reached for him, then sat back with a smile. The two American bodyguards were still seated on either side. Alessandro was standing in the aisle staring at one of them.

'*Mi chiamo Alessandro, e lei?*'

The man looked at him, smiled, and put out both hands helplessly. '*No capito.*' He glanced at Isabella for help.

'He asked you your name.'

'Oh. Steve. And you're . . . Alexandro?'

'Alessandro.' He corrected sedately, a mischievous gleam in his eyes.

'Okay, Alessandro. Have you ever seen one of these?' He pulled out an American fifty-cent piece, made it disappear, then promptly removed it from one of Alessandro's ears. The boy gave a delighted squeal and clapped his hands for more. A fifty-cent piece, a nickel, a quarter, then a dime appeared and disappeared while they struck up an awkward conversation, Alessandro chattering in

Italian and the large man communicating mostly in mime.

Again Isabella closed her eyes. It had all gone smoothly so far; all she had to do now was get through customs in New York and then back to Natasha's apartment, where she would take off all her clothes, sink into a tub of warm water, and hide for the rest of her life. She felt as though she'd been wearing the same clothes for the past week.

They had dinner, watched a movie and, except for two trips to the bathroom with Alessandro, they never left their seats. When they did, both guards casually came along. But Isabella was quick to notice that no one on the plane had shown an interest. Even the stewardesses seemed unimpressed. They were listed on the manifest only as I. and A. Gregorio, S. Connally, and J. Falk. Nothing exciting about that. Her long dark mink had drawn a look of approval from the chief steward, but even that was not remarkable. On the run between London and New York, they saw plenty of mink. Had they seen some of the jewellery carefully hidden at the bottom of her handbag they might have been more impressed.

'We'll be coming into New York in about half an hour,' the man named Steve leaned over to say. He spoke in a hushed, barely audible voice, and Isabella nodded her head. 'Mrs Walker will be waiting for you on the other side of customs. We'll go with you as far as her car.'

'Thank you.'

He looked at her cautiously, as soon as she looked away. He was almost certain he'd figured it out. They'd had a case like this two years before. A woman kidnapping back her children from their father, who had absconded with them to Greece. Something about the way she clung to the boy told him that something similar had happened to her. Damn shame to do that kind of thing to a kid too. He couldn't understand these rich people sometimes, yanking kids back and forth, like some kind of a game. But she looked like a nice woman, in spite of the occasional look of panic and the frown that too often altered her face. She had probably been scared shitless that her husband would catch on to her and she'd never get the kid out of France. That was all they knew of her, that she had been arriving in London from Nice. He turned his head slightly to watch her again as the plane began to descend.

'Another potty stop, Alessandro? Customs might take a long time.' His mother rapidly translated, but the child shook his head. 'Okay. Have you ever been to New York before?' Again Isabella translated. Alessandro shook his head, adding that he had thought they were going to Africa anyway. The tall, broad-shouldered American laughed and quickly fastened the boy into the seat. But Alessandro was watching his mother now and reached for her hand. Isabella held it in her own and gazed absently at the lights on the ground. It was four thirty in the afternoon, New York time, but in early February, evening had already come.

How different it was this time. She had last been to New York two years before. With Amadeo. Generally he did the American trips without her. She had preferred going to England and France. But that last time they had come to New York together, and it had been like a dream. They had stayed at the St. Regis, dined at Caravelle, and Grenouille, and Lutece. They had gone to an enormous party for American designers, attended several black-tie dinners, taken long walks in the park. This time there would be no St. Regis, no Lutece, no quiet, shared moments. She had left him now. She couldn't even wander with her memories anymore, see him in all the familiar corners of their home. There were no familiar corners. No familiar people. Only Natasha and her child and Isabella's own. Nothing that had been a part of Amadeo's life was left to her, and she was sorry suddenly that she hadn't brought something along. Something of his, to look at and touch and remember – something to remind her of the laughter and loving in his eyes. *Isabellezza*. She could still hear him call her name.

'Mamma! Mamma!' Alessandro was tugging at her sleeve. They were already on the ground. '*Siamo qui*.' We're here.

The two men looked at her quickly. 'Shall we go?' The plane hadn't even come to a halt yet, but they were already in the aisle. The man named Steve was handing her coat to her, the other one had Alessandro in his arms. The moment the plane came to a full stop, they were propelling her into the passageway. She felt for a moment as though she were still flying, nearly lifted off the ground between them, as they hurried along. Minutes later, when they arrived at customs, the other passengers were still straggling slowly from the plane.

The customs officer motioned to Isabella to open the bags. She unlocked them, flicking all four open as the bodyguards and Alessandro stood by.

'Purpose of your visit?'

'A family trip.' The customs agent cast an eye at the men on either side.

Jesus, what if he realises . . . if he recognises my name . . .

'What are these papers?' He looked at the two overstuffed bags.

'Some work I brought along.'

'You're planning to work over here?'

'Just on some private matters. Family matters.' He glanced again at the two suitcases and then began to dig his way through her clothes. But there was very little of interest, in Alessandro's bag or hers.

'All right, go on.'

They had made it. *She* had made it. Now all they had to do was find Natasha, and they could go home. For a moment she stood there, staring blankly, wondering if something had gone wrong and then she saw her, running toward them, her long blonde hair flying, floating silkily over a lynx coat. She was running, coming toward Isabella, and then suddenly they were in each other's arms, holding each other close, with Alessandro between them. He protested and then squealed as Natasha nibbled his neck.

'Ciao, Alessandro. How've you been?' She took him quickly from Isabella into her long lanky arms, and then the two women stood facing each other as hoarsely Natasha spoke to her. 'Welcome home.' And then she turned back to Alessandro. 'Do you know how heavy you are, kiddo? How about letting him walk to the car?' But quickly Isabella shook her head. His feet had barely hit the ground since Rome. It would be too easy for someone to sweep him off his feet, to grab him; he had been in someone's arms since they began the trip.

'It's all right. I'll carry him.'

'I understand.' And then she looked at the two bodyguards. 'We're out here.' The small tightly knit group moved as one body toward the exit and then toward the car. A Rolls-Royce with a chauffeur, and licence plates with initials Isabella didn't have time to see. Before she could catch her breath, they were whisked into the leather interior, the door had closed, the bags were stored, the men had waved, and the chauffeur pulled away from the kerb.

It was only then that Isabella realised they weren't alone in the car. There was another man in the front seat. She looked suddenly as he turned his head toward them and smiled. He was handsome and blue eyed, with a young face and silvery hair.

'Oh.' Isabella made only one small sound as he turned.

But Natasha was quick to pat her hand. 'It's all right

Isabella. This is my friend, Corbett Ewing.' He nodded and extended a hand.

'I didn't mean to frighten you. I'm awfully sorry.' They shook hands, and Isabella nodded stiffly. She hadn't expected to see anyone but the driver in the car. She looked at Natasha inquiringly, but Natasha only smiled and exchanged a look with Corbett. Then Isabella understood. 'How was the trip?' It was quickly obvious that he knew only that she had arrived from Rome. His look of casual ease as he sat there told her that he knew nothing of the potential terror of the trip. For an instant, but only that, she was annoyed at Natasha for bringing him along. She didn't want to have to make polite conversation all the way into New York. But it was also obvious that he had lent them the car, and perhaps Natasha had wanted him along. They seemed to understand each other, and Isabella realised that perhaps Natasha too had been cautious and needed his strength.

Isabella smilingly made the effort. She felt that she owed it to her friend. 'The trip was fine. But I think we're both . . . a little . . .' She suddenly faltered; she was so exhausted, she could barely find her words. '. . . we're both very tired.'

'I can imagine.' He nodded again, and after a few moments he turned to the front and spoke in low tones to his driver. But Isabella's fragile beauty hadn't escaped him before he turned away.

Chapter Thirteen

The Rolls-Royce limousine pulled up sedately in front of Natasha's building as the doorman and one porter rushed instantly to their aid. Isabella stepped out, holding Alessandro tightly by the hand, a look of bewilderment on her pale, ivory face. As she stood for a moment, looking up at the building and down the long tree-lined street, it dawned on her once again how very far from home she was. In another world, another lifetime. Only the day before she had worked at San Gregorio, and lived in the villa in Rome. And now she was here, at Natasha's on Park Avenue in New York. It was six o'clock in the evening, and crowds of New Yorkers were coming home from work. It was dark and the air was chilly, but everywhere about them was a kind of excitement, a cacophony of noises, a symphony of bright lights. She had forgotten how loud and how busy New York could be, somehow madder, even more exciting than Rome. As she stood briefly on the sidewalk, watching women in jewel coloured heavy wool coats and fur hats rush past, lost in the crowds of prosperous, energetic-looking men, she suddenly wanted to go somewhere, to go for a walk, get some air. She wanted to see them, to sniff out the town, and look in the shops. It didn't matter anymore that she had hardly slept at all in almost forty hours, that she had driven and flown halfway around the world. For a moment, just a moment, she wanted to come alive again, to be one of them. Natasha watched her as the doorman removed her luggage. And from where he stood on the sidewalk, Corbett was watching her too.

'Is everything all right, Isabella?'

She looked up at him carefully. 'Yes, fine. And . . . thank you so much for the ride.'

'Not at all.' And then he turned to Natasha. 'Will you two ladies be all right now?'

'Of course.' Natasha leaned toward him and kissed him on the cheek. 'I'll call you later.'

He nodded silently, watching them hurry inside and then, lost in his own thoughts, he climbed back into his car.

Natasha and Isabella marched rapidly through the lobby and crammed into the elevator en masse as a black-uniformed man in gold braid and white gloves manoeuvred the controls and the highly polished brass gate.

'Good evening, Mrs Walker.'

'Thank you, John. Good night.'

Natasha glanced at Isabella again as she fitted her key into the lock. 'You know, for a broad who's been travelling since God knows when this morning, you don't look half bad.' Isabella smiled in answer, and a moment later Natasha had opened the door, unleashing Ashley's barking excitement, Jason's frantic greeting, and Hattie's hello. The smells and sounds of the apartment overwhelmed Isabella as she came through the door. There was none of the palatial perfection of her villa on the Via Appia Antica, yet the apartment suited Natasha to perfection. Had Isabella designed a setting to show off Natasha's striking beauty, it would have been precisely what she saw now The living room was enormous, ice-white with dollops of richly textured cream, smooth white fabrics, white leather, white walls, long mirrored panels, and much chrome. There were stark glass tables that seemed suspended in thin air, delicate lighting, a white marble fireplace, and plants that hung airily from the ceiling to the floor. The large handsome modern paintings were the only splash of bold colour in the room.

'Do you like it?'

'It's exquisite.'

'Come on. I'll give you a tour. Or are you too dead to move?' The southern drawl was as gentle as ever, like a gentle southern breeze on a warm summer night. As always it seemed incongruous with Natasha's rapid pace, her determined step, her colourful language. She seemed to embody everything New York, until you heard the soft drawl, saw the big wistful blue eyes and the long golden hair.

Isabella was suddenly smiling and she wanted to see more. Alessandro had already disappeared with Hattie and Jason, the little brown spaniel yipping at their heels.

They had just entered Natasha's bedroom. Natasha sprawled into a chair. 'You hate it? Be honest. I don't know what happened to me when I did this room.'

'I know what happened. It's a dream.' The rest of the apartment was starkly modern, but in her bedroom Natasha had gone totally wild. In the middle of the room was a richly ornate antique four-poster, draped in clouds of silky white, with cushions and ruffles and wonderful little lace pillows, and a dressing table from a Scarlett O'Hara dream. There were two blue-and-white love seats near a tiny fireplace, and near a window was a beautiful wicker chaise longue upholstered in pale blue.

'It's so wonderfully southern, Natasha. Like you.' And then the two of them laughed again, as they had an aeon ago when Natasha was nineteen and Isabella twenty-one.

'C'mon,' Natasha said, 'there's more.' The dining room was done in restrained modern splendour with an enormous glass table, chrome chairs, and sideboards of thick glass. But here again Natasha had gone silently mad. The ceiling was painted blue and had been endowed with large white summery clouds.

'It's like a trip to the beach, isn't it?' She had done the

entire apartment with panache and humour, and somehow it also managed to look both spectacular and welcoming at the same time. A warm, cosy den managed to combine both modern wonders and old, coppers, velvets, more modern art, and a brightly crackling fire.

They peered briefly into Natasha's office and the large friendly kitchen with the bright yellow floor. Then Natasha looked at her, smiling, her eyes dancing for a moment as she stepped to one side. 'And if you'll walk down that hall, Isabella, I have a surprise.'

A month before it had been an empty maid's room, crammed with boxes and old skis. But after Isabella's first phone call Natasha had set to work with a vengeance. Now, as she swung open the door, she almost crowed at the look in Isabella's eyes. She herself had bought yards of fabric, a delicate rose silk a decorator friend had just brought back from France. With staples and tacks and delicate trimming, she had covered the walls in soft pink. A tiny French desk stood in the corner with a perfect little chair covered in the same rose. Some bookshelves, some plants, a beautiful little Oriental carpet in pale greens woven with shades of raspberry and the same dusty rose as the walls. There were two beautiful brass lamps on the desk and the table, a file cabinet she'd found that was actually covered in wood, and a tiny settee that had been irresistible, covered in velvet with cushions of the rose silk.

'My God, it almost looks like my boudoir.' Isabella stared at her and almost gasped.

'Not quite. But I tried.'

'Oh, Natasha, you didn't. How could you?'

'Why not? The phone has two lines. The file cabinet is empty. And I'll share my typist with you if you're very, very nice.' There was everything. Everything she could have possibly wanted. And more than that: there was a look to it, of something familiar, something warm, something from home. There were tears in her eyes again as she stared at it.

'You are truly the most extraordinary woman I know.'

Natasha squeezed Isabella's shoulders and walked back out to the hall. 'Now that you've seen your office, I'll show you your bedroom, but it's not quite so grand.'

'How could it be? Oh, Natasha, you're amazing.' Isabella was still speechless as they marched back down the main hallway the way they had come. On the way they passed Jason's room, where the boys were already tearing apart Alessandro's suitcase while Hattie ran a bath.

'*Va bène, tesòro?*' she called out to Alessandro from the door.

'*Sì, ciao!*' He waved happily at her and disappeared under the bed with Jason to go after the dog.

'You think your dog will survive?'

'Don't worry. Ashley's used to it. Here we are.' She opened the door and stepped in ahead of Isabella. The room was not as frilly as Natasha's nor as starkly modern as the rest of the house. It was warm and cosy and pleasant, done in rich bottle greens and antique French rugs. There were narrow glass tables and a dark green velvet chair. The bedspread was done in the same heavy velvet, and on the foot of the bed was a length of dark fur, folded neatly, like something from a baronial manor in a distant wintry land. A fire was burning in the marble fireplace. Dark red roses stood in a cut-crystal vase on a low table. In the corner was an armoire with magnificently panelled malachite doors.

'My God, that's a beauty. Where did you ever find that?'

'In Florence. Last year. Aren't royalties wonderful, Isabella? It's amazing what they can do for a girl.' Isabella sat down on the bed, and Natasha in the green velvet chair.

'Are you all right, Isabella?'

'I am.' She stared at the fire and for a moment she let her mind drift back to Rome.

'How was it?'

'Leaving? Difficult. Frightening. I was afraid every mile of the trip. I kept thinking something would happen. Someone would recognise us and find me out. I kept thinking . . . I worry about Alessandro . . . I suppose we couldn't have stayed in Rome.' For a moment, seeing Natasha so comfortable in her surroundings, she had longed for her own home in Rome.

'You'll go back.'

Isabella nodded silently in answer and then sought her friend's eyes. 'I don't know what to do without Amadeo. I keep thinking he'll come home. But he doesn't. He . . . it's hard to explain what it's like.' But she didn't have to. The pain of it was clearly carved in her heart, her soul, and her eyes.

'I suppose I can't really imagine,' Natasha said. 'But . . . you have to hold on to the good thoughts, the happy memories, the precious moments that make up a lifetime, and let the rest go.'

'How?' Isabella's eyes shot straight into hers. 'How do you forget a voice on a phone? A moment? An eternity of waiting, of not knowing, and then . . . How do you pick up the pieces, make it mean something again? How do you give a damn about anything, even your work?'

Before Natasha could answer, Alessandro and the puppy bounded in the door. 'He has a train! A real one! Just like the one Papa took me to see in Rome! Want to see it?' He was beckoning from the doorway, Ashley nibbling at his toes.

'In a minute, darling. Aunt Natasha and I want to talk for a while.'

Alessandro dashed off; Natasha watched him dart away. then answered the question.

'Alessandro, Isabella. Maybe that's all you hang on to for now. The rest will begin to fade in time. Not the good stuff, just the pain. It has to. You can't wear it for a lifetime, like five years ago's dress!'

Isabella laughed at the comparison. 'Are you suggesting I'm out of fashion?'

'Hardly.' The two women exchanged a smile. 'But you know what I mean.'

'*Ècco.* But, oh, Natasha, I feel so old. And there's so much I must do. If I can even manage to do it from here. God only knows how I'll cope with Bernardo from five thousand miles and over the phone.' She didn't want to explain the difficulties of their situation, but it all showed in her eyes.

'You'll do it. I'm sure.'

'And you don't mind too terribly much having a roommate?'

'I told you. It'll be like old times.'

But not quite, and they both knew it. In the old days they had gone out together, to restaurants, to operas, to plays. They had seen friends, met men, given parties. This was a very different time. Isabella would be going nowhere, except if it seemed safe for her to do so. Maybe, Natasha thought, they could go for a walk in the park. She had already cancelled most of her engagements for the next three weeks. Isabella didn't need to see her running in and out, going to cocktails, benefits, and all the latest shows. It startled her when Isabella spoke.

'I made a decision when we arrived tonight.' For a moment Isabella looked at her with a hint of laughter lurking in her eyes.

'What's that?'

'I'm going out tomorrow, Natasha.'

'No, you're not.'

'I have to. I can't live caged up here. I need to walk, to

get air, to see people. I watched them tonight as we drove through the city and pulled up at your door. I have to see them, Natasha. I have to know them and feel them and watch them. How can I make sensible decisions about my business if I live in a cocoon?'

'You could make the right decisions about fashion if you were locked in a bathroom for ten years.'

'I doubt that.'

'I don't.' For a moment there was war in Natasha's blue eyes. 'We'll see.'

'Yes, Natasha, we will.'

But as she said it she came alive again, and although it worried her, Natasha was relieved as she wandered back to her bedroom. Isabella di San Gregorio was not gone at all. At first she'd been worried, she wasn't sure how much of her friend had survived the ordeal. Now she knew. There was still fight there, and anger, and bitterness, and fear. But there was fire and life, and the diamond glints were still shining in the brilliant onyx eyes.

Having ascertained that the boys were surviving, she walked back to Isabella's bedroom to offer her dinner after she bathed and changed her clothes, but she only smiled as she stood in the doorway. Sprawled out on the green velvet bedspread, Isabella was dead to the world. Natasha pulled the fur cover over her, whispered 'Welcome home,' turned off the lights, and softly closed the door.

Chapter Fourteen

Wrapped in a blue velvet robe with a tall mandarin collar, Isabella wandered sleepily into the hall. It was very early. A wintery dawn sun cast shimmering daggers across the skyscrapers of New York. She stood at the living room window for a moment, thinking of the city that lay at her feet – a city that drew the successful, the dynamic, the fiercely competitive, and those destined to win. A city for people like Natasha – and she had to admit, for herself. But it was not the city Isabella would have chosen; it lacked the decadence, the laughter, and sheer charm of Rome. Yet it had something else; it shone brightly like a river of diamonds, and she watched as it seemed to beckon to her.

She walked softly into the kitchen, opened the cupboards, and found the makings of what Natasha called coffee. It was not what she would have served at home. But once she had made it, it was pungent and familiar and reminded her of their life together twelve years before. Scents always did that for her – one fragrance, a distant aroma, and she could see again all that she had long ago seen: a room, a friend, a moment, a date with a long-forgotten man. But this was no time for dreaming. She glanced at the kitchen clock and knew that her day had begun. It was six thirty in the morning. And six hours later than that in Rome. With luck she would catch Bernardo in his office, before lunch, staggering under the weight of what lay on his shoulders now. She took the cup of coffee to her pretty little office and smiled to herself as she switched on a light. Natasha, sweet Natasha. How kind she was.

How much she had done. But the tenderness in her eyes rapidly faded as she prepared for the business at hand.

As the operator put through the connection to Italy, Isabella unzipped one of her two overstuffed bags, pulled out a thick pad and two brightly coloured pens. She had just enough time to sit down and take another sip of her coffee as the receptionist at San Gregorio answered the phone.

The operator asked for Bernardo, as nervously Isabella began to tap the soft carpet with the tips of her well-polished toenails. She was careful to keep silent so the girl at San Gregorio wouldn't have a clue as to the identity of the caller. She had time for only one hasty doodle, and then he was on the line.

'Yes?'

'*Ciao, bravo.* It's me.' *Bravo* . . . roughly translated: good guy, patient one. More than anyone the name suited him.

'It went well?'

'Perfectly.'

'How do you feel?'

'Tired. A little. Still a little in shock, I suppose. I don't think I realised till I got here just what it all means. You're just lucky I was too tired to get on the next plane for home.' She felt a wave of homesickness overwhelm her and suddenly she wanted to reach out to him.

'You're lucky. I'd have given you hell and sent you right back.' His voice sounded grave, but Isabella laughed.

'You probably would have. Anyway we're stuck with it now, this madness we've concocted. We'll just have to make the best of it for as long as I'm here. Now tell me, what happened? Everything smooth over there?'

'I just sent you a clipping from *Il Messaggero*. Everything has gone according to plan. You are now in residence, as reported, in our penthouse suite.'

'And everything else?'

'Mamma Teresa took it badly at first, but I think now she understands. She thought you should have taken her with you. But she seems resigned. How's the baby?' The baby . . . she and Amadeo hadn't called him that in two years.

'Delighted. Perfectly happy. In spite of the fact that we didn't get to Africa.' They both laughed again, and Isabella was grateful that years before they'd installed a special line. It was used only by Isabella, Amadeo, and Bernardo, and now it would guarantee them freedom. There were no extensions where anyone could listen from anywhere in the house. 'Anyway now tell me. What's cooking? Phone calls? Messages? New orders? Any last-minute problems with the summer line?' It was to be unveiled soon. It was a hell of a time for Isabella to disappear.

'Nothing drastic has happened, except with the red fabric you ordered from Hong Kong.'

'What about it?' Her toes tensed as they played with the phone line snaking beneath her desk on the floor. 'They told me last week there was no problem.'

'They lied to you. They can't deliver.'

'What?' Her voice would have carried throughout the apartment, except that she had the foresight to close the door. 'Tell those bastards they can't do that. I won't buy from them again. Oh, Christ . . . no, never mind. I'll call them – dammit, I can't. It's thirteen hours later than here. But I can call them in twelve hours. I'll call them tonight.'

'You'd better work out some alternatives. Isn't there anything we can use here in Rome?'

'Nothing. Unless we use the purple from last season instead of the red.'

'Will that work?'

'I'll have to talk to Gabriela. I don't know. I'll have to see how that fits with the rest of the line.'

She knew instantly that it would create a whole different look for them. She had wanted a summer of primary colours this year. Bright shining blues, sunny yellows, the Hong Kong red, and plenty of white. If they used the purple, she'd need greens, oranges, maybe some of the yellow, only a little red. 'It changes the whole balance,' she said.

'Yes. But can it be done?'

She wanted to scream at him, 'Yes, but not from here!' 'What I'd like to know is how you can tell me nothing drastic has happened? The Hong Kong red is drastic.'

'Why don't you replace it with something from the States?'

'They didn't have anything I wanted. Never mind. I'll work it out later. What else? Any other happy little titbits for me?'

'Only one.'

'They're not delivering the pale green?'

'They already did. No, this is good news.'

'For a change.' But despite the sarcasm in her voice, Isabella's face had come alive. She didn't know how she'd do it, how she'd manage to make major fabric and colour changes in so little time, from so far away, but it brought her back to San Gregorio as she spoke to him. No matter where she was, she still had her business, and if she had to move mountains, she'd make the changes on time. 'So what's the good news?'

'F-B bought enough of the perfume to float the sixth fleet.'

'That's nice.'

'Don't get so excited.' Bernardo sounded like himself again. Tired, angry, annoyed.

'I won't. I'm sick of those bastards and their offers to buy us out. And don't bother me with that bullshit while I'm here.'

'I won't. What do you want me to tell Gabriela?' The chief designer was going to get ulcers when she heard the news. Changes? What changes? How can we make changes now?

'Tell her to stop everything till I call back.'

'That means when?'

'In September, darling. I'm on vacation, remember? What the hell do you think it means? I told you, I'll call Hong Kong tonight. And I'll work out alternatives today. I know every colour, every piece of fabric we have in stock.' And Bernardo knew only too well that she did.

'I assume this will affect ready-to-wear too.'

'Not so much.'

'But just enough.' His ulcer gave a familiar twinge. 'All right, all right. I'll tell her to hold it. But for God's sake, call me back.' The old irritation was back between them again. Insanely, it felt familiar and good.

'I'll call you after I talk to Hong Kong. About one o'clock.' She said it matter-of-factly, already scribbling a river of tiny well-organised notes. 'What does my mail look like?'

'There's nothing much.'

'Good.' Amadeo's secretary was answering all her mail from the top floor. 'I'll talk to you tonight. Call me if anything happens today.' But at his end Bernardo knew he would not. He could save it all till that night.

'You'll have plenty to keep you busy.'

'Mmm . . . hmm . . . I will.' He knew her well enough to know that she had already covered two sheets of her pad. 'Ciao.'

They hung up as though they were both seated in their respective offices at opposite ends of the same floor, and in her brand new office Isabella tore off her notes and spread them out before her. She had exactly twelve hours to replace that Hong Kong red. Of course there was always the chance that she could badger them into sending it, if they had it, if they could. But she knew she couldn't risk depending on them. Not anymore. She made another hasty note to herself for Bernardo. She wanted to cancel the account in Hong Kong. She had seen better fabrics in Bangkok anyway. In what concerned San Gregorio, Isabella was not one to be understanding or to be pushed around.

'You're up bright and early.'

Isabella looked up in surprise as Natasha's tousled blonde head poked throught the door. 'What happened to the days when you used to sleep till noon?'

'Jason. I had to learn to work in the daytime and sleep at night. Tell me something, do you always look like this at seven o'clock in the morning?' She was staring admiringly at the pale blue velvet dressing gown.

'Only when I go to work.' She grinned at her friend and pointed at the notes on the desk. 'I just talked to Bernardo.'

'How goes it in Rome?'

'Terrific, except I have to re-do half the summer collections before I call him back tonight.'

'Sounds like my rewrites. Jesus. Before you get started, can I fix you some eggs?'

Isabella shook her head. 'I've got to do some work on this before I eat. What about the boys? Are they up yet?'

'Are you kidding? Listen . . .' She put her finger to her lips, and they both smiled as they heard a distant shriek. 'Hattie's getting Jason dressed for school.' She looked gently at Isabella, walked into the room, and sat down. 'What are we going to do about Alessandro? Do you want him to stay home?'

'I – I don't know . . .' The clouds returned to her dark eyes as she frowned back at Natasha. 'I had planned to, but . . . I don't know. I'm not sure what to do.'

'Has anyone realised yet that you've left Rome?'

'No. Bernardo says it went perfectly. According to *Il Messaggero*, I have taken refuge at the top of the house.'

'Then there's no reason why anyone would suspect who he is. Do you suppose you could convince him not to tell anyone his last name? He could go to school with Jason and say he's our cousin from Milan. Alessandro . . .' She thought a moment. 'What about your grandfather's name?'

'Parel?'

'Parelli?' Natasha grinned at her creation. 'I spend half my life making up names. Every time I start a new novel, I start staring at the labels on anything at hand and I must have every name-the-baby book ever made. Well, how about it? Alessandro Parelli, our cousin from Milan?'

'And what about me?' Isabella was amused by her inventive friend.

'Mrs. Parelli, of course. Just give me the word and I'll call the school. As a matter of fact . . .' She looked pensive. 'I'll call Corbett and ask him if he has time to take them on his way to work.'

'Wouldn't that be something of an imposition?' Isabella looked concerned, but Natasha shook her head.

'If it were, I'd do it myself. But he loves doing things like that. He's always helping me with Jason.' She looked away for a moment, lost in her own thoughts. 'He has this thing about being helpful . . . about people who need him.' Isabella watched her, wondering if Natasha needed him enough. She seemed so independent. She would have smiled to know that it was the same thought that always crossed Corbett's mind.

'Well, if he wouldn't mind very much, it would be lovely. That way they wouldn't see me at the school.'

'That's what I was thinking.' She gnawed at a pencil. 'I'll call him.' And she disappeared before Isabella could say more. But since she had met him on the way in from the airport, Isabella had been wondering what lay between the silver-haired man and her old friend. It seemed a nice relationship, and the understanding between them was something that Isabella watched with envy now. But how serious were they? From Natasha, she knew she would gain no insight, not until she was ready to talk.

Natasha went to call Corbett and returned to say he'd be there shortly. The boys were up and tearing about.

'My God, will he be able to stand it?' Isabella winced and Natasha grinned.

'You will know how truly crazy the man is when I tell you that he'll love it. Even at this hour of the day.'

'Obviously a masochist.' But Isabella was smiling as she searched Natasha's eyes, but there was no answer there.

Natasha looked at her sympathetically in the kitchen as she made toast.

'Can you sleep today?'

'Are you kidding?' Isabella looked at her, horrified, and they both suddenly laughed. 'What about your work?'

'You'll hear me pounding away in half an hour. But not' – she grinned at her impishly – 'in anything quite as fancy as that.'

Isabella laughed. Natasha, she knew, possessed a uniform for working – jeans, sweat shirts, and woollen argyle socks. Suddenly Isabella realised she could do the same. She was suddenly invisible, non-existent, unknown.

'All right, Mrs. Parelli from Milan, I'll go call the school.' Natasha disappeared and Isabella went back to find her son.

She found him in the bedroom playing with Ashley, a big smile on his face.

'What are you so happy about?' She swept him into her arms with a kiss.

'Jason has to go to school today. I'm staying home with his train.' But Isabella plopped him back on his bed.

'Guess what? You're going to school too.'

'I am?' He stared at her in dismay. 'I can't play with the train?'

'Sure you can. When you come home. Wouldn't it be more fun to go to school with Jason than to stay here alone all day while I work?'

He thought about it for a minute and cocked his head to one side. 'Nobody will talk to me. And I can't talk to them.'

'If you go to school with Jason, pretty soon you'll be able to talk to everyone, and a lot quicker than if you sit here speaking Italian to me. What do you think?'

He nodded his head thoughtfully. 'Will it be very hard?'

'No different from your school in Rome.'

'We get to play all the time?' He looked at her delightedly, and she smiled.

'Is that all you used to do?'

'No, we had to do letters too.'

'How awful.' His expression said that he agreed. 'Do you want to go?' She wasn't sure what she'd do with him if he said no.

'Okay. I'll try it. And if I don't like it, we can both quit. Jason can stay home with me.'

'Aunt Natasha will love that. And listen, I have something to tell you.'

'What?'

'Well, it's all part of the adventure. We have to keep it a secret that we're here.'

He looked at her and then he whispered, 'Should I hide in school?'

She tried to keep her face serious and gently took his hand. 'No, silly. They'll know you're there. But . . . we don't want anyone to know who we are.'

'We don't? Why not?' He looked at her strangely, and she felt the iron mountain fall back on her heart.

'Because it's safer. Everyone thinks we're still in Rome.'

'Because of – of Papa?' His eyes were large and sorrowful now as they looked into hers.

'Yes. We're going to say that our name is Parelli. And that we're from Milan.'

'But we're not from Milano. We're from Roma.' He glared at her, annoyed. 'And we're di San Gregorio. Papa wouldn't like it if we lied about that.'

'No, and I don't like it either. But it's all part of the secret, Alessandro. We have to do it this way, but only for a little while.'

'Then can I tell them my real name at school?'

'Maybe later. But not now. Alessandro Parelli. They'll probably never even use your last name.'

'They better not. I don't like that one.' For a moment Isabella almost laughed. They'd probably call him Alessandro Spaghetti, as Natasha had done to her when they met.

'It doesn't matter what they call you, darling. You know who you are.'

'I think it's silly.' He tucked his legs under him and watched his friend. Jason was carefully tying knots in the laces of his shoes, which he had carefully put on. But on the wrong feet.

'It's not silly, Alessandro. It's necessary. And I will be very, very angry with you if you tell anyone our real name. If you do that, we'll have to go away again, and we won't be able to be with Aunt Natasha anymore, or Jason.'

'Will we have to go home?' He looked horrified. 'I haven't even used his train.'

'Then do as I tell you. I want you to promise me. Alessandro, do you promise?'

'I promise.'

'Who are you?'

He looked at her defiantly. 'I am Alessandro . . . Parelli. From Milan.'

'All right, darling. And remember that I love you. Now hurry up and get dressed.'

They could already smell Hattie making bacon in the kitchen. And Jason was staring down in confusion at his oddly clad feet.

'You have them on the wrong feet, sweetheart.' Isabella stooped down to give him a hand. 'Guess what? Alessandro is coming to school with you today.'

'He is? Oh, wow!' She explained to him about Parelli and that they were cousins from Milan. And then she remembered to tell the same thing to Alessandro.

'I'm his cousin? Why can't I say I'm his brother?' He had always liked the idea.

'Because you don't speak English, silly.'

'After I learn, then can I say that we are?'

'Never mind that. Just get your pants on. And wash your face!'

Twenty minutes later Corbett buzzed from downstairs. The boys were respectably clad in corduroy pants and sneakers with shirts and sweaters, woollen hats and warm coats. They had gobbled a quick breakfast and were off. As the door closed behind them Natasha looked at her faded T-shirt and wiped her hands on her jeans.

'Somehow I always wind up wearing whatever he was last eating. Alessandro sure looked cute.'

'He wanted to tell them he was Jason's brother.' Isabella sighed as they walked away from the door.

'Do you think he'll be able to keep his name a secret?' For a moment Natasha was worried.

'Unfortunately in the last four and a half months he has learned a great deal about secrecy, discretion, caution, and and danger. He understands that the first three are necessary to avoid the last.'

'That's quite a lesson for a five-year-old boy.'

'It is as well for a thirty-two-year-old woman,' Isabella

said, and as she watched her Natasha knew she spoke the truth.

'I hope you keep that in mind, spaghetti face. I wasn't exactly thrilled with your announcement last night that you wanted to go out. Alessandro is one thing, he's an anonymous child. There is nothing even faintly anonymous about you.'

'There could be.'

'What did you have in mind, seeing a plastic surgeon for a new face?'

'Don't be absurd. There is a way of carrying oneself when one wants to be seen. Of "being there", of commanding attention, and saying "Here I am". If I don't want to be seen, I don't have to be. I can wear a scarf, a pair of slacks, a dark coat.'

'Dark glasses, a beard, and a moustache. Right. Look, Isabella. Do me a favour. I have very delicate nerves. If you're going to start wandering around New York, I may have a nervous breakdown. In which case I won't be able to finish my rewrite, my next advance won't come in, my royalties will dry up, my publisher will can me, and my child will starve.'

But Isabella only laughed as she listened to her. 'Natasha, I adore you.'

'Then be a good friend. Stay home.'

'I can't do that. For God's sake, Natasha, if nothing else I need air.'

'I'll buy you some. I'll have it sent to your room.' She smiled, but she had never been more serious. 'If you start roaming around New York, someone will see you. A reporter, a photographer, someone who knows fashion. Christ, maybe even a reporter from *Women's Wear Daily*.'

'They're not interested in me. Only my collections.'

'Who're you kidding, darling? Not yourself, and not me.'

'We'll talk about it later.'

With the question of Isabella's venturing out still unresolved between them, they left each other for their separate worlds: Natasha, lost among her unruly papers, her many half-filled coffee cups, and her visions and characters and imaginary world; Isabella to her pad covered with minutely detailed notes, her carefully kept files, her long lists of the fabrics they currently had in stock, her swatches, her samples, her perfect memory of the summer line. Neither of them even heard the children come home at three thirty, and it was another two hours later when they met, each of them stiff, hungry, tired, in the kitchen.

'Christ, I'm hungry.' For a moment Natasha's accent seemed even more southern. Isabella looked tired, and there were soft shadows under her eyes. 'Did you eat today?'

'I didn't think to.'

'Neither did I. How'd it go?'

It had been gruelling, but she had made a contingency plan for the entire couture collection. 'I think we'll make it. We may not even have to use what I did today. But I couldn't take the chance.' She would only know for sure when she called Hong Kong at midnight.

They smiled at each other over their coffee as Natasha closed her eyes for a minute and Isabella stretched tired arms. Today had been a new experience for her. No buttons to push, no secretaries to command, no elevator to charge in and out of, investigating problems on every floor. No image to carry off, no aura, no magic, no spell. She had worn a black cashmere sweater and a well-worn pair of jeans.

'What are you doing tonight?' she asked Natasha.

'Same as you. Staying home.'

'Because you want to, or because of me?'

Isabella wondered how patient Corbett would be with Natasha's self-imposed sentence. It really wasn't fair to him.

'Don't be silly. Because I'm goddamn exhausted. And believe it or not, because I like to stay home. Besides, you're a lot more amusing than any of the invitations I've had in weeks.'

'I'm flattered.' But Isabella wasn't fooled by the blustering speech.

'Don't be. I'm surrounded by morons and bores, and people who invite me because they want to say that they know me. Ten years ago I was just another model from Georgia, and suddenly I'm 'A Novelist', 'A Writer', someone to decorate a dinner party.'

Dinner parties! Isabella had not been to one in months, and then she had never gone alone. It was never just Isabella, but Isabella and Amadeo, together. *We*, not *I*.

We were a kind of magical team, she thought. The two of us, who we were, what we were, what we looked like together. Like asparagus and hollandaise. It's difficult when you can no longer have both. Not as spicy, not as sweet . . . not as interesting . . . not as . . .

Suddenly sad again Isabella looked at Natasha with admiration – her brave friend who 'decorated' dinner parties unescorted and seemed always to have marvellous times. 'I'm nothing without him,' she whispered. 'All the excitement is gone. Everything that I was . . . that we were – '

'That's nonsense, you know. It may be lonely, but you're still what you always were. Beautiful, intelligent, an extraordinary woman, Isabella. Even alone. You were two wholes added to each other that made two and a half, not two halves that made one.'

'We were more than that, Natasha. We were one that made one. Superimposed, entwined, meshed, soldered, braided. I never quite knew where I began and he left off. And now I know . . . only too well . . .' She stared into her coffee, her voice whispery soft.

Natasha touched her hand. 'Give it time.'

But when Isabella looked up, her eyes were angry. 'Why should I? Why should I give it anything? Why did it have to happen to me?'

'It didn't happen to you, Isabella. It happened to him. You're still here, with Alessandro, with the business, with every part of you, your mind, your heart, your soul, still intact. Unless you let bitterness rob you, as you already think it has.'

'Wouldn't it do the same to you?'

'Probably. I probably wouldn't have the balls to do what you've done. To go on, to take over the business, to make it better, to keep running it even from over here. But that's not enough, Isabella. It's not enough . . . oh, God, baby, please . . . don't lose you.' Tears sprang up to her eyes as she looked at the dark-haired beauty, so tired, so suddenly bereft and alone. As long as she buried herself in her work all day, she wouldn't feel it. But sooner or later, even in the tiny maid's room office, the day had to end for her and she had to go home. Natasha understood.

Isabella stood up quietly, patted Natasha's shoulder, and walked silently back to her room. When she emerged again ten minutes later, she was wearing dark glasses, her mink coat, and another black wool hat. Natasha stopped short at the sight of her.

'Where the hell are you going?'

'Out for a walk.' It was impossible to see her eyes behind the glasses, but Natasha knew instantly that she had been crying.

For an instant the two women stood there, locked in battle without a single word. Then Natasha surrendered, overcome with sadness for her friend.

'All right. I'll go with you,' she said, 'but for chrissake, take off that coat. You look about as discreet as Greta Garbo. All you need is one of her hats.'

Tiredly Isabella grinned at her with a shrug that was pure Italian. 'This is all I brought with me, my only coat.'

'Poor little rich girl. Come on, I'll find you something.' Isabella trailed behind her as Natasha went to her closet and produced a red wool coat.

'I can't wear it. I . . . Natasha, I'm sorry . . .'

'Why not?'

'It's not black.' Natasha stared at her for a moment, not understanding, and then as she looked at her she knew. Before that she hadn't been sure.

'You're wearing mourning?' Isabella nodded. 'You can't just borrow the red coat?' The whole concept was new to her. The idea of wearing black dresses, black sweaters, black stockings. For an entire year.

'I'd feel awful.'

Natasha stared into her closet again and then muttered over her shoulder, 'Would you settle for navy blue?'

Hesitating for an instant, Isabella nodded and quietly took off the spectacular mink coat. Natasha pulled on a fox jacket, warm gloves, and a huge red fox hat. She turned to find Isabella smiling at her.

'You look marvellous.'

'So do you.'

It was amazing how she could do it. But she did. The navy blue coat was totally plain, and her black wool cap was hardly more exciting, but the ivory face and the deep set almond eyes were all she needed. She would have stopped traffic in the dead of night.

The two women left the apartment soundlessly. It was already dark outside. Natasha plunged ahead as the doorman swept open the door, and for a moment Isabella was startled by the bitter chill. She felt suddenly as though someone had punched her, hard, in the chest. She gasped for a moment and felt a crystalline haze of tears fill her eyes.

'Is it always like this in February? Somehow I only remember New York in the fall.'

'A blessed repression, my dear. Most of the time it's worse. Any place special you want to walk?'

'How about the park?' They were hurrying along Park Avenue. Natasha looked at her, shocked.

'Only if you're feeling suicidal. They have a quota to meet you know. I think it's something like thirty-nine muggings and two murders an hour.' Isabella laughed at her and suddenly felt her body come alive.

But it wasn't energy that spurred her feet forward, only tension and loneliness, and fatigue, and fear. She was so tired – of working, of travelling, of hiding, of missing him, and being brave. 'Try to be brave for just a little while longer.' She could still hear the words Amadeo had said to her when they had let him talk to her . . . that last night.

Her feet were already pounding the pavement. Natasha kept pace with her, but Isabella had forgotten she was there. '*Try to be . . . brave . . . brave . . . brave . . .*' It seemed to Isabella that they had covered miles when they finally stopped.

'Where are we?'

'Seventy-ninth Street.' They had gone eighteen blocks. 'You're not in bad shape, for an old broad. Ready to go home now?'

'Yes. But more slowly. How about walking somewhere more interesting?' They had passed block after block of buildings that looked like Natasha's, stone fortresses with awnings and doormen. Impressive but unexciting.

'We can walk over to Madison and look at the shops.' It was almost seven o'clock now. A dead hour when people were at home. That hour after work and before one went out for the evening. And it was really too cold for many

146

people to be window-shopping at night. Natasha glanced at the sky. There was a familiar chill in the air. 'I think it might snow.'

'Alessandro would love that.' They were walking slowly now, catching their breath.

'So would I.'

'You like snow?' Isabella looked at her in surprise.

'No. But it would keep you at home, without me having to run my ass off just to make sure you don't get out of line.'

Isabella laughed at her, and they walked on, past blocks of boutiques that housed delights from Cardin, Ungaro, Pierre D'Alby, and Yves Saint Laurent. There were art galleries and coiffures by Sassoon.

'Checking out the competition?' Natasha watched her, amused. Isabella was drinking it all in, her eyes sparkling with pleasure. She was a woman who loved every facet of her work.

'Why not? Their things are very pretty.'

'So are yours.'

Isabella executed a half bow as they strolled on. It was the Faubourg St.-Honoré of New York, a shimmering necklace of bright, priceless gems, strung together, enhancing each other, a myriad of treasures hidden in each block.

'You really love it, don't you?'

'What, New York?' Isabella looked surprised. She liked it. It intrigued her. But love . . . no . . . not yet. Even after her year there she had been glad to go back to Rome.

'No. Fashion. Something happens to you, just looking at clothes.'

'Aahhh . . . that.'

'Christ, I'd have gone nuts it I'd had to go on modelling.'

'That's different.' Isabella looked at her wisely, the keeper of secrets rarely bestowed.

'No, it's not.'

'Yes, it is. Modelling is like a lifetime of one-night stands. There are no love affairs, no tender lovers, no betrayals, no broken hearts, no marriages, or precious offspring. Designing is different. There is history, drama, courage, art. You love the clothes, you live with them for a while, you give birth to them, you remember their fathers, their grandfathers, the dresses of other collections, other times. There is a romance to it, an excitement, an . . .' She broke off, then laughed at herself. 'You must think I'm mad.'

'No. That's how I feel about the people in my books.'

'Nice, isn't it?' The two women looked at each other in perfect understanding.

'Very.'

They were almost home. As they rounded the corner on to Park Avenue Natasha felt the first flakes of snow.

'See, I told you. Not that I suppose that will keep you at home.' But there was no harm in this. They could walk like this in the evening. It hadn't been risky after all.

'No, it won't. I couldn't have stayed in the apartment. Not for very long.'

Natasha nodded quietly. 'I know.'

She also knew that Isabella would not be satisfied forever with a brief evening stroll.

Chapter Fifteen

'Mamma! *Guardi!* . . . It snowed!'

And indeed it had. A foot-deep blanket covered the entire surface of New York. And from the cosy warmth of the apartment all four of them watched the swirling storm. It hadn't stopped since Natasha and Isabella had returned to the apartment the evening before.

'Can we go play in it?'

Isabella glanced at Natasha, who nodded and offered to lend them the appropriate clothes. School was of course closed. The city had come to a complete stop.

'We'll go after breakfast.' Isabella glanced at her watch. And after she called Bernardo in Rome. She had reached Hong Kong too late the previous evening and she hadn't dared call him that night. She absented herself from the boys quickly, closed the door to her office, and picked up the phone.

'Where were you last night? I figured you'd call me around four.'

'How charming. My manners are not as bad as that, Bernardo. That is why I waited till this morning.'

'Kindly signora.'

'Oh, shut up.' She was smiling, and in a good mood. 'The Hong Kong fabric is hopeless. We'll have to go with the alternate plans.'

'What alternate plans?' He sounded baffled.

'Mine of course. Did you tell Gabriela to hold everything?'

'Obviously. That's what you wanted. I practically had to pick her up from a dead faint on the floor '

'Then you should thank me. In any case I worked out everything yesterday. Now, do you have pen and paper?'

'Yes, madame.'

'Good. I've got it all worked out. First the couture collection, then we'll do the rest. Starting with number twelve, the red lining is now yellow. The fabric number in our storeroom is two-seven-eight-three FBY . . . Fabia-Bernardo-Yvonne. Got that? Number sixteen, seventeen, and nineteen . . .' On she went until she had covered the entire line. Even Bernardo was stunned.

'How in God's name did you do that?'

'With difficulty. By the way, the additional pieces in the ready-to-wear collection won't cost that much more. By using fabric we've got in stock, we're saving a hell of a lot of money.'

Indeed they were, Bernardo thought with admiration. And she had spelled out every single bloody fabric. She knew every piece, every roll, the yardage available, the textures, the shades.

'And if thirty-seven in the couture line looks awful, tell her to skip it,' Isabella continued. 'We probably ought to just forget it and only leave it in as number thirty-six in the blue.'

'Which one is that?' He was overwhelmed. In a day she had done the work of a month. In one morning she had salvaged the entire summer line. Only in speaking to Gabriela again the previous evening had he realized how potentially disastrous the absence of the fabric from Hong Kong could have been.

'Never mind which one that is. Gabriela will know. What else is new?'

'Today, nothing. Everything's quiet on the home front.'

'How nice for you. In that case I'm taking a vacation today.'

'You're going out?' he sounded horrified

'Only to the park. It's snowing. Natasha and I just promised the boys.'

'Isabella, be careful.'

'Obviously. But believe me, there won't be another soul.'

'Why don't you just let Allessandro go with Natasha? You stay home.'

'Because I need some fresh air, Bernardo.'

He began to speak, but she cut him off.

'Bernardo, I love you. Now I have to go.'

She was curt, cheerful, and unnerving as she blew him a kiss and hung up the phone. He didn't like it. He didn't like it at all. There was a little too much spunk in her voice again. And at this distance he had no control. He just hoped that Natasha was smarter than Isabella and wouldn't let her go out for more than an occasional brief stroll after dark. Then he laughed to himself. There was one way to keep her out of trouble, and that was to heap more work on her, like the massive endeavour of the day before. It was inconceivable that she had actually done it.

'Are you ready?' Isabella looked at the two little boys bundled up like snowmen, Jason in a red snowsuit, Allessandro in a bright yellow spare.

They were off to the park instantly, and within half an hour the boys were sliding down little hills on Jason's sled. Slipping, whooshing, squealing along, laughing, and throwing snow. After the sledding they got into a snowball fight, and quickly Isabella and Natasha joined the fun. Only a few brave souls had been hardy enough to come out in the cold.

The four weathered it for almost two hours, and then happy and sodden they were ready to go home.

'Hot baths for everyone!' Natasha shouted as they came in the door. Hattie had hot chocolate and cinnamon toast waiting and a fire going in the den. The snowstorm continued for another day, and the boys didn't have to go to school all week as businessmen snowshoed to their offices and housewives resurrected skis to get to the store.

But for Isabella the holiday was a brief one, and after the day of sledding she returned to her office in the back of Natasha's apartment with a fresh batch of problems from Rome. Two of the more important alternate fabrics had been accidentally destroyed by a flood in the storeroom the week before. Their number-one model had quit and everything had to be fitted again. Minor problems, major headaches, disasters and victories, a month filled with a blessed mountain of work in which Isabella could hide, except for the evening walks with Natasha. They had now become a ritual without which Isabella thought she couldn't live.

'How long are you going to go on like this?' They had just stopped for a light on Madison Avenue. Isabella had been peering into boutique windows, examining the spring displays. It was March, and the last snows had finally come and gone, though it was still wintry cold and there was almost always an icy wind.

Her question caught Natasha by surprise. 'What do you mean? Go on like what?'

'Living like a hermit, baby-sitting for me? Do you realize you haven't been out once in the evening during the five weeks we've been here? Corbett must be ready to kill me by now.'

'Why should he?' Natasha looked baffled as she stared at her friend.

But Isabella was amused at her feigned innocence. She had long since understood. 'Certainly he must expect a little more of your time.'

'Not as a rule, thank you. We keep our lives very much

to ourselves.' Natasha looked faintly amused. But this time it was Isabella who stared.

'What the hell do you mean?' She wasn't angry at Isabella, just confused.

But Isabella answered with a slow smile. 'I don't expect you to be a virgin, you know, Natasha. You can be honest with me.'

'About what?' And then suddenly Natasha was grinning. 'About Corbett?' For a long moment she laughed until tears came to her eyes. 'Are you kidding? Oh, Isabella . . . did you think? . . . Oh, Jesus!' And then she looked at her friend, amused. 'I can't imagine anything less appealing to me than getting involved with Corbett Ewing.'

'Are you serious? You're not involved with him?' Isabella looked stunned. 'But I had assumed . . .' And then she looked even more puzzled. 'But why not? I thought that you two – '

'Maybe you thought, but Corbett and I never thought. We've been friends for years and we'll never be anything more. He's almost like a brother and he's my very best friend. But we're both two basically very high-powered people. As a woman, I'm not gentle enough for Corbett, not fragile or helpless enough. I don't know, I can't explain it. He always says I should have been a man.'

'How unkind.' Isabella looked disapproving.

'Doesn't Bernardo say unkind things to you?'

Isabella smiled in answer. 'At least every day.'

'Exactly. It's like brother and sister. I can't imagine anything different with Corbett.' She grinned to herself again, and Isabella shrugged, feeling a little silly.

'I must be getting old, Natasha. All my perceptions are off. I truly assumed right from the beginning . . .' But Natasha just grinned and shook her head. And Isabella was pensive for a long moment as they walked along. She was suddenly thinking of Corbett Ewing in a very different light.

They didn't speak again until they approached the building and Natasha noticed Isabella smiling as they walked along.

'You should have gone to the opera ball, you know,' Isabella said. 'It would have been fun.'

'How do you know?'

'We have a marvellous one in Rome.'

'I mean how do you know there was one here and that I was invited to it?'

'Because I'm an excellent detective and the invitation didn't quite burn.'

Suddenly there were tears in Natasha's eyes. Her lies, her 'sacrifice', had been a disservice to her friend. 'All right,' she said, throwing her arm around Isabella's shoulders and hugging her briefly. 'You win.'

'Thank you.' Isabella marched into the building with a look of victory and an awesome glint in her eye.

Chapter Sixteen

Isabella turned the light off in her office. It was eight o'clock in the evening and she had just made her last call to rome. Poor Bernardo, it was two in the morning for him, but the summer collection had just opened and she had to know how it had gone.

'Exquisite, *cara*,' he had said. 'Everyone declared it a marvel. No one understands how you could do it with the pressure you've been under, with the difficulties, with everything.' While she listened to him, her eyes had glowed.

'It didn't look too peculiar with all those new colours instead of the red?' Working this way, on paper, from a distance was a little bit like being blind.

'No, and the turquoise lining in the white evening coat was sheer genius. You should have seen the reaction of the Italian *Vogue*.'

'*Va bène*.' She was happy. He had given her every detail until at last there was nothing left that she didn't know. 'All right, darling, I guess we've done it. I'm sorry I woke you. Now go back to bed.'

'You mean you don't have any other projects for me at this hour? No frantic instructions about your new ideas for the fall?' He missed her, but his need was fading. It had been good for both of them – her escape had been an escape for him too.

'*Domani*.' Tomorrow. For a moment her eyes clouded over. The fall . . . would she have to design the collection from here then? Would she never be able to go home? Two months. It had already been two months since she had come to the States. Two months of hiding and running her business from five thousand miles, on the phone. Two months of not seeing the villa, not sleeping in her own bed. It was already April. The month of sunshine and gardens and the first burst of springtime in Rome. Even in New York the weather had been a little warmer as she had strolled every evening to the edge of the park and a few times to the East River to catch the parade of joggers and sturdy-looking little boats. The East River was not the Tiber, and New York wasn't her home. 'I'll call you in the morning,' she told Bernardo. 'And by the way, congratulations on the soap.'

'Please. Don't even mention it.' It had taken four months to do the research, another two to put it on the market. But at least it had paid off. They had just received an order for half a million dollars from F-B, of course.

Bernardo was describing the orders, but she wasn't listening. The soap. Even that reminded her of her last day with Amadeo. That fateful day when she had argued with Bernardo and then left them to run off to lunch. It had been almost seven months. Seven long, lonely, work-filled months. She dragged her attention back to Bernardo.

'What's it like in New York now by the way?' he was asking.

'Still cold, perhaps a bit warmer, but everything is still very grey. They don't see spring here until May or June.'

He didn't tell her that the garden at the villa was in full bloom. He had been there to check on things only a few days before. Instead he said, '*Bène, cara.* I'll talk to you tomorrow. And congratulations!'

She blew him a kiss and they hung up. *Congratulations.* In Rome she would have watched with terror and fascination as they opened the show. She would have stood by, breathless, suddenly unsure of the colours, the fabrics, the look, unhappy with the jewellery, the music, and the models' perfectly done hair. She would have hated every moment, until the first *mannequin* stepped on to the grey silk runway. Then, after it had begun, she would have felt the thrill of it as she did each season. The sheer excitement, the beauty, the madness of the high-fashion world. And when it was over, she and Amadeo would have winked at each other secretly from across the murderously jammed room and then found each other later for a long, happy kiss. The press would have been there, and there would have been rivers of champagne. And parties in the evening. It was like a wedding and a honeymoon four times a year.

But not this year. Tonight she was in blue jeans, in a tiny one-room office, drinking coffee, and very much alone.

She closed the door to her office and glanced at the kitchen clock as she walked past. She heard the boys in the distance and wondered why they weren't in bed. Alessandro had learned English, not perfectly, but enough to be understood. When he wasn't, he shouted to compensate for it, as though otherwise he might not be heard. The odd thing was he rarely spoke it. It was as though Alessandro needed his Italian as a reminder of home, of who he really was. She smiled to herself as she walked past their room. They were playing with Hattie, had the television going, and Jason had just set up his train.

She had missed her walk tonight. She had been too nervous, waiting to call Bernardo, wondering what had happened at the opening of the collections that day. And she was growing tired of the familiar route now anyway, even more so now that Natasha didn't always come along. She had picked up her life again, and in the evenings Isabella was often alone. Natasha was going to be out again that evening. A benefit ball.

Pausing at her own doorway, Isabella stopped for a moment and then walked slowly to the end of the hall to Natasha's door. It was nice to see her looking pretty again, wearing bright colours, doing something elegant or surprising with her long blonde hair. It brought fresh life to Isabella, so tired of looking in the mirror and seeing her own face, her dark hair pulled back, and the constant sobriety of her austere black clothes on her ever thinner form.

She knocked softly once and smiled as Natasha muttered, 'Come in.' She had long tortoise-shell hair-pins clenched in her teeth, and her hair was already swept in a swirl of loose Greek curls, which cascaded softly from a knot on the top of her head.

'That looks pretty, madame. What are you going to wear?'

'I don't know. I was going to wear the yellow one until Jason checked it out.' She groaned again as she jabbed in another of the long pins.

'Don't tell me, fingerprints?' Isabella glanced at the discarded yellow silk.

'Peanut butter with his left hand. Chocolate ice cream with his right.'

'Sounds delicious.' She was smiling again.

'Yeah, maybe, but it looks like hell.'

'What about this one?' Isabella went into her closet and came out with something familiar and pale blue. She had thought of Natasha when she bought the fabric. It was the same colour as her eyes, a kind of lavender with a bluish hint.

'That? It's gorgeous. But I never know what to wear with it.'

'What about gold?'

'Gold what?' Natasha looked at her quizzically as she finished her hair.

'Sandals. And a touch of gold in your hair.' She was staring at her as she did the models at their fittings for the collections in Rome. Eyes narrowed, feet wide apart, seeing something different than what actually was. Creating her own magic with a woman, a dress, an inspiration.

'Wait! You're going to spray my hair gold?'

Natasha shrank at the frilly white dressing-table, but Isabella ignored her and disappeared. She was back in a minute with a needle and some very fine gold thread.

'What's that?'

She threaded the needle as Natasha stared.

'Sit still.' She wove it in airily with a deftly moving hand, clipping thread, making the ends disappear, and working miracles with the needle again until it was done, creating only an impression, as though mixed in with Natasha's own hair she had grown little shimmering wisps of gold.

'There.'

Natasha stared at her reflection in astonishment and grinned.

'You're amazing. Now what?'

'A little of this.' She set down a box of powder, transparent, translucent, shimmering with tiny flecks of gold. The impression it created was one of dazzling beauty, a shining lustre to an already lovely face. Then she disappeared into Natasha's closet and came out with gold sandals with low heels. 'You'll look like a goddess when I'm through.'

Natasha was beginning to believe her as she strapped her own forgotten sandals to invisibly stockinged feet.

'Nice stockings. Where'd you get them?' Isabella looked down with interest.

'Dior.'

'Traitor.' Then, thoughtfully, 'Don't apologize. They look nicer than ours.' She made a mental note to say something to Bernardo. It was time they did something new and different about theirs. 'Now . . .' She pulled the dress out of its plastic case and grunted with satisfaction as she dropped it perfectly without disturbing a hair on Natasha's head. She zipped her up in businesslike fashion and walked around to the front, tucking, smoothing, approving. The dress was one of hers. She had done it for their spring line, only three years before. For jewellery she picked from among her own things a ring of pale mauve amethysts, edged with diamonds and set in gold. There was a pair of tiny, delicately fashioned ear-rings, and a bracelet as well. It was a remarkable set. 'Where did you ever get it?'

'Amadeo bought it for me in Venice last year. They're nineteenth century, I think. He said the stones are all imperfect, but the setting is remarkably fine.'

'Oh, Jesus, Isabella. I can't wear this. Thank you, but, darling, you're nuts.'

'You bore me. Do you want to look lovely or don't you? If not, you might as well stay here.' She closed the necklace around Natasha's throat. It fell to precisely the right depth of the necklace, sparkled dazzlingly from the pale mauve chiffon folds. 'Here, put these on yourself.' She held out the ear-rings after closing the bracelet on Natasha's wrist. 'You look marvellous.' Isabella gazed at her in sheer delight.

'I'm scared stiff. What if I lose them, for chrissake? Isabella, please!'

'I told you, you bore me. Now go out and have a good time.'

Natasha glanced in the long mirror and smiled at Isabella and her own reflection. The doorbell rang almost instantly, and a stockbroker in a dinner jacket arrived to claim his date. Isabella went to her room and waited until she heard the door close again. There had only been a soft knock before Natasha left with him, and a hastily whispered thanks.

And with that, Isabella was left with the sounds of the

boys again, and the whoosh and whistle of Jason's little toy train.

She looked at her watch half an hour later, and went to kiss them both in their bed. Alessandro looked at her strangely. '*Non esce più, Mamma?*' You don't go out any more?

'No, darling. I'd rather stay here with you.' She turned out the lights for them and went to lie down on the fur throw on her bed. '. . . *non esce più, Mamma? . . . No, caro. Mai.*' Never. Maybe never again.

She tried to sleep as she gazed at the fire, but it was useless. She was still too nervous, too excited, too on edge after the day of waiting for news of the collections in Rome. And she hadn't had any air all day long. Hadn't walked. Hadn't run. With a sigh at last she turned over, looked into the fire, and then stood up. She went to find Hattie, in her room watching television, her hair in curlers and a copy of *Good Housekeeping* near her bed. 'You'll be home for a while?'

'Yes, Mrs Parelli. I'm not going out.'

'I'm going for a walk then. I'll be back very soon.'

Isabella closed the door again and returned to her own room. The borrowed navy blue coat hung in her closet now, and she no longer needed the wool hat. She shrugged quickly into the coat and picked up her bag, glancing around the room for a moment as though she were afraid to leave something behind. What? Her handbag? Her compact? Long white kid opera gloves? She looked down sombrely at the jeans that she wore, and for an instant a pang of jealousy shot through her. Natasha. Lucky Natasha. With her benefits and her gold sandals and her beaux. Isabella smiled to herself when she thought back to their conversation about Corbett.

She should have known Corbett was not Natasha's type. He couldn't be handled easily enough. She looked at herself in the mirror then, angrily, and whispered, 'Is that what you want?' She didn't, of course. She knew she didn't. Not a stockbroker in horn-rimmed glasses. 'Ah, then it's a beautiful one you want.' She accused herself as she softly closed the door. 'No! No!' was her answer. But what did she want then? Amadeo, of course. Only Amadeo. But as she thought it, a brief vision of Corbett flashed into her head.

That night she walked further than she ever had, her hands jammed into her pockets, her chin tucked into the collar of the coat. What was it she wanted? Suddenly she wasn't sure. She wandered more slowly past the now too familiar shops. Why didn't they change the windows more often? Didn't anyone care? And didn't they know that they were still using last year's colours? And why wasn't it spring? She found fault with all of it as she pushed the vision of Natasha repeatedly out of her head. Was that it then? Was she only jealous? But why shouldn't Natasha have a good time? She worked hard. She was a good friend. She had opened her home and her heart to Isabella as no one ever had. What more could she possibly want from her? To keep her locked at home the way she herself was?

Suddenly, in spite of herself, she knew the answer only too well. It wasn't Natasha's imprisonment she wanted, but some freedom of her own. That was all. She dug her hands further into her pockets, jammed her chin even further down, and walked on endlessly until, for the first time, she was downtown. No longer in the cosy, residential safety of the sixties; or the distinguished sobriety of the seventies; or even the decorous boredom of the eighties; not to mention the dubious, shabby gentility of the nineties, where she had now and then strayed; but the other way this time, past the bustling fifties, its restaurants, its excited diners, its screeching taxis, and its far larger shops. Past department stores with overdone windows, and Tiffany's with its glittering goodies, Rockefeller Center with its still hopeful skaters, and St Patrick's with its lofty spires. She walked all the way down to Forty-second Street, to the office buildings, the less fashionable stores, and the drunks. Everything seemed to be careering past her at a speed that reminded her of Rome. At last she turned back towards Park Avenue, and past Grand Central Station, she stood looking straight up Park. Lined on either side of her were skyscrapers, towering monuments of glass and chrome, where fortunes were aspired to, ambitions fulfilled. It took her breath away as she stared at them; the tops of the buildings seemed to lead straight to heaven. Slowly, thoughtfully, Isabella walked home.

She felt as though she had opened a new door that night and there was no way she could close it again. She had been crouching, hidden in a maze, locked behind an apartment door, pretending that she was living in a village far from the city's excitement. But she had seen too much that night, felt the nearness of power, success, money, excitement, ambition. By the time Natasha came home, she had made up her mind.

'What are you still doing up, Isabella? I thought you'd have been asleep for hours.' She had seen the light in the living-room and wandered in, puzzled.

Isabella shook her head briefly, smiling a little at her friend. 'You look wonderful tonight, Natasha.'

'Thanks to you. Everyone loved the gold in my hair; they couldn't figure out how I'd done it.'

'Did you tell them?'

'No.'

'Good.' She was still smiling. 'One has to have a few secrets after all.'

Natasha watched her, worried. Something had changed tonight. There was something about the way Isabella sat there, about the way she looked, and the way she smiled. 'Did you go out for a walk tonight?'

'Yes.'

'How was it? Did anything go wrong?' Why did she look like that? There was something peculiar about her eyes.

'Of course not. Why would anything go wrong? It hasn't yet.'

'And it won't. As long as you're careful.'

'Ah, yes.' She looked wistful. 'That.' She suddenly raised her head with a look of power and grace that suggested that she should have been the one wearing the gold threads in her hair. 'Natasha, when are you going out again?'

'Not for a few days. Why?' Dammit. She was probably lonely and bored. Who wouldn't have been? Particularly Isabella. 'As a matter of fact I was thinking of staying home for the rest of the week, with you and the boys.'

'How dull.'

That was it then. Natasha should have known. She had got too swept up in it all again, taken Isabella too much at her word.

'Not at all, silly. In fact' – she yawned prettily – 'if I don't stop running around like this, I'm going to roll over and die.' But Isabella was laughing at her, and Natasha didn't understand.

'What about the film premiere you were supposed to attend day after tomorrow?'

'What film premiere?' Natasha widened her eyes and looked spectacularly dumb, but Isabella only laughed more.

'The one on Thursday. Remember? The benefit for the heart foundation or whatever it is!'

'Oh, that. I thought I wouldn't go.'

'Good. I'll use your ticket.' She sat back and almost crowed.

'What? I hope you're kidding.'

'No, I'm not. Want to get me a ticket?' She grinned at Natasha and crossed her legs under her on the couch.

'Are you nuts?'

'No. I walked downtown tonight, and it was wonderful. Natasha, I can't do this anymore.'

'You have to. You know you have no choice.'

'Nonsense. In a city the size of this one? No one will know me. I'm not saying I'm going to start parading around, going to fashion shows, and having lunch. But some things I can do. It's insane to hide like this here.'

'It would be insane not to.'

'You're wrong. At something like your film premiere I can slip in and slip out. After the cocktails, the gathering. I can just watch the movie and the people as I come and go. What do you think? That I can design clothes for women of fashion without setting foot out of my house and getting a feeling for what's working, what isn't, what they like, what looks good on them, without even seeing what's being worn? I'm not a mystic, you know. I'm a designer. It's a very down-to-earth trade.'

But the speech wasn't convincing, and Natasha only shook her head.

'I can't do it. I can't. Something will happen. Isabella, you're mad.'

'Not yet. But I will be. Soon. If I don't start getting out. Discreetly. With caution. But I can't go on like this for much longer. I realised that tonight.' Natasha looked woebegone, and Isabella patted her hand.

'Please, Natasha, no one even suspects that it's not I at the top of the house in Rome.'

'They will if you start showing up at film premieres.'

'I promise you, they won't. Will you get me the ticket?' She suddenly wore the pleading eyes of a child.

'I'll think about it.'

'If you don't, I'll get it myself. Or I'll go somewhere else.

Somewhere out in the open, where I'm sure to be seen.' For a moment her dark eyes glinted viciously, and Natasha's own blue ones suddenly blazed.

'Don't blackmail me, dammit!' She jumped to her feet and paced around the room.

'Then will you help me? Please, Natasha . . . please . . .'

At the sound of her friend's words Natasha turned slowly to face her again, looked at the haunted eyes, the narrow, pale face, and even she had to admit that Isabella needed more than the apartment and an occasional walk up Madison Avenue in the dark. 'I'll see.' But Isabella was tired of the game now; her eyes caught on fire and she jumped to her feet.

'Don't bother, Natasha. I'll take care of the matter myself.' She marched towards the back of the house. In a moment Natasha heard her close her door. Slowly she turned off the lights in the living-room and looked at the city outside. Even at two in the morning, it was alive, busy, bustling; there were trucks, taxis, people; there were still horns and voices, excitement and turmoil outside. It was why people flocked to New York, why they couldn't stay away. She herself knew that she needed what it gave her, needed to feel its tempo beating like the pulse in her veins. How could she deny it to Isabella? But perhaps in not denying it to her, if the kidnappers found her again, she could cost Isabella her life. On silent feet Natasha walked slowly down the hall. She stood outside Isabella's doorway and then gently knocked. The door opened quickly, and the two women stood there, silent, face to face. It was Natasha who spoke first.

'Don't do it, Isabella. It's too dangerous. It's wrong.'

'Tell me that when you have lived like this, in terror, in hiding, for as long as I have. Tell me you'd be able to go on.'

But Natasha couldn't tell her that. No one could.

166

'You've been very brave, Isabella, and for such a long time.'

'*Brave . . . for just a little while longer.*' The echo of Amadeo's words caught Isabella unexpectedly and lodged in her throat. With tears in her eyes she shook her head. 'I haven't.'

'Yes, you have.' They were still whispering. 'You've been brave and patient and wise. Can you be for a little while longer?'

Isabella almost cried out at the words as frantically she shook her head from side to side, whispering to Amadeo, as well as her friend. 'No. No, I can't.' And then she stood very straight, very tall, and looked at Natasha boldly, the tears suddenly gone. 'I can't be brave for a little while longer. I've done this for as long as I can.'

'And Thursday?'

Isabella looked at her, smiling slowly. 'The premiere? I'll be there.'

Chapter Seventeen

'Isabella! . . . Isabella! . . .' There was a frantic knocking as
Natasha stood in front of her door.

'Wait a minute! I'm not ready yet. Just a second . . .
there . . .' She slipped into her shoes and clipped on her ear-
rings, glanced at herself quickly, and pulled open the door.
Natasha was waiting, dressed for the evening in a beige
Chinese evening coat lined in the palest peach satin. The
trousers she wore under it were mocha-brown velvet, all
the colours brought together in brown-and-peach brocade
shoes. And she was wearing coral ear-rings that peeked
through her blonde hair. Isabella looked her over
admiringly and smiled in pleasure as she approved. 'My
dear, you look marvellous. And it's not even one of mine!
Where did you get that sensational outfit?'

'In Paris last year.'

'Very handsome.'

But suddenly it was Natasha who looked and approved,
startled into silence as she saw the familiar figure standing
regally in the centre of the room.

It was the old Isabella, and for a moment Natasha was
breathless, under the spell. This was Isabella di San
Gregorio as she had once been. Amadeo's woman and the
brightest star in all of Rome.

It was not only what she wore, but the way she wore it,
and the angle of the long, ivory neck, so delicately carved,
the sweep of her perfectly combed and knotted dark hair,
the shape of her tiny ears, the depth of the remarkable
black eyes. But now Natasha gasped at what she was
wearing, so simple and so stark. One totally plain stretch of

black satin which fell from her shoulders to her toes. A tiny V at the neckline, the smallest of cap sleeves, and the richness of the heavy black satin, which exposed only the tips of black satin shoes. Her hair was swept into a knot, her arms totally bare, and her only jewellery was a pair of large onyx ear-rings set in diamonds, as bright as her shining eyes.

'My God, it's gorgeous, Isabella!' It was perfectly simple, perfectly plain. 'It must be one of yours.'

Isabella nodded. 'My last collection, before . . . we left home.' There had been a long pause. *Before Amadeo disappeared.* It was from the same collection as the green satin dress she had worn that night, waiting for him to come home.

'What are you wearing over it? Your mink coat?' Natasha was hesitant. The coat was sure to draw attention. Yet, even in totally plain black satin, Isabella was a woman everyone would see.

But Isabella was shaking her head, this time with a tiny look of pleasure, the hint of a smile.

'No, I have something else. Something from the collection we opened this week. Actually,' she said over her shoulder as she fumbled in the closet for a moment, 'this is only a sample, but Gabriela sent it to me to show me how well it worked. That was the box you picked up at your agent last week. In the collection we lined it in turquoise, to be worn over purple or green.' And as she spoke she emerged from the closet again, wearing a creamy white satin coat. With the black beneath it she looked even more striking than before.

'Oh, God.' Natasha looked as though she'd seen a ghost.

'You don't like it?' Isabella was stunned.

'I love it.' Natasha closed her eyes and sat down. 'But I think you're crazy. You're crazy. You'll never be able to pull this off.' She opened her eyes again, staring at Isabella

169

ın the remarkable white coat and the strikingly simple black gown. The whole outfit was so simple and so beautiful that it shrieked of haute couture. And one look at her face, so pale and so revealing, and the game would be over. The whereabouts of Isabella di San Gregorio would be instantly known. 'Is there any even faintly human chance I can talk you out of this?' Natasha stared at her glumly.

'None.' She was in command again. The princess of the House of San Gregorio in Rome. She glanced at the watch she had left on the table, then back at her friend. 'You'd better hurry, Natasha, you'll be late.'

'I should be so lucky. And you?'

'Just as I promised. I'll stay here until precisely nine-fifteen. I'll get into the limousine you rented for me, go straight to the theatre, have the driver check with the ushers if the movie has started, and if it has done so, on schedule at nine-thirty, I'll hurry inside. I'll sit in the aisle seat you reserved for me and depart the instant the house-lights come on at the end.'

'The instant *before* the house-lights come on. *Don't* wait for the credits, or for me. Just get the hell out. I'll come home later, after the dinner.'

'*Ècco.* And when you get back, I shall be here, and we can celebrate a perfect evening.'

'Perfect? A thousand things could go wrong.'

'But nothing will. *Va, cara.* You'll be late for the cocktail.'

Natasha stood as though paralysed. Isabella was smiling at her. She didn't seem to understand anything, how great a risk she was running, how easily she could be recognised, the furor it would cause if her residence in New York became known.

'Does Bernardo know what you're up to?'

'Bernardo! Bernardo is in Rome. And this is New York.

Here I am only a face in the fashion magazines. Not everyone keeps up with fashion, my dear. Or didn't you know?'

'Isabella, you're a fool. You don't just design dresses for French countesses and rich women from Rome and Venice and Milan. You have an entire American line, men's wear, ready-to-wear, cosmetics, perfumes, soaps. You are an international commodity.'

'No. I'm a woman. And I can't live like this anymore.'

They had been over it one hundred and three times in the past two days, and Natasha's arguments were wearing thin. The best she'd been able to do was come up with a reasonably safe plan. And with luck it would work if Isabella came late enough, left early enough, and sat quietly in her seat in between. Maybe, just maybe, it would be all right.

'So are you ready?' Isabella was looking at her sternly, as though urging a reluctant debutante to attend her first dance.

'I wish I were dead.'

'Don't be foolish, darling.' She kissed Natasha's cheek softly. 'I'll see you there.'

Without another word Natasha stood up to go; she paused for a moment in the doorway, shook her head, and then left as Isabella sat down again, smiling to herself and impatiently tapping one black satin shoe on the floor.

Chapter Eighteen

The limousine Natasha had rented was waiting in quiet black splendour outside the door. It was precisely nine fifteen. Isabella walked out to the kerb. The air on her face felt wonderful, and for once she didn't even mind the cold. The driver closed the door behind her with a thud as Isabella settled herself carefully on the seat, the white coat spread around her like a coronation robe.

They drove decorously through Central Park and then headed downtown to the theatre, as Isabella silently watched the other cars pass by.

Oh, God, she was out at last. In silks and satins, in perfume and evening clothes. Even Alessandro had looked at her with excitement and squealed with glee as he kissed her goodnight carefully, holding both hands, as instructed, in mid-air. 'Just like with Papa!' he had shouted.

But it wasn't just like with Papa. For a moment Isabella's thoughts flew back to Rome. The days of going to parties in the Ferrari, of rushing home from the office to chatter and dress for a ball, her mind still in a work-battered daze, of Amadeo singing in the shower as she laid out his dinner jacket and disappeared into her dressing-room to emerge in grey velvet or blue brocade. It was foolish, an 'empty life', someone had once told her, but it was also their world. They had conquered it together and they enjoyed it, sharing their laughter and their success with amusement and pride.

It was different now. The seat next to her was empty. There was no one but the driver in the long black car. No one to talk to when she got there, no one to laugh with when at last she got home, no one to shine for and smile at Her head had been just a little higher because he had been there.

Her face was suddenly very sober as they halted outside the theatre. The driver turned in his seat to look at her.

'Mrs Walker mentioned something about my going in to see if the movie has already started.'

He left her in the limousine and went to see if all was ready.

She felt her heart begin to race a little, as it had at her wedding when, in a cloud of white lace and veiling, she had been Amadeo's bride. But it was foolish to feel like that now. She was only going to a movie. And this time she was wearing black. And she was no longer Amadeo's bride, but his widow. It was too late to hesitate though. The chauffeur had already returned to help her from her car.

In the darkened theatre Natasha was frantic. A party of seven had taken over the first seven seats along the aisle, and all her excuses – 'I'm sorry, would you mind terribly? My cousin . . . she has a terrible cold . . . here in a minute . . . coming late . . . may not feel well and have to go . . .' – were useless. No one heard her, the group was too unwieldy and too large. A fat man from Texas – 'in oil, darlin'' – in a dinner jacket and a Stetson had had too much to drink. 'Bad kidneys, darlin', you know.' It had been impossible to move him from his seat on the aisle. Beside him were his white-brocaded wife, their hosts, and next to them the financial editor of *The Times* of London, yet another very social couple, and at last Natasha with her spare seat. She wanted to kill Isabella. The plan had been lunacy from the start. Isabella would have to climb over everyone; it was going to be impossible to keep her from being seen. She sat glowering, waiting for the film to start, hoping Isabella would develop smallpox or at least typhoid, maybe even malaria, on her way to the car.

'You look happy tonight, Natasha. What happened to you, they cancel your new book?'

'I should be so lucky.' She glanced across the empty seat at Corbett Ewing.

'You look mad as hell.' He glanced with amusement at the man in the white dress Stetson in the aisle seat. 'Problems with Texas?' Corbett Ewing looked at her with dancing blue eyes and a broad grin.

'I was trying to save the seat for a friend.'

'Aha! So you're in love again. Goddamn it, every time I go out of town, I seem to miss my chance.'

Natasha smiled. But he suddenly realised that she was concerned. And as he watched her he understood who the friend had to be. As he thought of her he felt his heart race.

'Where've you been?' Natasha tried to make idle chitchat but the worry was still in her eyes.

'Tokyo mostly. Then Paris, London. And last week Morocco. God, that's a beautiful place.'

'So I hear. How's business?' With Corbett that was like asking the White House chef, 'How was lunch?' Corbett was constantly brewing some of business and industry's major deals.

'All right. How's your book?'

'Finished, finally. I've decided that I'm not really a writer. Just a rewriter. I spend six weeks cooking them up and six months boiling them down.'

'Actually, that's about how it works with me.' They both fell silent for a time, watching the crowds.

And then, without any notice, Corbett moved into the empty seat. Natasha looked at him, startled, and gestured to him to move back.

'I can't see there.' He looked at her sweetly.

174

'Corbett . . . will you please move!' Her voice was urgent. but his smile only widened as he shook his head.

'No, I won't.'

'Corbett!' But at that moment the lights suddenly dimmed. Natasha went on urging him in the darkness, and behind them a row of dowagers complained.

'Ssshhh!'

At precisely that moment the usher's flashlight appeared at the end of the aisle. Natasha looked up, startled. At least Isabella was right on time. She was standing in momentary confusion, staring down at the man in the white hat.

'Hi, darlin', you must be Natasha's cousin. Now isn't that a nice coat.' It was spoken in a loud stage whisper as the dowagers came alive again, and the Texan introduced Isabella to his wife. Isabella murmured pleasantly and glanced down the row of seats. Natasha signalled to her, and Isabella nodded, progressing slowly over seven pairs of feet and knees.

'I'm sorry . . . oh . . . sorry . . . terribly sorry.' She had reached Natasha, who only pointed silently to the empty seat . . . Isabella nodded, glanced at Corbett, climbed over both of them, settled her coat around her and sat down. The movie was just beginning and the theatre was very dark, but as she sat there she turned to Corbett, and they exchanged a smile. At first she was too excited to watch the movie; instead she found herself staring up and down the long dark aisles. What did they look like, who were they, what were they wearing, and could they possibly understand how good it felt to be out? She was smiling to herself in the darkness, staring happily at the back of elaborate hair-dos and well-barbered heads. At last she let her eyes be drawn by the movie and sat happily, almost childlike, enjoying what was happening on the screen. How long had it been since she'd even been to a movie? She thought for a moment. Early September, with Amadeo. Seven months . . .

she heard herself utter a small happy groan. The film itself was delightful, and she was enchanted by its beauty and the humour of the two stars. She watched, engrossed, until the curtain went down slowly and the house-lights began to come up.

'Is it over?' Isabella glanced at Corbett in confusion, not satisfied that the story had been resolved. But he was smiling at her, amused, and pointed at the words on the screen almost hidden by the gold tassels of the heavy curtain still swinging closed.

'It's only intermission.' And the smile deepened. 'It's nice to see you, Isabella. Let's go to the lobby for a drink.'

But as Isabella nodded, Natasha's hand was instantly on her arm, and her eyes held Corbett's with a dark frown.

'I think she should stay here.'

He paused for an instant, looking with interest at Isabella and then with concern at his old friend. He wanted to tell her to relax a bit, that he was neither a masher nor a rapist, but this wasn't the place nor the time. He turned again to Isabella. 'Would you like me to bring something back?' But Isabella only shook her head, smiling politely, and sat down again in her seat.

As soon as he had left, Natasha moved closer, wishing once again that she hadn't agreed to let Isabella come.

Isabella only smiled at her and patted her hand. 'Don't look so worried, Natasha. Everything is fine.' She was getting the chance she had so desperately wanted. To watch the people, to look at the gowns, to hear the laughter, to be 'there'. And suddenly Natasha saw her standing, looking slowly around.

She hissed at her fiercely. 'Sit down.'

But Isabella was Isabella, and before Natasha could stop her, she had begun to slide slowly in the opposite direction, towards the other aisle. 'Isab – . . . goddamn . . .' She whispered to herself through clenched teeth, standing up quickly, apologising, avoiding toes in elegant slippers, and trying to stay close to Isabella. But the instant they had joined the throng in the aisle, Isabella seemed to be swept from her on a current of people who swirled between then, laughed gaily, tried not to spill drinks, and tugged at Natasha's long sleeves.

'Natasha! Darling! I missed you at – '

She muttered quickly, 'Later,' and pressed on. But she was a good distance behind Isabella now, cascading into the lobby with the others, where a crowd pressed around the makeshift bar.

'Changed your mind?' It was Corbett Ewing, suddenly towering above Isabella as she looked up at him with a smile.

'Yes, thank you.'

'Would you like a drink?'

'No, I – ' Far behind her Natasha was suddenly staring, a look of panic in her eyes. She waved frantically to Corbett, who only waved back.

Natasha did not return the smile but gazed frantically at Isabella. She had to get to her. She motioned to her to turn around. Isabella did so, puzzled, wondering if there was something special she should see. It was Natasha who saw the danger approaching, in the form of two reporters, one from *Women's Wear Daily* and the other from the People section of *Time*. The woman from *WWD*, spiderlike in a black jersey dress, had stared at Isabella for a moment, knit her brows, and then was attempting to move closer, having whispered something to the man she had in tow. Meanwhile Isabella was smiling at Corbett and casting Natasha an embarrassed look.

Natasha was still not able to get near her. She wanted to kick them, bite them, shove them aside. She had to get to Isabella, before the two reporters, before . . .

177

It was too late. A double flash exploded in Isabella's eyes. She wheeled suddenly, frightened, briefly blinded by the lights. She grabbed at Corbett's arm just as Natasha reached her and pulled her to her side.

Corbett was still standing there, startled, his drink in his hand, his powerful body blocking the reporters who had momentarily been shoved aside. Natasha grabbed his arm then, shouting above the din.

'Get her out of here for God's sake! Now.' She grabbed his drink from him, and both his arms were around Isabella like a fortress as another flash of light went off in her face. Before she knew what had happened, he had propelled her half-way across the room. Dimly Isabella heard the murmur that had gone up in the lobby. Corbett held her arm tightly, and they ran out of the lobby to his Rolls-Royce. Isabella had not said a word, but as she ran with him something told him that this was not new to her. They barrelled into the car. As the door was still closing Corbett was shouting, 'Get us the hell out of here.' It was only then that the reporters came hurtling after them through the door. Corbett grinned. Football in college still paid off now and then. And he had to admire Isabella. She had come the distance with him, without ladylike pretensions about high heels or falling or what she might be doing to her dress. She sat on the seat now, without speaking, trying to gather her wits and catch her breath. They had already turned the corner, and the reporters were left gaping at the kerb.

'Are you all right?' Corbett turned to her now, opening a compartment and pulling out a brandy decanter and one glass.

'How convenient.' And then, smiling faintly, 'Yes. I'm fine.'

'Does this happen to you often?' He handed her the glass, and she took it.

'Not in a while.'

He looked at Isabella and noticed the hand that trembled as she held her glass. At least she was human, despite the composure. She was no longer even out of breath. 'Natasha didn't tell me where I should take you. Do you want to go home? Or would it be safer at my place?'

'No, our place will be fine. And I apologise for – for the ugly scene.'

'Not at all. My life is extremely dull by comparison.' He gave the address to the chauffeur. But he was suddenly unnerved by what he had seen of Isabella. Despite the composure, there was a look of despair on her face. 'I don't mean to make light of it. It must be very unnerving. Is that why you left Italy? Or is this something that only happens to you here?' His voice was gentle as he settled back next to her on the seat.

'No. This . . . it happened at home too. I – I'm sorry but I can't explain. It's very awkward. I'm only very sorry to have spoiled your evening. You can just drop me off and go back.'

But that was not at all what Corbett Ewing had in mind. There was something rare and strange about this woman that touched his heart. Something hidden, something remarkable and oblique. She had regal bearing, beauty, he could see in her eyes that there was humour and wit, but there was also something else, something buried, something more. Pain, sorrow, loneliness, he had seen it now, with her dark, smouldering look. He sat very quietly for a moment, then as they turned into the park he spoke easily again.

'How's my friend Alessandro?' They exchanged a smile, and Corbett was pleased to note that the mention of the boy seemed to unbend her.

'He's very well.'

'And what about you? Bored yet?' He knew that she

179

rarely left the apartment, except for brief walks with Natasha. He didn't understand it, but it seemed to be all she did. But now she shook her head vehemently with a smile.

'Oh, no, not bored! I've been so busy!'

'Have you?' He looked intrigued. 'Doing what?'

'Working.'

'Really? Did you bring your work with you?' She nodded. 'In what line?'

For an instant she was stumped. But she came up with an answer quickly. 'With my family. In . . . art.'

'Interesting. I'm afraid I can't claim anything as noble as my line of work.'

'What do you do?' Obviously something very successfully, she thought, as her eyes gently wandered over the wooden-and-leather interior of the new Rolls.

'A number of things, but mostly textiles. At least that's what I prefer. The rest I leave to the people I work with. My family began with textiles a long time ago and that's what I've always liked best.'

'That's interesting.' For a moment there was a light in Isabella's eyes. 'Are you particularly involved in any one kind?' She was dying to know if she bought from him but she didn't dare ask. Perhaps she could glean the information from something he said.

'Wools, linens, silks, cottons. We have a line of velvets that upholsters most of this country, and of course man-made fibres, synthetics, and some new things we're developing now.'

'I see, but not dress fabrics then.' She looked disappointed. Upholstery wasn't her bag.

'Yes, of course. We do garment fabrics too.' Garment. She cringed at the hideous word. Garment. Her dresses weren't garments. That was Seventh Avenue. What she did was haute couture. He couldn't decipher the look in her eyes but he was amused just the same. 'We probably even made the fabric for the dress you have on.' He allowed a rare burst of pride to show in his voice, but she looked at him then, haughty, the princess from Rome.

'This fabric is French.'

'In that case I apologise.' Amused, he backed down. 'Which brings to mind something far more important. You never told me your last name.'

She hesitated only for an instant. 'Isabella.'

'That's all?' He smiled at her. 'Just Isabella, the Italian friend?'

'That's right, Mister Ewing. That's all,' She looked at him long and hard, and he nodded slowly.

'I understand.' After what he had glimpsed at the theatre, he knew she had been through enough. Something very difficult had happened to this woman, and he wasn't going to pry. He didn't want to frighten her away from him.

They pulled up at that moment in front of Natasha's door, and with a small sigh Isabella turned to him and proffered her right hand. 'Thank you very much. And I'm terribly sorry to have spoiled your evening.'

'You didn't. I was just as happy to get out of there. I always find benefits a bore.'

'Do you?' She looked at him with interest. 'Why is that?'

'Too many people, too much small talk. Everyone is there for the wrong reasons, to see their cronies and not to benefit whatever cause. I prefer seeing my friends in small gatherings where we can hear each other talk.'

She nodded. In some ways she agreed with him. But in other ways evenings like that one were in her blood.

'May I see you inside, just to make sure no one is lurking in the halls?'

She laughed at the suspicion, but gratefully inclined her head.

'Thank you. But I'm quite sure I'm safe here.'

As she said it something told him that that was why she had come to America. To be safe.

'Let's just make sure.' He walked her to the elevator and then inside. 'I'll just take you up.'

Isabella said nothing until the elevator stopped, and then suddenly she felt awkward; he had been so incredibly nice.

'Would you like to come in for a moment? You know, you could wait for Natasha until she comes home.'

'Thank you, I'd like that.' They closed the door. 'Why didn't she come back with us, by the way, instead of staying to play *Meet the Press*?' That had puzzled him as he had run with Isabella, thinking of what Natasha had just said.

Isabella sighed as she looked at him. She could at least tell him that much. 'I think she felt it would be wiser if no one knew I was with her.'

'That's why you came in late?' She nodded, and he said, 'You lead a very mysterious life, Isabella.' He smiled, not asking further questions, as they sat down on the long white couch.

The rest of the evening passed quickly. They chatted about Italy, about textiles, about his home. He had a plantation he had bought in South Carolina, a farm in Virginia, and a house in New York.

'Do you keep horses in Virginia?'

'Yes, I do. Do you ride?'

She grinned at him over their brandies. 'I used to. But it's been a long time.'

'You and Natasha will have to bring the boys down there sometime. Would you have time for that before you go back?'

'I might.' But as they began to speak of it Natasha marched through the door. She looked wilted and exhausted and she looked Isabella straight in the eye.

'I told you you were crazy to try it. Do you have any idea what you've done?' Corbett was startled for a moment at the look on her face and the vehemence of her tone. But Isabella did not appear to be ruffled. She motioned to Natasha to sit down.

'Don't get so excited. It was nothing. They took some pictures. So what?' She tried to conceal her own worry and held out a warm hand.

But Natasha knew better. She turned her back in fury, and then stared at Corbett and then Isabella, as she pulled up the satin tunic and sat down.

'Do you have any idea who they were? *Women's Wear*, *Time* magazine. The third one was the Associated Press. And I think I might even have caught a glimpse of the society editor from *Vogue*. But the fact is, you ass hole, that it wouldn't have mattered if it was a twelve-year-old boy with a Brownie. Your game is up.'

What game? What was happening? Corbett was intrigued. He looked at both women and was quick to speak.

'Should I go?'

Natasha answered him before Isabella could. 'It doesn't matter, Corbett. I trust you. And by tomorrow morning the whole world will know.'

But Isabella was angry now. She stood up and walked around the room. 'That's absurd.'

'Is it, Isabella? You don't think anyone remembers you? You think in two months everyone has forgotten you? Do you really feel that safe? Because if you do, you're a fool.'

Corbett said nothing. He only watched Isabella's face. She was frightened, but determined, and she had the look of someone who had taken her chances, lost the first hand, and was not going to give in or quit. He wanted to comfort her, to tell her he'd protect her, to tell Natasha to settle down. His voice was deep and gentle when at last he spoke. 'Maybe nothing will come of it.'

Natasha only glared at him furiously, as though he had been part of the original plot. 'You're wrong, Corbett. You don't know how wrong you are. By tomorrow it will be in all of the papers.' She looked unhappily at Isabella. 'I'm right, you know.'

Isabella stood very still and spoke very softly. 'Maybe not.'

Chapter Nineteen

Corbett Ewing sat in his office, staring at the morning paper in despair. True to Natasha's predictions, it was all in the news. He was reading *The New York Times*. 'Isabella di San Gregorio, widow of the kidnapped and subsequently murdered couturier, Amadeo di San Gregorio . . .' It went on to explain once again every possible detail of the kidnapping and its eventual unhappy outcome. More interestingly it described in intricate detail how she had disappeared and it had been thought that she had taken refuge in a penthouse atop her couture house in Rome. There was a brief line, questioning if she had in fact been in the States all along, or if she had slipped away after the successful opening that week of San Gregorio's spring line. The article went on to mention that it was not known where she was staying and that discreet enquiries of prominent people in the fashion world had turned up nothing. Either they were co-operating in keeping her whereabouts secret or they didn't know. Signore Cattani, the American representative of San Gregorio in New York, said that he had heard from her more frequently than usual in recent months, but that he had no reason to believe that she was in New York and not Rome. There was also a mention of the fact that she had been seen at the film premiere escorted by a tall, white-haired man, that they had made good their escape together in a black chauffeured Rolls. But his identity had been uncertain. The reporters' interest had centred on their shock at seeing Isabella, and although one of the reporters had been under the impression that he was indeed a familiar face, no one had actually thought to check him carefully, and all they had of him in the photographs was his back as they ran.

Corbett sighed, set down the paper, sat back in his chair, and swivelled slowly around. What did she know of him? What had Natasha said? He wished that, of all the women in the world, she were anyone but who she was. He sat, looking dejected, glancing at the paper, and then at his hands. Slowly his thoughts turned from his own worries to hers. Isabella di San Gregorio. It had never dawned on him before.

Natasha's cousin from Milan! He smiled to himself at the story and then smiled more broadly as he put together the rest of the pieces and remembered the whole silly game . . . he had told her he was in textiles . . . she had told him her family was in art. Yet she knew something about fabrics. And the way she bridled when she had told him that the satin for her outfit was surely not his but had been bought in France! He understood everything better now: the secrecy, their flight from the benefit, and Isabella's eyes filled with fear, as though she had lived that scene only too often, as though she had been haunted by it for much too long. Poor woman. What she must have gone through. He found himself also wondering how she managed to run her business from New York.

One thing was certain: Isabella di San Gregorio was a remarkable woman, a woman with talent and beauty and soul, but he wondered now if he would ever get to know her. If he even had a chance. He realised that there was only one answer, and it had to come from her. That night he would tell her. He couldn't take a chance of her finding out later and having it taint what he felt for her, what he wanted to help her do. If she'd let him. If she'd even speak to him again.

With a long sigh of resignation Corbett Ewing stood up

and left his desk. He looked far up Park Avenue to where he knew Isabella hid, in Natasha's apartment, with her child and Natasha's, and then he sat down again and picked up the phone

Isabella was still talking to Bernardo in Rome. He had first got the news at noon. His secretary had brought him the afternoon paper, which he read in horror, his eyes flaming, but without saying a word. He had called Isabella at six in the morning, and at seven, and now again, just after ten.

'All right, goddamn it! So what! I did it! There's no changing that now. I'll go back into hiding. No one will know if I'm still here. I can't bear it any longer. I work night and day. I eat with the children. I take short walks after dark. No people, Bernardo. No one to look at and laugh with and talk to. No one intelligent to talk business with. The only excitement in my evenings is provided by Jason's electric train.' Her voice pleaded with him, but Bernardo didn't want to hear.

'All right, go ahead, make a spectacle of yourself. Expose yourself. But if something happens to you or Alessandro, don't come crying to me, because it'll be your own goddamn fault.' And then suddenly he took a long breath and slowed down. At the other end he could hear Isabella crying softly into the phone. 'All right, all right, I'm sorry . . . Isabella, please . . . but I was so frightened for you. It was such a foolish thing to do.' He lit a cigarette and then stubbed it out.

'I know.' She sobbed again and then tiredly wiped her eyes. 'I just felt I had to. I really didn't think anyone would see me or that there would be any harm.'

'Do you understand differently now? Do you realise how visible you are?'

She nodded miserably. 'Yes. I used it love it. Now I hate it. I'm a prisoner of my own face.'

'It's a beautiful face, and I love it, so stop crying.' His voice was gentle.

'So what do I do now? Come home?'

'Are you crazy? It would be worse than last night. No. You stay there. And I'll try telling them that you only left here after the collection and you're coming back to Europe. I'll hint to them something about France. That will make sense to them because of your mother's family there.'

'They're all dead.' She sniffed loudly and blew her nose.

'I know that. But it makes sense that you'd have ties there.'

'You think they'll believe it?'

'Who cares? As long as they don't see you out in public again, you're safe. No one seems to know where you're staying. Did Natasha leave the party with you?' He prayed for a moment that one of them had been smarter than that.

'No. A friend of hers took me home. She left separately.'

'Good.' He paused for a moment, trying to sound offhanded. 'And by the way, who was the man in the photograph?' That was all he needed. For her to get involved with someone over there.

'He is a friend of Natasha's, Bernardo. Relax.'

'He won't tell anyone where you are?'

'Of course not.'

'You're too trusting. I'll get busy here with the press. And Isabella, please . . . for God's sake, *cara*, use your head and stay home.'

'*Capisco, capisco*. Don't worry. Now I understand. Even here I'm a prisoner. More so even than I was in Rome.'

'One day that will be over. You just have to be patient for a while. It's only been seven months since the kidnapping, you know. In a few months, in a year, it will be old news.' Old news . . . she was thinking that she would be old news by then too.

'Yeah. Maybe. And Bernardo . . . I'm sorry to give you so much trouble.' She suddenly felt like a very naughty child.

'Don't worry. I'm used to it. I'd be lost without it by now.'

'How's your ulcer?' She smiled into the phone.

'Doing beautifully. I think it's growing bigger and stronger every hour.'

'Stop that. Take it easy, please, will you?'

'Yeah. Sure. Now get to work on those problems with the ready-to-wear for Asia, and if you get bored, you can start on the summer line.'

'You're too good to me.'

'*Ecco*. I know. I'll call you later if anything else comes up. Nothing should if you keep your door closed and stay home.'

'*Capisco*.' They said ciao and hung up. At her end Isabella felt resentful. Why should she have to stay home, and what right did he have to tell her not to trust Corbett? She stepped out of her office, wandered into the kitchen, and found Natasha pouring herself a cup of coffee and looking grim.

'Did you have a nice chat with Bernardo?'

'Yes, lovely. But do me a favour, not you too.' Natasha had been quick to storm into her room at seven, with the newspaper in her hand and a look of fury still on her face. 'I don't think I can take any more today. I made a mistake. I was over-confident. I shouldn't have gone out last night, but I did. I had to. I couldn't stand it anymore. But I realise now that I have to stay in the background at least for a while.'

'What's he going to tell the press?'

'That I was here for a few days and that I'm going to live in France.'

'That ought to keep them scouting around Paris for a

189

day or two. And you, what are going to do?'

'What I have been doing. My work and not much else.'

'At least one nice thing happened out of all that ruckus last night.' She watched Isabella intently.

'What?' Isabella looked blank.

'You ran into Corbett again.' Natasha paused, watching her face. 'And may I say that you made quite a hit.'

'With Corbett? Don't be silly.' But as she turned away Natasha was sure she saw her blush.

'Do you like him?' There was a long silence. 'Well?'

But slowly Isabella turned to her with a warm light in her eyes. 'Natasha, don't push.'

She nodded. 'I think he might call you.' Isabella nodded silently in answer, but her heart did a little leap as she went back to her office and closed the door.

Chapter Twenty

Isabella was still in her room, dressing for dinner, when Corbett arrived. From behind her closed door, as she listened, she heard the delighted shrieks of Jason and in a moment the equally pleased giggles of her own son. She smiled to herself. It wouldn't do him any harm to see a man for a change. It had been too long since he had been around Bernardo, and unlike her own home, Natasha didn't have any men working in her household. Alessandro had contact with only females, which lately had made him miss his father all the more.

Isabella zipped up the black wool dress she was wearing, smoothed her black stockings, and slipped into black suede shoes. She put on black enamel and pearl ear-rings and ran a hand over her dark, severely worn hair. She grinned to herself as she flicked the light off. The swan had turned into an ugly duckling again. But it didn't matter. She wasn't trying to woo Corbett Ewing, and like Alessandro, it would do her good to have a male friend.

When she walked quietly into the living-room, she found him besieged by both boys, who had just opened two large packages that had yielded identical firemen's hats equipped with flashing lights and sirens with two firemen's coats to match.

'Look, we're firemen now!' They donned their equipment and zoomed around the room. Alessandro was obviously delighted to see Corbett again, and the shrieking from the sirens was appalling, as Natasha winced.

'Lovely gift, Corbett. Remind me to call and thank you tomorrow morning at six o'clock.'

He started to answer and then saw Isabella standing across the room. He rose quickly, looked at her nervously, and walked towards her to take her hand. 'Hello, Isabella. How are you?' But her eyes told him how she was. She was tired. Exhausted. But he found himself struck by her beauty again. She would have been surprised to hear it, but he decided that she looked even more so in the stark black wool, without the magnificence of satins and the striking white coat. 'You must have had quite a day.' He rolled his eyes sympathetically, and she smiled as she followed him into the room and sat down on the couch.

'Oh, I survived it. One always does. What about you?'

'For me it was easy. All they knew about me was that I had white hair. The only thing they didn't say was that I was an elderly gentleman –' He started to say more but the boys cut him off.

'Look, look, it squirts water!'

'Oh, no!' Jason had discovered that there was a little pipe fitted somewhere into the hat that could be filled with water and subsequently used to douse all of one's friends.

'Corbett, I may never speak to you again!' Natasha groaned and announced to the boys that it was time for bed.

'No, Mommy . . . Aunt Isabella . . . no . . . please!' Jason looked at them pleadingly, but Alessandro simply moved in closer to Corbett's knees. He was staring at him with interest while Jason continued to play with the hat. Isabella had never seen him so quiet, and from a little distance she watched. Corbett had noticed it too and he turned to smile at him and casually put an arm around the small shoulders.

'What do you think of all this, Alessandro?'

'I think it is . . .' He groped for the right English, 'very fun. I like very much the hat.' He stared up at Corbett admiringly and grinned.

'I thought they were pretty good too. Would you like to come and see a real firehouse with me sometime?'

'For firemans?' He looked at Corbett and then at his mother with awe. 'You go too?' Isabella nodded, noticing that Alessandro now spoke in English to her too.

'Of course. I meant both of you. What do you say?'

'*Si!*' But that was too much for him. He spent the next five minutes rattling frantically to his mother in Italian. There were lengthy discussions about how wonderful American firemen must be, what they wore, how big their trucks were, and whether or not they really used a brass pole.

'*Non so . . . non so . . . aspetta . . .* wait, we'll find all that out!' Isabella was laughing with him, and she watched with amusement as he shifted his seat from next to hers on to Corbett's knee.

'We will go soon?'

'I promise!'

'Very good.' He clapped his hands and took off in hot pursuit of Jason, and moments later they were banished to their room, despite begging, pleading, protests, and outraged comments that it was too early for firemen to go to bed. When at last they were gone, the room was strangely quiet.

Corbett watched Isabella once again. 'You have a lovely boy.'

'I'm afraid he's a little eager for male company, as you probably observed.' But after what Corbett had undoubtedly read in the papers that day, there was no need to hide the truth. 'In Rome he had one of my business associates who is his godfather. Here he has' – she looked at Natasha – 'only us. It's not quite the same thing. But you needn't feel obliged to take him to a firehouse. The gifts you brought are marvellous. You've done more than enough.'

'Don't be silly. I'd love it. Natasha can tell you. Jason is one of my best friends.'

'Fortunately,' she confirmed it, 'since his charming father never shows up.' She and Isabella had discussed that often in the past two months. But Jason seemed happy anyway, and having another child around was doing both boys a lot of good. It made up for other lacks, other losses, as neither of their mothers could.

'I'll work it out for some time this week. Maybe this weekend, if you're all free.' But as he said it Isabella looked at him and laughed.

'Oh, yes, we're quite free.'

Corbett was glad that she was laughing. After what he had read that day, he was not sure how she still could. But as he watched her he realised how very strong she was. She was bruised, she was lonely, but she was undaunted, and there was still laughter there, and fire, and a certain indestructible joy. He smiled at her openly and then raised an eyebrow.

'Tell me, Isabella,' he said, 'would you like to hear some more from me about textiles tonight? Or shall we just discuss art?' He was laughing at her now too. In a moment they were all laughing, and the atmosphere in the room was easy and free.

'I'm sorry. I couldn't help it. But what you told me was very interesting. Even if we do buy most of our satins in France.'

'That's your mistake. But the least you could have done was tell me that you were in fashion or something related to the trade.'

'Why? I was enjoying what you had to tell me. And you were absolutely right about everything except synthetics. I hate using them in couture.'

'But you do use them in ready-to-wear, don't you?'

'Obviously. I have to, for durability, and the price.'

'Then I'm not so far off.' They launched into an intricate discussion of chemicals and colours. Quietly Natasha left them. When she returned, the conversation had moved on to Asia, the difficulties of doing business there, the climate, the financial arrangements, problems of exchanges, open markets, all highly specialised terms, until at last Hattie announced dinner and Natasha yawned.

'I adore you both, but you're boring the hell out of me.'

'I'm sorry.' Isabella was quick to apologise. 'It's just very nice to have someone to talk to about business for a change.'

'I'll forgive you.'

Corbett smiled at his hostess.

The three of them had a delightful evening. They made their way to lemon soufflé and then finally espresso as Hattie passed a small silver platter covered with mints.

'I shouldn't.' Natasha sounded like Scarlett O'Hara as she plopped four of the tiny candies into her mouth.

'Neither should I.' Isabella hesitated, but then shrugged. 'But why not? According to Natasha and Bernardo, I'm going to be in hiding for the next ten years anyway, so I might as well get enormous and fat. I can let my hair grow to my ankles . . .'

Natasha quickly interrupted, 'I didn't say ten years. I said one.'

'What difference does it make? One year? Ten? Now I know how people feel when they're sentenced to prison. It never seems real until you've living it, and once you are, it's difficult to believe it will ever stop. It just goes on and on and on until one day it's over, and by then it probably doesn't matter any more.' She looked serious as she stirred her coffee and Corbett watched.

'I don't know how you stand it. I'm not sure I could.'

'Apparently I don't stand it very gracefully or I'd never have indulged in that fiasco last night. Thank God for you,

Corbett, or I would have been thrown to the wolves, and by now I wouldn't even be able to stay here at Natasha's. I'd have to be hiding alone with Alessandro some place else.' The three of them were considerably sobered by the thought.

'I'm glad I was there then.'

'So am I.' She looked at him openly, and slowly she smiled. 'I'm afraid I was very foolish. But also very lucky. Thank you again.' She had come to her senses, but he was shaking his head.

'I didn't do anything. Except run like hell.'

'That was enough.' For a moment their eyes met across the table, and he looked at her with a warm smile. Reluctantly they left the dining-room and returned to the living-room to sit by the fire. They chatted about Natasha's books, the theatre, travel, and events in New York, and for a moment Natasha looked worried seeing a look of longing come into Isabella's eyes. Corbett understood quickly, and for a moment they were all quiet. And then Natasha stood up lazily and turned her back to the fire.

'Well, you two. I think I'm going to be rude for a change. I'm tired.' But she knew also that Corbett had wanted to speak to Isabella alone. Surprised, Isabella waited for Corbett to suggest that he should go, but he didn't. He stood to kiss Natasha, and then they were alone.

He watched her briefly as she looked absently into the fire, the glow lighting her face softly, the light reflecting in her large dark eyes. He wanted to tell her how lovely she looked, but knew instinctively that he could not.

'Isabella . . .' His voice was whisper-soft, and she turned her face towards his. 'I'm awfully sorry about last night.'

'Don't be. It was inevitable, I suppose. I only wished that it could be different.'

'Natasha's right, you know. Eventually, it will be.'

'But not for a very long time.' The laughter had faded, and she looked at him wistfully. 'In some ways I've been spoiled.'

'Is that sort of thing important to you, like last night?'

'Not really. But people are. What they're doing, what they look like, what they think. It's very difficult suddenly living without them in my own tiny world.'

'It needn't be quite as tiny as this.' He glanced around the softly-lit living-room and turned his eyes to hers with a smile. 'There are ways for you to get out without being seen.'

'I tried that last night.'

'No, you didn't. You walked right into the bull-ring, dressed like the matador, and when everyone noticed you, you were surprised.'

She laughed at the comparison. 'I hadn't thought of it quite that way.'

He laughed softly too. 'I'm not sure if I said just the right thing. But you can get out of here. You can go for drives in the country. For long walks. There's no need to lock yourself up here entirely. You need it. You need to get out.'

She stretched unhappily, trying to quell the yearning in her heart.

'Will you let me take you out sometime? With Alessandro perhaps? Or alone?'

'That would be very nice.' She sat very still for a moment and looked into his eyes. 'But you don't have to, you know. You're very kind.'

He wouldn't take his eyes from hers. He shook his head softly, then looked away. 'I understand more than you think I do. I lost my wife a long time ago. Not as shockingly as you lost your husband. But it was intolerably painful in its own way. I thought I would die without her in the beginning. One loses all that is familiar, all that matters, everything that really counts. The one person who knows how you think, how you laugh, how you cry, how you feel, the person who remembers the favourite jokes of your childhood, the worst fears, the person who knows it all, who has the key. Suddenly you're left alone and you're certain that no one will ever understand again.'

'And do they?' Isabella watched him, fighting back tears. 'Does someone else learn the language, understand the secrets; does anyone ever really care again?' She was thinking, *Will I ever care again?*

'Eventually I'm sure there is always someone. Maybe the secrets aren't quite the same, maybe they laugh differently, or they cry more, or their needs are differently geared to yours. But there are other people, Isabella. As much as you don't want to hear it, it's something you should know.'

'Have there been for you? Anyone who could replace her?'

'In some ways no. But I haven't really been open to it, not unlike you. What has happened though is that I've learned to live with it. It doesn't hurt every day. But then again I didn't lose my home, my country, my whole way of life as you have right now.'

She sighed softly. 'The only two things I haven't lost are my business and my child. Which is why I'm here. There was a false alarm about Alessandro, and I decided that I couldn't live that way any more.'

'But you still have those two things, and no one can take them from you. Not the business and not the child. They are both safe here with you.'

'Alessandro is, but I worry about the business a great deal.'

'I don't think you have to. From what I've read of it, it seems to be quite secure.'

'For now. But I can't run it this way forever. You of all people must understand that.'

He did, better than he wanted to tell her. After what she had just told him, he couldn't say more. He felt a weight settle on his shoulders as he warmed his hands at the fire.

'Eventually there are changes you can make. You can open a larger office here. You can divide your administration in such a way as to allow you to run it from anywhere. But only if you have to. And this probably isn't the right time.'

'I plan to go back to Rome.'

He nodded sagely in answer, saying nothing. Then softly: 'In time I'm sure you will. And in the meantime you're here. I'd like to help you make the most of that. The one thing that saved me when Beth died was my friends.'

Isabella nodded her understanding; she knew that only too well.

'Corbett . . .' She looked at him with tears suddenly shining in her eyes. 'Do you ever get over the feeling that any day now she's coming home? I don't think anyone understands it. But I keep feeling that, as though he were only on a trip.'

He smiled gently and nodded. 'In some ways he is. I believe that one day we'll all meet again. But now we have this life to make better. We have to make the most of it while we're here. But in answer to your question, yes, I used to feel that Beth was only out for a while, for a few hours, away for a couple of days, visiting, shopping, somewhere. I'd hear the elevator, or a door would close in my apartment, and I'd think "She's home!" And a minute later I'd feel even worse than before. Maybe it's a game that we play with ourselves to keep from knowing the truth. Or maybe it's just hard to break old habits. Someone comes home every day and you think that they will forever. The only thing that changes in the end is eventually that someone no longer comes home. What it does is make you very grateful for what you have, while you have it, because now you know how brief and ephemeral it sometimes is.' They sat quietly again for a while as the ashes in the fire dimly glowed.

'Seven and a half months is not very long. But it's long enough to be very lonely and to realise that you really are on your own.'

'It frightens me sometimes. No, that's not true. It terrifies me.'

'You don't look very terrified to me.' She looked calm, pulled together, and able to handle almost everything, and he was sure that in the last seven and a half months she had. 'Just don't let people push you. Go at your own pace.'

'I don't have a pace. Except in my work. That's the only life I have now.'

'Now, only for now. Don't forget that. It's not forever. Remind yourself of that every day. If it gets unbearably painful, tell yourself that it is only right now. When I lost Beth, a friend told me that – a woman. She said that it was a little bit like having a child. When you're in labour and it gets unbearable, you think it will go on forever, that you'll never survive. But it isn't forever, it is only a few hours. And then it's over, finished, behind you. You've done it, you've arrived.'

She smiled at the comparison. She had had a hard time when Alessandro was born. 'I'll try to remind myself.'

'Good.'

And then she looked at him questioningly. 'Do you have children, Corbett?'

But he shook his head. 'Only those I borrow occasionally from friends.'

'That may not be such a bad arrangement.' She grinned at him. 'You may feel that way, especially after you've gone to the firehouse with Jason and Alessandro.'

'I'll enjoy it. Now what about you?'

'What about me?'

'Would you like to go for a drive tomorrow?'

'Aren't you working?' She looked startled.

'It's Saturday. Are you?'

'I'd forgotten. And I was going to but' – she looked warmly at him – 'I'd love to go for a drive. In broad daylight?'

'Of course.' He looked momentarily victorious.

'There are curtains in the backseat of my car. We can draw them until we get a little way out of town.'

'How mysterious.' She was laughing again, and Corbett stood up as she held out her hand. 'Thank you, Corbett.' He was going to tease her about being formal, but decided that it would be wiser not to. He shook her hand then and walked to the door.

'I'll see you tomorrow, Isabella.'

'Thank you.' She smiled again as the elevator reached them. 'Good night.'

This time when he left her he was smiling, but a tremor of fear ran through him when he remembered all that he hadn't said.

Chapter Twenty-One

The next day they drove into Connecticut for the day, hidden deep in the secrecy of his curtained Rolls, chatting about business again, this time about her grandfather's couture house in Paris and then once again about Rome.

'How do you know so much about all this?' She looked at him intently as they drove beneath trees that were just beginning to show leaves.

'It's no different than any business. Whatever the commodity you deal in, the concepts are often the same.' The idea intrigued her. She had never even thought of applying what she knew of her business to anything else.

'Are you involved in a great many undertakings?' But she already knew from his extensive knowledge that he was. She thought it strange how close-mouthed he was about business – most men were so eager to talk about nothing else.

'Yes.'

'Why don't you tell me more about them?'

'Because they would all bore you. Some of them even bore me.' She laughed with him and stretched happily as they got out of the car.

'If you only knew how long it's been since I've walked on grass and seen trees. And finally, finally, there's a little green here. I thought it was going to be grey forever.'

He smiled at her gently, 'See. it's the same thing. Nothing is forever, Isabella. Nothing good, and nothing bad. We both know that by now. You can't chop down a tree because it isn't yet in bloom. You have to wait, nurture it, love it. In time it revives again.' He wanted to tell her, 'So will you.'

'Perhaps you're right.' But she was too happy to think of the past now. She just wanted to breathe deeply and enjoy the country and her first taste of spring.

'Why didn't you bring Alessandro?' He looked down at her.

'He and Jason had a date with some friends in the park. But he told me to be sure and remind you about the firehouse.' She wagged a finger at him, laughing. 'I told you so!'

'I've already arranged it. For Tuesday afternoon.'

'You're a man of your word then.'

He looked at her seriously. 'Yes, Isabella, I am.'

But she knew that already. Everything about him suggested the man of honour, someone you could rely on and trust with the secrets of your heart. She hadn't met anyone like him in years; it had been even longer since she had opened up to anyone as she had to him. Her only confidants had been Amadeo, Bernardo, and Natasha. But she had lost Amadeo, and she and Bernardo, well, she and Bernardo were not talking about personal matters anymore. There was too much distance between them, and, too, she was feeling herself withdraw from him and he from her. So she was left with Natasha, and now Corbett. It was amazing how in a few short days she had come to trust him and all that he said.

'What were you thinking?'

'That it's strange how comfortable I feel with you. Like an old friend.'

'Why is that so strange?' They stopped at a fallen tree and sat down. His long legs were stretched out before him, crossed at the ankles; his broad shoulders were encased in fine English tweed. He looked amazingly young, despite the prematurely white hair.

203

'It's strange only because I don't know you. Not really, not who you are.'

'Yes, you do. You know all the essentials about me. Where I live, what I do. You know that I've been Natasha's friend for years. You know other things. I've also told you a great deal.' He was referring to Beth, his lost wife. Isabella nodded quietly and then looked up at the trees, her long neck arched skyward, her hair hanging down her back. He was smiling at her; for a moment she looked like a child on a swing.

He was intrigued by her, by her great beauty, and her diamond-sharp mind, the delicate elegance combined with the rare strength and the power of command. She was all contrasts and rich shadings, with mountains and valleys and textures that he loved. 'Why do you always wear black, Isabella? I've never seen you wear a colour, except that night; the coat you wore was white.'

She looked at him simply. 'For Amadeo. I'll wear black like this for a year.'

'I'm sorry. I should have known that. But people don't do that any more in the States.' He looked upset, as though he had said something he shouldn't have, but Isabella smiled.

'It's all right. It doesn't upset me. It's a custom, that's all.'

'You even wear black at home.' She nodded. 'You must look marvellous in colours though – dove colours, and pale peach, and bright blues, and magenta – with your dark hair . . .' He looked dreamy and boyish. She laughed.

'You should be a designer, Corbett.'

'Sometimes I am.'

'Like with what?' Her eyes grew serious as she straightened her head to look at him more closely. He was an interesting man.

204

'Oh, I picked out some designs for an airline once.' He was afraid to say much more

'Was it successful?'

'The airline?'

'No, the design. Did it look well?'

'I thought so.'

'You used your textiles?' He nodded, and she seemed to approve.

'That was good business. I try to use interchangeable things once in a while between my ready-to-wear and my couture. It's not always easy though because of the fabrics. But I do it when I can.'

'Where did you learn all this?' He was fascinated, and she smiled.

'My grandfather. He was a genius. The one and only Jacques-Louis Parel. I watched him, I listened, I learned from him. I always knew I'd be a designer. After I spent a year here, I set up my own design studio in Rome.' That was how she had met Amadeo, how it had all begun.

'Congenital genius then.'

'Obviously.' With a grin she picked a tiny wildflower.

'And humility too.' He put an arm easily around her shoulder and stood up then. 'How about some lunch?'

'Can we go somewhere?' She looked delighted, but he quickly shook his head.

'No.' For a moment her eyes fell.

'I was stupid to ask.'

'We'll come back this summer. There's a nice restaurant just over that hill. But in the meantime, Isabella, I made some provisions.'

'You did?'

'Of course. You didn't expect me to starve you, did you? I have a little more sense than that. Besides, I get hungry too, you know.'

'You brought a picnic?'

'More or less.' He held out a hand to her, and she got up from the log, dusting off her black skirt and pulling the black blazer closer around her as they walked back to the car. Corbett drove to a nearby lake, stopped, and unpacked a large leather bag. The picnic consisted of pâté, Brie, French bread and caviar, cookies and pastries and fruits.

She looked at it all delightedly, spread out on the little table he had popped out of a compartment on the back of the front seat. 'My heavens, this is gorgeous. The only thing missing is the champagne.'

He bowed from his seat and looked mischievously at her. 'You spoke too soon.' He opened the bar again and withdrew a large bottle resting in a bucket of ice. He set out two glasses.

'You think of everything.'

'Almost.'

She played with Alessandro through a rainy Sunday and was grateful that it hadn't rained the day before. On Monday she worked for fifteen hours, and on Tuesday she spent the day making calls to Hong Kong and Europe, to Brazil, and to Bangkok.

She was in the kitchen in bare feet and blue jeans, sipping coffee, when the doorbell rang. She looked up startled. It was ten minutes too early for it to be the boys. Hattie was marketing, and Natasha had told her she'd be gone all day. With a puzzled look Isabella went to the front door and looked through the tiny peep-hole and then grinned. It was Corbett, also wearing an old sweater and jeans.

'How could you forget something so important? It's firehouse day, of course!'

Isabella looked embarrassed. 'I forgot.'

'Are the boys here? If not, I'll have to take you. The firehouse will never forgive me if we don't show up. I'll just say you're my niece.' His eyes wandered over Isabella appreciatively, suddenly noticing the long thin legs and the narrow hips.

'The boys will be home in five minutes, and they'll be thrilled. And how are you?'

'I'm fine. What are you two up to? Working as usual?'

'Of course.' Isabella looked at him grandly and then beckoned him back towards her office door. 'Would you like to see the beautiful office Natasha gave me when I arrived?' She was like a little girl showing off her room. And he followed her willingly and whistled when he stepped inside. 'Isn't it lovely?'

'It certainly is.' Her work was spread out on the table, mountains of papers, and the floor was covered with neat stacks of designs. 'This must take some getting used to. I imagine you have a little more space in Rome.'

'Just a bit.' She smiled to herself, thinking of the enormous offices she and Amadeo had shared on the fourth floor. 'But I'm managing.'

'It looks like you are.'

At that moment the boys arrived, with whoops at discovering that he was there. Ten minutes later they had left again, with Corbett, and they didn't return for another two hours.

'How was it?' Isabella was waiting for them when they got home, and they told her in every detail. Alessandro announced to her excitedly that there really was a brass pole, calling it over his shoulder as Hattie finally dragged him off for a bath. 'And more to the point,' she said to Corbett when they were alone, 'how are you? Exhausted?'

'A little. But we had a wonderful time.'

'What a good sport you are. Would you like a drink?'

'Please. Scotch and water on a lot of rocks.'

'Very American.' She cast him a look of mock disapproval and went to Natasha's white marble bar.

'What should I be drinking?'

'Cinzano, Pernod, or maybe kir.'

'I'll remember that next time. But frankly, I prefer Scotch. She handed it to him, and he grinned. 'Where's Natasha?'

'Dressing for dinner and a gallery opening.'

'And you, Cinderella?'

'The usual. I'm going out for my walk.'

'You're not afraid to do that, Isabella?' He looked at her with sudden concern.

'I'm very careful.' She didn't even stroll back on Madison Avenue anymore. 'It's not very exciting, but it helps.' He nodded.

'May I join you tonight?'

She answered quickly. 'Sure.'

They waited until he had finished his drink and Natasha had left for the evening before they went out. They covered her usual route and a bit more, jogging part of the way and strolling the rest of the way home. She always felt better once she'd done that. As though her body were crying out for exercise and fresh air. It still wasn't enough, but it was better than nothing.

'Now I know how those poor little dogs feel, locked up in apartments all day.'

'I feel that way in my office sometimes.'

'Yes.' She looked at him reproachfully. 'But you can get out.'

He seemed to be thinking about something then as they returned to the apartment, but the boys set upon them quickly, in their pyjamas now, with freshly washed hair, and the moment was lost. Isabella watched him with them for half an hour as they wrestled and played. Corbett seemed to be having a good time. He had a lovely way with children, as he did with everyone. But it pleased her to see the children with him. He was their only man. Hattie finally arrived on the scene though and despite frantic protests took them both off to bed.

'Do you want to stay for dinner?'

'I'd love it.'

In the kitchen they ate a cosy dinner that Hattie had left for them to serve themselves -- fried chicken and corn on the cob – and dripped butter over their plates. After dinner they wandered to the back of the house and settled down in Natasha's pleasant little den. Isabella put on some music, and Corbett comfortably stretched his long legs.

'I'm awfully glad I went to that benefit last week. Do you know I almost didn't go?'

'Why not?'

'I thought I'd be bored.' He laughed at the thought of it, and Isabella did too.

'Were you?'

'Hardly. And not for an instant since then.'

'Neither have I.' She smiled at him easily and was surprised when he took her hand.

'I'm glad. I'm so sorry for what you've been through. I wish I could change all that.' But he couldn't, and he knew it. Not yet.

'Life isn't easy sometimes, but as you said, we always survive.'

'Some do, some don't. But you're a survivor. So am I.'

She nodded, agreeing. 'I think my grandfather taught me that. No matter what happened, what went wrong, he picked himself up and did something better immediately afterwards. Sometimes it took him a little time to catch his breath, but he always managed to do something spectacular. I admire that.'

'You're a great deal like him,' he said, and she smiled her thanks. 'Why did he finally sell the business?'

'He was eighty-three and tired and old. My grand-mother was dead, and my mother had no interest in the business. I was the only one left. And I was too young. I couldn't have run Parel then. Though I could now. Sometimes I dream of buying it back and merging it with San Gregorio.'

'Why haven't you?'

'Amadeo and Bernardo always insisted that it didn't make sense.'

'Does it? To you?'

'Maybe. I haven't totally ruled it out.'

'Then maybe one day you'll buy it.'

'Maybe. One thing's for sure: I'll never sell out what I have.' She was referring to San Gregorio.

'Was there a question of that?' He looked away as he asked her.

'Not for me. Never. But my director, Bernardo Franco, keeps trying in that direction. He's a bloody fool. I'll never sell.'

Corbett nodded knowingly. 'I don't think you should.'

'One day the business will belong to Alessandro. I owe him that.' Again Corbett nodded, and the conversation turned to other things – music and travel, the places they had lived as children, and why Corbett had never had a child.

'I was afraid I wouldn't have time for one.'

'And your wife?'

'I'm not really sure she was the type. In any case she agreed with me, and we never had one, and now it's a little too late.'

'At forty-two? Don't be absurd. In Italy men much older than you have children all the time.'

'Then I'll run out and have one immediately. What do I do? Put an ad in the paper?'

Isabella smiled at him from the opposite end of the tiny couch. 'I shouldn't think you'd have to do anything as drastic as that.'

He smiled softly. 'Maybe not.' And then, not even knowing how it happened, she saw him draw closer, put his hands on her shoulders. She felt herself drift into his arms. The music was playing in the distance and there was a pounding in her ears as Corbett kissed her and she clung to him as to a life raft in a heavy surf. He kissed her gently and she felt it deeply as she sensed her whole body reach out for him until she pulled away with a little lurch.

'Corbett! No!' She startled herself but was quickly comforted by the look in his eyes. It was a look of gentle loving from a man she trusted, with whom she felt totally safe. 'How did that happen?' Her eyes were misted with tears of confusion and, perhaps, a touch of joy.

'Well, let's see, I slid along the couch here, then I put my hand here . . .' He was laughing at her kindly, and she couldn't do anything but laugh too.

'That was terrible, you shouldn't do that, Amadeo – ' Suddenly she stopped. There was no Amadeo. Quick tears rose to her eyes. But he took her back in his arms and held her close to him as she cried.

'No, Isabella, don't. Don't look behind you, darling. Think of what I told you. The pain won't go on forever. This is very, very new.'

But he was grateful as he held her that Amadeo had been gone for almost eight months. It was long enough for her to be ready, to at least consider someone else.

'But I shouldn't, Corbett.' She pulled away from him slowly. 'I can't.'

'Why not? If it's not something you want too, then we won't even talk about it again.'

'It's not that, I like you . . .'

'Is it too soon? We'll go slowly. I promise. I don't want you to be unhappy, not ever again.'

She smiled at him gently then. 'That's a lovely dream. Nothing is forever, remember? Nothing good, and nothing bad.'

'No, but some things are for a very long time. I would very much like that with you.'

Without knowing why she said it, she found herself saying, 'So would I.'

He smiled at her then. They drank brandy, listened to the music, and sat on the floor like children. It was easy to be with him, and she was happy, happier still when he kissed her again. This time she didn't argue, and she didn't want him to stop. Finally he glanced at his watch, looked at her warmly, and stood up.

'I think, my darling, it's time for me to go home.'

'So early? It can't be more than ten o'clock.'

He shook his head. 'It's almost one thirty, and if I don't get out of here now, I'm going to attack you.'

'Rape?' She said it with amusement. She was back in control.

'We could start with that. It has a nice ring, don't you think?' His blue eyes were twinkling wickedly, and she laughed.

'You're impossible.'

'Maybe, but I'm mad about you.' He reached a hand out to her and pulled her up. 'Do you know that, Isabella? I haven't felt like this for years.'

'And before that?' She was still playing. She was so happy suddenly that she wanted to fly.

'Oh, before that I fell in love with a girl named Tillie Erzbaum. She was fourteen and had a fabulous chest.'

'How old were you?'

He considered it thoughtfully. 'Nine and a half.'

'Then you're forgiven.'

'Thank God.'

They walked slowly to the door and he kissed her again as they said goodnight.

'I'll call you tomorrow.' She smiled at him happily. 'And what about our walk? May I join you tomorrow?'

'I think that might be arranged.'

When she woke up the next morning, she was horrified at what she'd done. She was a widow. In her heart she was still a married woman. What was she doing kissing him all night on the den floor? Her heart pounded each time she thought of it, and she felt sorrow mixed with unfamiliar guilt. When he called her, she hid in her office and told Natasha in a brusque voice through the door that she was too busy to take calls from anyone, even him. But it wasn't his fault, she reasoned, as she tried fruitlessly to lose herself in her work. It wasn't his fault at all. She had been as eager as he for those kisses, as surprised as he at her responses, and much more so at what she felt stirring deep in her soul. But Amadeo . . . Amadeo . . . It was true then. Amadeo was not coming back again.

'Where are you going?' Natasha looked at her in surprise as she hurried towards the front door.

'I'm going for my walk early. I have too much work to do tonight.' She glanced nervously at Natasha, and her voice was sharp.

'All right. You don't have to get so uptight about it. I just asked.'

She was back at five o'clock, but still shaken, still nervous, still shocked at what she'd done. Then, suddenly, as she came up in the elevator she realised that she was being a fool. She was a grown woman, she was lonely, and he was a very attractive man. So she had kissed him. So what? But when she opened the door to the apartment, she jumped when she saw him standing in the middle of the room. As usual the children were playing around his legs, and Natasha was sprawled out on the couch, surrounded by books and papers, trying to chat with Corbett in spite of the din.

'Hi, Isabella. How was your walk?' Natasha called out.

'Fine.'

'I hope it did something for you. You were in one rotten mood when you left.'

She nodded, and Corbett grinned. But there was nothing too familiar, nothing possessive or uncomfortable about the look in his eyes.

'Did you have a rough day?'

She nodded again, trying to smile at him, and she relaxed a little at the continued look of comfortable friendship in his eyes. Maybe she had made too much of it. Maybe he wouldn't pursue it after all. It had been the brandy, the music, but it could still be forgotten; it wasn't too late. And then she found herself smiling and sprawled like Natasha in a chair. Natasha was yelling for Hattie while the boys and Corbett played. Hattie appeared a moment later, and Natasha waved the boys away.

'Jesus, I love them, but sometimes they drive me nuts.'

Corbett relaxed in a chair, let out a sigh, and grinned. 'Don't you two ever play rough with them? They've got more energy than brand-new box springs.'

'We read them stories.' Natasha looked at him in amusement. 'And play games.'

'Then buy them a punching bag or something. No, come to think of it, I guess they don't need one. They have me.'

His eyes met Isabella's, this time with a more pointed look. 'You already went for your walk?'

She nodded. 'Yes.'

'Okay. Then show me what you did in your office today. You promised yesterday, remember?' And before she could object, he had taken her hand and pulled her to her feet. Not wanting to make a scene in front of Natasha, she walked quickly to her office. Corbett closed the door.

'Corbett, I –'

'Wait a minute before you say anything. Please.' He sat down in a chair and looked at her kindly. 'Why don't you sit down?'

She did so, like an obedient schoolgirl, relieved only that he hadn't swept her expectantly into his arms.

'Before you tell me what you're thinking,' he went on, 'let me tell you what I already know. I've been through this. I know what it's like. And it's awful, so at least let me share what I learned. If I'm not entirely crazy, I left here last night and you were as happy as I was. But sometime – maybe last night, maybe this morning, maybe not even till tonight, though I doubt that – you started thinking. About your husband, about what used to be, about still being married. You felt guilty, frightened, crazy.'

Isabella stared at him in amazement, not saying a word, but her eyes very wide.

'You couldn't even understand why you'd done it, you could barely remember who I was. But let me tell you, darling, that's natural. It's something you have to go through. You can't run away from it now. You're lonely, you're human, you didn't do anything terrible or wrong. And if you had been the one who'd been kidnapped, your husband would be going through exactly the same thing right now. It takes about this long to feel again, to thaw out, and then you've got all the same feelings you've ever had before and no one to share them with. But now you've got me. You can either try it, very, very slowly, or you can run like hell and hide in your guilt and your feelings of still being married for the rest of your life. That's not an ultimatum. You may just not want me. I may not be the right one. If that's what you're thinking, I'll understand it. But don't run away from what you feel, Isabella . . . You can't go back.' He stopped then, almost breathless, and Isabella looked at him, stunned.

'But how did you know?'

'I went through it. And the first time I kissed a woman I felt as though I had defiled Beth's memory, as though I had betrayed her. I was torn apart. But the difference was that I didn't give a damn about that woman. I was just lonely and horny and tired and sad. I care about you, though. I love you. And I hope to hell you can care about me.'

'How do you understand everything like that?' She looked at him in amazement from across the room. And he smiled at her lovingly, easily, straight from the heart.

'I'm just very smart.'

'Ah, and humble!' She was suddenly smiling again, and enjoying teasing him.

'In that case, we happen to be evenly matched. Is that why you went out walking without me?'

'I wanted to run away from you. To have finished my walk before you got here.'

'That was smart.' But he didn't look hurt by it, nor did he look amused. He simply understood.

'I'm sorry.'

'Don't be. Do you want me to leave now? It's all right, Isabella, I'll understand.'

But she shook her head and held out her hand. He walked to her and took it, looking down into the bottomless black eyes.

'I don't want you to go. I feel stupid now. Maybe I was

wrong.' She clung to him as the children did, and gently he took her hands and knelt beside her, holding them in his own.

'I told you we'd go slowly. I'm not in a rush.'

'I'm glad.' And with that she put her arms softly around his neck and hugged him, childlike. They held each other that way for what seemed like a very long time, and this time it was Isabella who moved her hand slowly, touched his chin and his eyes and his lean, handsome face. It was she who took the first step this time and whose lips sought his, gently at first then hungrily. And it was she who trembled when they stopped.

'Take it easy, darling.'

But she was smiling again. 'What was it you said about rape?'

'If you rape me, I'll punch you.' He looked like offended virtue itself as she laughed. Then he was smiling again. 'Want to go for a drive?' he looked hopeful, but he didn't want to push.

'You brought the car?'

'No, I was planning to steal one. Of course I did. Why?'

'Then I'd love it.' She paused. 'What will we tell Natasha?'

'That we're going out for a drive. Is that so wrong?'

She looked at him sheepishly. 'I still feel guilty.'

But he smiled gently at her. 'Don't worry about it. Sometimes so do I.'

They bid Natasha a casual au revoir and went out for a drive, down to Wall Street, to the Cloisters, and then through the park. Settled against the plush upholstery, sitting close to him, she felt protected from the world.

'I don't know what happened to me today,' she said.

'Don't worry about it, Isabella. It's all right.'

'I suppose so. Do you suppose I'll ever be sane again?' She looked at him, smiling, half in jest, half in truth.

'I hope not. I like you like this.'

She smiled at him tenderly. 'I like you too.'

But Isabella knew that she more than liked him two weeks later when Natasha was away for the weekend with the boys.

'You mean they just left you?' He looked infinitely sorry for her when he came by on Saturday afternoon for tea. He had planned to sit with her for a few hours and maybe go for a walk, and he had been hoping that perhaps Natasha was going out. He enjoyed his time alone with Isabella, but it was even more precious to him because it was so rare. They were always surrounded by children, or Natasha, or even Hattie, the maid. 'Where did they go?'

Isabella smiled in amusement as she handed him a cup of Earl Grey. 'Just to some friends of Natasha's in Connecticut. It'll do the boys good.'

He nodded slowly, but it wasn't the boys he was thinking of as gently he reached for her hand. 'Do you realise how quiet it is here, and how seldom we're alone?'

She sat there thinking, and slowly her mind drifted back to Rome. She had had so much space in her home there, so much room to herself, so many hours of her own time. 'I wish you had known me then.' She said it dreamily as he watched her eyes.

'When, Isabella?'

'In Italy . . .' She said it softly and then looked up at him with a soft blush. 'But that doesn't make any sense, does it?' In Italy, in the good days, she had been married. Corbett would have had no place in her life.

But he understood what she was thinking. It was normal that now and then she should long for her home. 'Do you have a wonderful house there?'

She smiled and nodded, and then told him about

Alessandro's Christmas carousel as her eyes danced. She looked so lovely as she told him that he put down his cup and took her in his arms.

'I wish I could take you back there . . . take you home, if that's what you want.' And then he spoke very softly. 'But maybe one day home will be here?' But she didn't really think so; she couldn't imagine spending the rest of her life anywhere except Rome. 'Do you miss it awfully?'

She shrugged and smiled. 'Italy is . . . just Italy. There's nothing like it anywhere in the world. Crazy people, crazy traffic, good spaghetti, wonderful smells . . .' As she said it she found herself thinking of the narrow back streeets not far from San Gregorio, of women nursing babies in doorways and children running out of church, of the birds singing in the tree-tops in her garden . . . just thinking of it brought tears to her eyes.

And as he watched her Corbett felt sympathy for her tear at his heart. 'Do you want to go out for dinner tonight, my love?' It was the first time he had called her that and she smiled, but slowly she shook her head.

'You know I can't.'

But he thought for a moment. 'Perhaps you can.'

'Are you serious?'

'Why not?' His eyes danced with mischief now. He had a plan. 'There's a funny little Italian restaurant I used to go to, way downtown. No one "respectable" ever goes there.' He grinned. 'We could probably dash in for a quick dinner, and no one would have any idea who you were. And it's so Italian that it's bound to feel like home.' For a moment he wondered if that would make things worse, but he had a feeling that wouldn't be the case, and he was going to see to it that she had a marvellous time.

Like a fellow conspirator he waited in the living-room while she got dressed. She emerged giggling, in black slacks and sweater, with a black Borsalino fedora pulled low over one eye.

'Do I look mysterious?' She was laughing, and so was he. 'Very much so!'

He even had the Rolls parked a few doors away, and they slipped unnoticed into the restaurant, where they gorged and Isabella chatted happily with their waiter as they drank inexpensive Roman wine.

'Promise you won't tell Natasha! She'd kill me for this.' Her eyes sparkled, and he agreed.

'I couldn't tell her. She'd probably kill me first.' But he didn't feel nervous about Natasha. He knew that Isabella was safe, and when they had had their fill of pasta and the simple red wine, they drove slowly home with a brief detour through the park. 'Happy?' She nodded and settled her head against his shoulder. She had put her hat on the seat beside her, and her raven hair lay softly against his coat. He touched it gently, and then her cheek with his hand. And his eyes never seemed to leave her as he and Isabella went slowly inside.

'Do you want to come in for coffee?' She looked at him invitingly, but it wasn't coffee either of them had in mind.

He nodded and followed her inside, but once in the hallway, Isabella never bothered to put on the lights. She found herself instantly in Corbett's arms and in the darkness felt herself throbbing with a passion that she had long since forgotten, as Corbett pressed his mouth down on hers. Breathlessly they walked hand in hand to the bedroom, and without turning on the lights, Corbett undressed her and she him, and their bodies joined at last. It seemed hours later when she turned on a small light and smiled at him as he lay in her bed. She looked around the room at the debris of their clothes, and she started to laugh.

'What's so funny, my darling?'

'We are.' She looked down at him and then kissed him softly on the neck. 'You can't trust us at all. My room-mate goes away for the weekend, and what do we do? We run out for dinner and then we come home and make love.'

He pulled her slowly back to him again. '... and then we do it again ... and again ... and again ...'

Chapter Twenty-Two

April and May sped past them very quickly. When the weather permitted, they went walking every evening, or they went on drives. Sometimes they took Alessandro to the country and watched the look of wonder in his eyes as he played in grass, and built castles on still deserted beaches. And once or twice they took Natasha with them. For the first few weeks she had tried to pretend that she didn't know what was happening, but at last she had asked. And Isabella had nodded girlishly as she laughed and admitted that she and Corbett were in love.

She was obviously immensely happy, and whenever Natasha saw Corbett, so was he. But it was also clear to Natasha that aside from Isabella's delight about her romance she still had major worries with her work.

It was a warm, balmy evening when Corbett arrived at the house with a hansom cab to take Isabella for a drive. She laughed when she saw it, and they rode around in it for two hours.

'So how was work today, sweetheart?' He pulled her closer to him and looked down into the dark eyes.

'Terrible. Bernardo is giving me trouble again.'

'The new line?'

'No, that's already settled. We open next week. It's everything else. Plans for the winter, cosmetics, fabrics, I don't know. He's impossible right now.'

'It could be that there's too much on his shoulders with you over here.'

'What are you suggesting?' She looked at him tiredly. 'That I go home?'

'Hardly. I've always thought though that there are things you could change.'

'I know, but I can't now. Not while I'm here.' The way she said it made her think of Rome again, which was something she hated to admit to Corbett now. They had clung to each other as though it would be forever, but sooner or later she would have to go home. And Corbett's business would always keep him in the States. *Nothing is forever*, she thought to herself, and then pushed the words from her mind.

'Well, don't worry about it. Things will probably settle down in a few days.'

But they didn't. For the next two weeks, matters only got worse. Blow-up after blow-up after argument after fight. Isabella was sick of it. She told Bernardo that one morning on the phone. He seemed to have separated himself from her and seemed, in fact, better able to handle his feelings for her.

Oh, Bernardo, she thought to herself more than once. *If only it could be you I love. Life would be so much simpler*.

'Be sensible for chrissake and sell out.'

'Ah, no, that again! Listen, Bernardo, I thought we settled that before I left!'

'No, we did not. You just refused to listen to reason. Well, I've had it up to here. Gabriela is doing the work of ten people, you change the goddamn fabrics every time we turn around, you don't understand a thing about marketing cosmetics, and I get stuck cleaning up after you every goddamn time.'

'Is that right, then why don't you have the balls to quit like a man instead of telling me to sell out? Maybe the problem is with you, and not with the business! It's you who makes the problems between us all the time, you who won't do what I tell you. Why don't you do what I ask you to do for a change instead of shoving F-B down my throat everytime I open my mouth?'

The rage of Italian continued from Isabella's office. 'I won't listen to this anymore. And if you don't stop it, I'm coming home,' she shouted. 'The hell with all that garbage about danger. You're running my business into the goddamn ground.' It wasn't a fair accusation and she knew it, but the level of frustration between them had surged tidal-wave high. She had been in the States for five months and the charm of doing business this way was beginning to wear very thin.

'Do you have any idea of what you're doing, Isabella? Have you ever even listened to the F-B people? No. Of course not. You would rather sit on your ass over there and insult me and hang on to your business and your ego and save face.'

'The business is perfectly solid and you know it.'

'Yes, I know it. But the fact is I can't do it alone anymore, and you still can't come home. Circumstances, Isabella, circumstances. Your grandfather ran into circumstances too, and he was smart enough to sell out.'

'I never will.'

'Of course not.' She could hear the acid in his voice. 'Because you're too proud to, despite that fact that F-B and IHI and Ewing have all been begging me for you to sell out. Well, in point of fact not lately,' he went on, 'but I know damn well all I have to do is pick up the phone and call them and you'd have yourself a deal.'

There was no answer to what he'd said to her. Isabella was shocked nearly speechless.

'Who?'

'What are you talking about?' She wasn't making sense suddenly, and he was confused.

'I'm asking you who's been offering to buy us.' Her voice had the ring of cold steel.

'Are you crazy? I've been telling you since last October and you ask me who?'

'I don't give a damn. Tell me now. Slowly.'

'Farnham-Barnes.' He spoke to her as though she were retarded.

'And who else?'

'No one. What's wrong with you? F-B. F-B. F-B. And they belong to IHI.'

'And what was that other name?'

'What? Ewing? He's chairman of the board of IHI. The offer originally came from him.'

'Oh, my God.'

'What is it?'

'Nothing.' She was shaking from head to foot.

The picnics. The walks, the dinners – the firehouse . . . they flashed before her eyes – what a fine joke on her. It was a love affair – his love affair with the House of San Gregorio.

'Should I call them?'

'No. Do you understand me? Never! Cancel our dealings with F-B as of today. Call them, or I'll do it myself!'

'You are crazy!'

'Listen to me, Bernardo, I am not crazy and I've never been more serious in my life. Call F-B and tell them to drop dead. Now, today. *Finito*. No more offers, no more orders. Nothing. And get yourself ready. I'm coming home this week.' She had just decided. The nonsense had gone on for long enough. 'If you still think it's necessary, hire two guards, but that's all. I'll call you and let you know when I'm arriving.'

'Are you bringing Alessandro?' Bernardo was shocked. She was speaking in a voice that he hadn't heard in years.

Maybe never. She was suddenly ice and daggers, and he was glad he wasn't in the same room with her or he'd have feared for his skin.

'I'm not bringing Alessandro. He can stay here.'

'How long will you be here?' He didn't even argue. He knew there was no point. Isabella was coming home. *Punto.* Period. *Finito.* And maybe she was right. It was time.

'For as long as I have to be to whip you and everyone else there back into line. Now call Farnham-Barnes.'

'You're serious?' He was truly shocked now.

'I am.'

'*Capito.*'

'And tell them to get the penthouse ready. I'll stay there.' Without further ado she hung up on him.

'How dare you!' Isabella marched into the tiny room and stood glaring at Natasha.

'What?'

'How dare you!'

'How dare I what?' Natasha looked at her in sudden terror. Isabella stood before her, trembling from head to foot, her face white as paper, and her hands clenched at her sides.

'You set me up!'

'Isabella? You're not making sense!' Had she cracked up then? Was the strain of the business too much for her? But as Natasha watched her, it was clear that she had something very definite on her mind. She sat down suddenly, eyeing Natasha, an evil smile of fury hovering on her face.

'Let me tell you a little story then,' Isabella said. 'Perhaps after that we'll both understand. Last October, after my husband died – you know, Amadeo – perhaps you remember him? Well, he died, the victim of a brutal kidnapping . . .'

226

Natasha stared at her. If this was madness, it was calculated madness, cold and furious, with every word dipped in bitterness. Frightened, she watched her. There was nothing to do now but let her go on.

'He left me with his business, a large and successful couture house in Rome. We also do ready-to-wear, cosmetics, lingerie, I won't bore you with the list. I took over the business, worked my ass off, and vowed to myself and Amadeo that I would keep the business strong, until one day our son could take over, in twenty-five or thirty years. But lo and behold, my right-hand man, Bernardo Franco, first proposes marriage.' Natasha was shocked, but Isabella pressed on. 'And then announces to me that an American business named Farnham-Barnes wants to buy me out. No, I tell him. I'm not selling. But he pushes and he pushes and he tries and he tries. Unsuccessfully. I won't sell. So, miraculously, one day a phone call comes, telling me that my son has been kidnapped too. Only, fortunately, it is a hoax. And my son is fine. Bernardo then tells me that my life and the child's are not safe in Rome. I must leave, he tells me. So I call my friend Natasha Walker in New York, whom, as it so happens, he has screwed once or twice when she was in Rome.' Natasha began to argue, but Isabella held up a hand. 'Let me go on. I then call my friend Natasha, who invites me to stay with her. An elaborate plan is concocted to keep me safe and to run the business from Natasha's apartment in New York. Wonderful. Bernardo tries once again to get me to sell to F- B and I won't. I fly to America, with my son, and my friend Natasha picks us up at the airport, with a friend in a very pretty Rolls-Royce. I then live with Natasha, I run my business, Bernardo drives me crazy, and every time he has the opportunity he bugs me to sell out. I still hold my ground. But I become friends with the man at the airport, Mister Corbett Ewing. Conveniently "my friend",' – she dripped venom on the words – 'Natasha, invites me to join her at a film premiere. I go, and whom should I be sitting next to, but Mister Corbett Ewing, who only happens to be the chairman of the board of IHI, which owns Farnham-Barnes, which wants to buy me out. Happy coincidence, no? I spend three months being pumped about my business, being courted, being primed by this monster, this user, this villain, who wants to buy my business and will apparently do anything to do it, including pretending to be in love with me, playing up to my child, and using my "friends". Natasha, of course, invites him over night and day and is thrilled when we "fall in love". And what happens, then, my dear, do you get a commission from Corbett when he marries me and convinces me to sell to him?'

Natasha looked at her in astonishment and slowly stood up. 'Do you mean what you're saying?'

Isabella was like ice now. 'Every word. I think Bernardo arranged the hoax about Alessandro to get me out of the way, he used you to send me over here, and you saw to it that Corbett Ewing got close to me! It was all very handsomely done, but it's useless, because I will never sell out. Never! Not to Corbett, not anyone, and I think what you all did is disgusting! Do you hear me, damn you? Disgusting! You were my friend!' There were tears of rage and disappointment in her eyes now, and Natasha dared not approach.

'Isabella, I did nothing. Nothing! It was you who wanted to come here. You who wanted to go to that damned premiere. I didn't want you to do it. What do you think, that I tipped off the press? Oh, Jesus!' She sat down again and ran a hand through her tangled hair.

'I don't believe you. You're lying, like Bernardo. Like *him.*'

'Look, Isabella, please. I know this is difficult, and the

228

way you tell it, everything fits, but it just happened that way, no one planned it, certainly not Corbett.' There were tears running down her face now. 'He loves you, I know that. He was distraught when he found out who you were after the premiere. He came here the day after to tell you; he talked about it with me. He was afraid that something like this might happen. But he didn't tell you. I don't know why, but something happened that night that made him change his mind. He was afraid of losing you before he had a chance, and he hoped that if it ever came out, by then you might understand.'

'Understand what? That he slept with me to steal my business? I understand that perfectly.'

'For chrissake, listen to me.' Natasha was sobbing and holding her head in both hands. 'He loves you, he didn't want to lose you. When he found out who you were, he told his men at F-B to drop their offer and never ever mention his name.'

'Well, Bernardo just did.'

'Was it a new offer, or was he still referring to the old one?'

'I don't know, but I'll inform myself about it when I go to Rome. Which brings up my only further question. You say you're my friend — well, I have no one to turn to no matter what I think the truth is — will you keep Alessandro for me while I go home?'

'Of course. When are you leaving?' Natasha looked shocked.

'Tonight.'

'For how long?'

'A month, two months. As long as it takes me. I don't know. And keep that bastard away from my child while I'm gone. When I return, I'll work out another arrangement. If I am not going back to Rome permanently, I'll find a place of my own.'

229

'You don't have to do that, Isabella.' Natasha had crumpled on to her bed, crushed.

'Yes, I do.' She started to leave the room, then stopped for a moment. 'Thank you for keeping Alessandro for me.' She loved Natasha. They had been through much together. No matter what the truth was.

Natasha was still crying. 'I love him, and I love you. What are you going to say to Corbett?'

'Just what I told you.'

She called him then, and he was there an hour later, looking scarcely better than Natasha had when she was through.

'Isabella, all I can tell you is that I tried to tell you so many times. But something always intervened.' He looked at her, heartbroken, from a seat half-way across the room. He didn't dare to come near her. 'I'm horrified it came out this way.'

'You had to push and pump and prime and find out and dig inside my head for all you could learn about the house. Well, do you know enough now? It won't do you a bit of good, you know. I'm not selling, and I had Bernardo cancel all our dealings with Farnham-Barnes as of today.'

'There has been no offer from F-B to San Gregorio in over three months.'

'I'll have to check that out. But it makes no difference. You were smart enough not to make offers while you were "courting" me, maybe you figured that I was smart enough to find you out. But then what? What did you have in mind, Corbett, to marry me and charm me out of San Gregorio? You never stood a chance.'

'What are you going to do now?'

'I'm going back to Rome and kick everyone's ass right back into line.'

'And then what? Come back here to hide again? Why

230

don't you bring the business with you? That's the only thing that makes any sense.'

'Never mind what I do with my business. You've already said and done enough.'

'Then I'll go now. But you must know one thing, Isabella. What happened between us was real, it was honest, I meant every bit of it.'

'It was a lie.'

'I wasn't. I love you.'

'I don't want to hear it!' She stood up and smiled at him viciously. 'Nothing lasts forever, Corbett. Remember? Not even a lie. You used me, dammit! You took my heart and my body and my vulnerability, and you used me, just to add another notch to your corporate belt. San Gregorio. Well, you got me, but you won't get the rest.'

'I can't say I never wanted the rest. Before I met you, I did. But not after that. Never for an instant after that.'

'I will never believe you.'

'Then I'll say goodbye.'

She watched as he walked unhappily out of the room. But she was already in her room packing when he waved his car away and walked alone, rapidly, head bent, back to his office.

Chapter Twenty-Three

The plane touched down at Leonardo da Vinci Airport at 11.05 the next morning. Bernardo and two guards were waiting as she came out of customs, and the greeting she gave Bernardo showed affection as well as strain. She looked exhausted, having not slept a wink on the flight. It had been painful leaving Alessandro, awkward leaving Natasha, and all she had wanted to do was get away.

She had cried halfway to Rome. He had betrayed her. They had all betrayed her. Bernardo, Amadeo, Corbett, Natasha. All the people she trusted. All the people she loved. Amadeo, by dying; Bernardo by his efforts to make her sell out; and Corbett – she couldn't bear thinking of it. She wondered how she would begin again, how she would even function anymore.

As she came through customs with two small suitcases she looked tiredly into Bernardo's eyes. It was hard to believe that she hadn't seen him in five months. It felt more like five years.

'*Ciao, Bellezza.*' He thought as he looked at her that the five months she'd spent in New York hadn't been very kind. She looked frail, thin, and ravaged, and there were deep circles carved under her eyes. 'Do you feel well?' He was worried.

'Only tired.' For the first time in twenty-four hours she smiled.

He could sense the strain in her all the way into Rome. She was unusually reticent as she gazed silently and painfully out the window of the limousine.

'Nothing has changed much.' He tried to make small

talk. He didn't want to talk business in front of the guards.

'No, but it's warmer.' She remembered how cold it had been the night of her flight.

'How's Alessandro?'

'He's fine.'

Isabella longed to see the villa but she knew she wasn't ready to. Not yet. And she had business to do at the house. It made more sense for her to stay there. There was more to it, though she could only barely admit it to herself. Having given her body to Corbett, she hadn't wanted to return to the bed she and Amadeo had shared. Now she had betrayed him too. And for what? A ruse. A lie.

She felt her heart patter softly as they pulled up in front of the heavy black door. She wanted to cry out, but all she did for a moment was stare at it. Then she was out of the car and striding into the House of San Gregorio as though she had never been gone. No one had been warned of her coming, but she knew it would be all over Rome by that night. She didn't give a damn. Let them haunt her, let them set off flashbulbs in her face; she didn't give a damn about that either. Nothing would ever bother or surprise her, not anymore. Out of long habit she inserted her key in the elevator and pushed the fourth-floor button as Bernardo watched her, stricken, unhappy.

Something dreadful had happened to her, he realised. She was dead inside. That pale, ivory face he loved so well was like a mask. He had never seen her like this, not even during those awful hours when they had waited, not during the funeral or even on her flight into exile. The Isabella he had known for years was no more.

From the end of the fourth-floor hall she walked to the door of the stairs to the penthouse, Bernardo following up the short flight of stairs. It was then that she finally sat down, that she took off the black fedora she had worn, and seemed to relax.

'Allora, va bène, Bernardo?'

'I'm all right, Isabella. What about you? You've been gone for five months and you come home and act like I have leprosy.'

Maybe you do, she thought. She said only, 'Did you call F-B?'

He nodded. 'It made me ill, but I did. Do you know what that will do to our figures?'

'We'll make it back by next year.'

'What happened yesterday?' He didn't dare argue with her now. She looked too tired, too frail.

'I learned something very interesting.'

'And what was that?'

'That a friend of Natasha's, whom I also thought had become my friend, had been using me. To buy the business. You may recognize the name, Bernardo. Corbett Ewing. I wasn't amused.'

Bernardo looked at her, shocked. 'What do you mean, "using" you?'

She spared him the details. 'I never realised who he was. But Natasha knew, of course. And you did. I have no idea if you all concocted this thing together. I have no way of knowing; there is no way I ever will know. I'm not sure if that's why you insisted that I get out of Rome. It doesn't matter anymore, Bernardo. I'm home now. It's really Ewing who's the villain. The matter has been settled. I'm not selling. And I've made a decision that I should have made awhile ago. It has taken me some time.'

Bernardo wondered what was coming. His ulcer twinged miserably, and he waited for her news.

'I'm moving the main part of the business back with me, to the States.' It had been Corbett's suggestion. But, remarkably, he'd been right.

'What? How?'

'I haven't worked that out yet. The couture will stay

234

here. Gabriela can run it. I can fly over several times a year. That end of the business doesn't need my constant supervision. The rest of it does. Otherwise it's impossible, it's too much of a strain on you . . . and on me.' She smiled again, but weakly, and watched Bernardo as he absorbed the shock. 'We'll work it out together while I'm here. But I want you to come with me. No matter what has happened, I need you. You've always been my friend and you're too good to lose.'

'I'll have to think about it. This comes as a bit of a shock. I don't know, Isabella . . .' But with her words she was only confirming what he already knew. He was only her friend and employee. She would never let him be more. And he realised something else. He was glad. She would always have been too much for him to handle as a lover. She was going on about her plans.

'I can't live over here any more, not with Alessandro. You were right about that. I can't take that chance. There's no reason why we can't run the entire international end from New York. And' – she hesitated again 'I've decided to take Peroni and Baltare with me, if they'll go. Of our four under directors they're the only two who speak English. The other two will have to go. But we can talk about the rest later. And I'll say one thing.' She sighed softly and looked around. 'It's nice to see something familiar for a change. I've been damn tired of being so far from home.'

'But you've decided to stay there. Are you sure?'

'I don't think I have a choice.'

'Maybe not. What about the villa?'

'I'll close it and keep it. That belongs to Alessandro. He may come back here to live one day. But it's time I set up a home for him over there. And it's time I stopped hiding. It's been nine months since Amadeo died, Bernardo. It's enough.'

235

He nodded slowly, trying to understand it. Nine months. And how much had already changed.

'What about Natasha? I gather then that you two have had a falling-out?'

'You gather correctly.' She didn't volunteer more.

'You really think that Ewing was trying to push you?'

'I'm as sure as I'll ever be. Perhaps you know more about that than I do. I'll never know that either.'

It was shocking. She trusted no one now. She was suddenly bitter and cold. It made him uncomfortable and it frightened him.

What he saw in the next three weeks did nothing to change his mind.

Isabella made her announcements to the directors and checked every inch of the House of San Gregorio, going from room to room to office to stock room to desk to file, on every floor. Within three weeks she knew everything that was happening and all that she wanted to know. The two under directors she'd asked to join her in New York had agreed to do so, and she had decided to hire two American under directors to work with them there. The rest of the staff was being shuttled and divided. Gabriela was immensely pleased. She would be almost autonomous now in the couture end, overseen only by Isabella, who trusted her completely. But it was there that Isabella's trust stopped. She was suspicious, untrusting, and the greatest change of all was that she didn't even fight with Bernardo anymore. She was no longer an easy woman to work for, and she was suddenly a woman whom everyone feared. Her axe could fall anywhere. Her black eyes saw everything, her ears heard it all. She seemed to have got over her suspicions of him – but she was distrustful of everyone else.

'Well, Bernardo, where do we stand?'

She watched him over lunch in her office. For only a moment he wanted to touch her hand. He wanted to free her from this hideous spell, to assure himself that she was still human, to reach out to her. But he wasn't sure if anyone could anymore, not even he. The only time her voice warmed was on the phone with Alessandro; she had promised him in her phone call that morning that she was coming home soon.

'We stand remarkably well, Isabella.' Bernardo let the moment pass with a small sigh. 'Considering the kind of changes we're making. I'd say you've done splendidly. We ought to be able to set up offices in New York in another month.'

'That means late July, early August. It'll do.' And then came the final question. The one he'd been dreading for weeks. 'And you?'

He hesitated for a long moment, and at last he shook his head. 'I can't.' She stopped eating, put her fork down, and stared. For an instant she looked like the old Isabella, and he was almost relieved.

'Why not?'

'I've thought about it. But it would never work.' She waited in silence while he went on. 'You're ready to run it by yourself. You understand the business as well as I do, better in fact than even Amadeo did. I don't know if you realise that.'

'That's not true.'

'Yes, it is.' He smiled at her, and she was touched. 'And I wouldn't be happy in New York. I want to be in Rome, Isabella.'

'And do what?'

'Something will come along. The right thing. In time. I might even take a long vacation, go somewhere, spend a year in Greece.'

'You're crazy. You couldn't live without the business.'

237

'Everything has to come to an end.'

She looked at him thoughtfully. 'Nothing is forever.'

'Precisely.'

'Will you think about it for a while longer?'

He almost agreed to it and then he shook his head again. It was pointless. It was over. 'No, *cara*, I won't. I don't want to live in New York. As you said when you got here, it's enough.'

'I wasn't referring to you.'

'I know that. But it's time for me now.' Suddenly, as he looked at her, there were tears in her eyes. The drawn, tired face with the big black eyes crumpled. He moved to sit next to her on the leather couch and took her in his arms. '*Non piange, Bellezza. Isabellezza . . .*' Don't cry.

Isabellezza . . . At the sound of the word she turned her head and broke into sobs.

'Oh, Bernardo, there is no Isabellezza anymore.'

'There will always be. For me. I will never forget those times, Isabella. Nor will you.'

'But they're over. Everything's changed.'

'It has to change. You're right to change it. The only thing you're wrong to change is you.'

'But I'm so confused.' She stopped for a moment to blow her nose in his handkerchief as he gently ran a hand over her dark hair.

'I know you are. You don't trust anyone anymore. It's natural after what happened. But now you have to put it away. You have to stop before you let it destroy you. Amadeo is gone, Isabella. But you can't let yourself die too.'

'Why not?' She looked like a heartbroken little girl as she sat next to him and blew her nose again.

'Because you're too special, Bellezza. It would break my heart if you stayed like this, angry, unhappy, distrustful of

238

everyone. Please, Isabella, you have to open up and try again.'

She didn't tell him that she had done that and been hurt more than she ever had before.

'I don't know, Bernardo. So much has changed in the last year.'

'But you'll see. You'll find in time that some of them have been good changes too. You're making the right decision taking the business to America.'

'I hope so.'

'What are you doing about the villa, by the way?'

'I'll start packing up next week.'

'You're taking everything with you?'

'Not all of it. Some things I'll leave here.'

'Can I help you?'

Slowly she nodded. 'It would make it much easier. I've – I've been afraid to go back.'

He only nodded and smiled as she blew her nose for a last time.

Chapter Twenty-Four

The car turned into the gravel driveway and came to a halt outside the familiar front door. Isabella looked at it thoughtfully for a moment before she stepped out. The house looked larger to her somehow, and the grounds seemed strangely quiet. For a moment it was like returning from a long trip. She expected to glimpse Alessandro's face at the window and then a minute later see him come bounding out to meet her, but he didn't. No one came. Nothing stirred.

Bernardo stood soundlessly behind her as she began to walk slowly towards the house. In the five weeks that she had been in Rome, she had never come out here. In a way, in her heart, she hadn't really been back. She had come to Rome to minister to her business. But this was something different, something private, a piece of the past. And she herself had known that she wasn't ready to see it. Now that she was back again, she was grateful that she wasn't alone. She glanced over her shoulder then with a soft smile, remembering Bernardo. But the dark eyes weren't smiling; they looked unhappy and distant as she looked around her and then rang the bell. She had her key with her but she didn't want to use it. It was like visiting someone else now. Someone she had once been.

Bernardo watched as a maid opened the door and Isabella stepped inside. He had warned them. Signora di San Gregorio was coming home. The information was met with trepidation and excitement: with Alessandro? Forever? There had been a flurry of planning – what rooms to open, what meals to prepare. But Bernardo had been quick to dispel the illusions. She won't be staying there, and she will be alone. Alessandro was still in America. And then he had dealt the last blow. She'll be closing the house.

But it wasn't the same anymore anyway. The central figures of the household were already gone. Mamma Teresa had left in April, understanding at last that her charge would be gone for too long. Bernardo had spoken to her openly, the risks were too great. He would be gone for a year maybe, perhaps a little less, or probably more. She had gone to a family in Bologna, with three daughters and two little boys. She had never quite recovered from the way Isabella had left her, without even warning her that she was taking Alessandro away from her, in the dark of night, leaving his bed empty and his room locked, and the woman who had protected and loved him far behind. Luisa had taken a job for the summer in San Remo, with people for whom she had worked once before. And Enzo had retired; his room in the garage was empty. The three stars of the household had long since tearfully gone. Now there were only the lesser lights to help Isabella.

Bernardo had ordered countless boxes, which had been left in the front hall. Isabella saw them as soon as she entered. Silently she stood and looked at them, but her eyes drifted away from them. She seemed to be waiting – for familiar noises, for sounds she had heard there, for voices that were no more. Bernardo watched her, hanging carefully back. She put down her light linen jacket and began to walk slowly down the long hall. Her footsteps rang out emptily. Had it only been five months since the night she'd fled with Alessandro? Five months since she had crept down that hall, collecting suitcases and Alessandro in his red sleepers, whispering 'sshhh' and promising adventure? '*Are we going to Africa, Mamma?*' She smiled to herself and wandered into the living-room. She glanced at the blue Fabergé clock that she had looked at so intently that night she had waited for Amadeo, when they were expected for dinner at the Principessa's house – the night he had been so late, the night he had disappeared. She sat down heavily on the chaise longue near the window, staring emptily at Bernardo.

'I don't even know where to begin.' Her eyes were full and heavy, and he nodded, understanding.

'It's all right, Bellezza. We'll do it slowly, room by room.'

'It will take years.' She looked out to the garden. The carousel she had given Alessandro for Christmas was shrouded in canvas, its chimes and music silent. Tears came to her eyes, but she smiled.

Bernardo watched her, remembering that night, as he was. He fumbled in his pocket and pulled something out that he held in his hand.

'I never gave you this last Christmas. I was afraid it would make you too unhappy if I gave you a gift.' Christmas with Amadeo had always been an extravaganza, jewellery and funny objects, little treasures and remarkable books she had coveted, tiny wonders she had always loved. There had been no way Bernardo could have made that up to her, and he had been afraid to even try. But he had gone to Alfredo Paccioli and he had bought her something that now, five months later, he held out to her. 'I felt awful afterwards not giving you anything.' Silently he felt for the now familiar pocket watch that had been Amadeo's. He always wore it.

He handed her the small package. She took it, her eyes filling, and sat down again with a very small smile.

'You don't need to give me presents, Bernardo.' But she took it and opened it, then she looked up at him, speechless with emotion. It was a large gold ring with the seal of San Gregorio carefully engraved in it, impeccably carved in a smooth face of black stone. It was onyx, and its proportions were perfect on her long slender hand. She slipped it on

242

above her wedding ring, her eyes wide and mist-filled again.

'Bernardo, you're crazy . . .'

'No, I'm not. Do you like it? He smiled at her from where he stood, looking very young to her, almost like a boy.

'It's perfect.' She gazed at the ring again.

'If you like it half as much as I do my pocket watch, I'll be happy.'

Without saying more, she rose and went to him. They hugged each other for a moment, and he felt her heart beating as he held her close.

'Thank you.'

'*Va bène, Bellezza*. Sshhh. No, don't cry. Come on, we have work to do.' They pulled apart slowly, and he took off his jacket and unclasped his cuff links as she watched. 'Where do we start?'

'My bedroom?'

He nodded, and hand in hand they walked determinedly down the hall. She was dividing everything into three categories. The things she would leave in the house under dustcovers, to be retrieved by her one day perhaps, or put to use in the house if Alessandro ever opened it again, if as a grown-up he came back to Rome. The things she would pack and send to America. And precious objects that couldn't be left there, but would have to be put in storage. Of those, she decided, there were few. Things were either worth taking with her or could be left here at the house. Things like the grand piano, and some of the large antique furniture that had been in Amadeo's family for years, but of which neither of them had ever been very fond. Most of the rugs she was leaving in storage. They may not fit in her new rooms. The curtains would stay on the windows they were made for. The sconces and the chandeliers would stay. She didn't want to leave holes and gaping openings in the house. When Alessandro came back one day, she

243

wanted it to still look like a home, not a barracks that someone had ransacked, preparing for flight.

'*Allora.*' She looked at him. '*Avanti!*'

He smiled at her, and they began to pack. First her bedroom, then Alessandro's, then her boudoir; then finally they stopped for lunch. The sacred shrine was being dismantled, the boxes were piling up endlessly in the hallway, and Isabella was satisfied as she looked around. It was a good opportunity to weed out her favourite things from the ones she didn't really care about. Bernardo had watched her carefully, but there had not been a single tear since they had started. She was in command of herself again.

They sat in the garden, eating lunch. 'What are you going to do about the carousel?' Bernardo said. He was munching on a prosciutto and tomato sandwich. Isabella poured them both a glass of white wine.

'I can't take it. I don't even know where I'll be living. We may not have a garden.'

'If you do, let me know. I'll have it packed up.'

'Alessandro would love that.' She looked at Bernardo. 'Will you come to visit us?'

'Of course I will. Eventually. But first' – he looked victorious – 'I'm going to Greece.'

'You've decided then?'

'It's all settled. I rented a house last week on Corfu, for six months.'

'And after that?' She took another sip of wine. 'Maybe you should come to New York and look it over.'

He shook his head. 'No, Bellezza, we both know we've made the right decisions. I'll do something here.'

'For one of my rivals?' Her look of concern was only half serious, but again he shook his head.

'You don't have any, Isabella. And I couldn't bear to work for second best after you. I've already had five offers.'

'Jesus, have you? From whom?' He told her, and she was derisive.

'They make garbage, Bernardo. No!'

'Of course, No! But something else may come up. There's been one offer that intrigues me.' He told her. It was the largest designer of men's wear in Italy, who also did private fittings in London and France.

'Wouldn't that bore you?'

'Maybe. But they need someone to run it. Old man Feleronio died in June, the son lives in Australia and is a doctor, the daughter knows nothing about the business. And,' he looked at her mischievously, 'they don't want to sell it. They want someone to run it for them, so they can go on living like kings. Eventually I think they'll sell, but maybe not for another five or ten years. It would give me a lot of freedom to do what I want.' He smiled at her.

'Go ahead, say it. Something you never had with me.'

'I wouldn't have respected you as much if you'd taken a back-seat. And there's no reason for you to, you know more about this business than anyone in Europe.'

'And the States,' she added proudly.

'And the States. And if you do half as good a job teaching Alessandro, San Gregorio will go on for the next hundred years.'

'Sometimes I worry about that. What if he doesn't want it?'

'He will.'

'How can you know?'

'Do you ever talk to him about it? He sounds more like fifteen than five. He may not quite have your eye for design and colour, but the workings of it, the genius, the machinery of San Gregorio, it's already in his blood. Like Amadeo. Like you.'

'I hope so.' She made a mental note to talk to him about it more when she got back. 'I miss him terribly,' she said, and I think he's getting angry. He wants to know when I'm coming home.'

'When are you?'

'In another month. It's just as well. Natasha took a house in East Hampton for the summer. He can be at the beach there while I finish here and then when I look for an apartment in New York.'

'You're going to be awfully busy. You have to find temporary office space   the boys are going to be arriving over there two weeks after you do – not to mention finding permanent space, an architect to do it, a place for you and Alessandro to live – '

'While *you* sit on your ass in Greece!'

He grinned at her. 'I've earned it, you monster.'

'Come on,' she said, 'let's go back to work.'

They worked until eleven o'clock that evening, dividing treasures in the living-room, packing what they could, and leaving the rest for the professional packers. Red labels marked what was going with her, blue ones what was staying in Rome, green ones what was going into storage. Then there were the left-overs, the inevitable throwaways that surface in everyone's life when they move. Even for Isabella, with her Louis XV and her marble and her Fabergé, there were still broken toys, things that she hated, books she didn't want to keep, and dishes that were cracked.

Bernardo dropped her off that night at the House of San Gregorio and picked her up again the next day. For the next three weeks they stopped work early, arriving back at the villa by two o'clock and leaving after midnight. By the fourth week the job was done.

Isabella stood for a last, lonely moment, amid the mountain of boxes stacked up neatly in the living-room and the hall. A sea of red labels, the treasures she was sending to New York. The house suddenly echoed strangely; the lights were off. It was after two o'clock in the morning.

'Are you coming?' Bernardo was already waiting in the driveway.

'*Aspetta!*' she shouted. Wait. Even as she thought. For what? Was he coming? Would she hear his footsteps? The man who'd been gone for ten months. She whispered softly in the darkness. 'Amadeo?'

She waited, listening, watching, as though he might come back to her and tell her his disappearance had all been a joke. That she should stop everything and unpack. There hadn't really been a kidnapping . . . or there had been, but it was someone else they had killed. She stood there, trembling, alone, for a minute that seemed like an hour. Then, tears streaming from her eyes, she closed the door softly and locked it. She held the door-knob for a last time, knowing that she would never be back.

Chapter Twenty-Five

'You'll come to see me? You promise?' She was clinging to Bernardo at the airport. They had both been crying. Now he dabbed at her eyes with his handkerchief and brushed roughly at his own.

'I promise.' He knew how nervous she suddenly was about running the business alone in New York. But she was staffing it wisely. Peroni and Baltare were unimaginative but solid. Isabella didn't need anyone with imagination, she had enough for them all. 'Kiss Alessandro for me,' he said.

She was crying again. 'I will.' It had been an unbearable week of goodbyes. At the villa. At the house. With Gabriela, whom she would see on her next trip to Rome in three months. But still there was the constant pain of leaving, and now Bernardo. In some ways it was like leaving as she had six months before. But this time it was in broad daylight, from the Rome airport, the two bodyguards looked bored, and there had been no more crank calls. It was finally over. Even Bernardo had agreed that she would be safe now being seen in New York. It was no secret that the business was moving, and there would be photographs and phone calls from the press. But the police had assured her that she was no longer in any real danger. She had to be reasonable, and perhaps a little careful with Alessandro, but no more so than anyone in her position. She had learned the lesson well. Painfully well.

She kissed him for a last time, and he smiled at her, once again through his own tears.

'*Ciao, Isabellezza*. Take care.'

'Ciao, Nardo. I love you.'

They hugged one last time, and she got on to the plane. Alone this time, without bodyguards, in first class, with her name on the manifest. Her eyes were streaming with tears.

She slept for three hours, then submitted to a brief dinner, taking some papers from her briefcase and smiling at the prospect of seeing Alessandro. She hadn't seen him in two months.

When the plane landed in New York, she went quickly through customs, without fear this time. She remembered the last time she'd come into New York, exhausted, terrified, her jewellery hidden in her handbag, the bodyguards beside her, and her child in her arms. Today the customs officers dismissed her with a wave, and she muttered a quick 'thank you', passing through the gate, her eyes combing the airport.

Then she saw them, Natasha and the children, waiting, and she ran towards them and took Alessandro in her arms.

'Mamma! . . . Mamma!' The whole airport was filled with his clamouring. She held him tightly in her arms.

'Oh, darling, how I love you . . . oh, and you look so brown. Bernardo said to kiss you.'

'Did you bring my carousel?' His eyes were wide and happy, a reflection of her own.

'Not yet. If we find a house with a garden, I'll have them send it, but you're almost too big for it, you know.'

'Carousels are for babies.' Jason looked at them disgustedly, all that kissing and hugging. That kind of stuff wasn't appropriate for a man. But Isabella kissed him anyway, and tickled him, and he suddenly laughed.

'Wait till you see what I've brought you two!' There were shrieks of excitement and more laughter, and Isabella looked up at Natasha. Her face sobered, but she smiled gently. 'Hello.'

For an instant Natasha hesitated, and then they went into each other's arms. 'I've missed you, too, you know.'

'So have I. It was horrible not having a room-mate.' They both laughed again. Natasha knew as they walked along together that she was no longer angry. The light of anguish had somewhat dimmed in her friend's eyes.

'I almost dropped dead when you said you were moving the business. What did they say in Rome?'

'The same thing. The only one who thought it was wonderful was Bernardo. He knew I was right to do it. It's going to be a mad-house for a while. I have a million things to do.' She groaned just thinking of it.

'I'll help you.'

'Aren't you staying out in East Hampton?' They all looked brown and healthy from their month in the sun.

Natasha nodded. 'Yes, but I can leave the boys with Hattie.'

Isabella nodded slowly. 'All right.' She had some fences to mend with Natasha. The business with Corbett didn't matter so much anymore. Maybe Natasha's intentions had been good. But it didn't matter. Isabella didn't want to know. The subject was closed between them. This time there was no Rolls, only the ordinary limousine Natasha sometimes rented, with the driver who had taken Isabella to the disastrous premiere in April. Isabella smiled at him. It seemed a thousand years before.

They went back to the apartment. The boys opened their packages, shouting and laughing, trying on sweaters and funny hats, throwing pieces of new games, and playing with their toys.

At last Isabella smiled shyly at Natasha, holding out a package. 'This one is for you.'

'Come on, Isabella. Don't be silly.'

'Never mind. Open it.' It was the cream of the new

winter couture collection, which had opened in June. It was a soft blue cashmere dress with a matching blue coat. Natasha held it up in front of the mirror, looking awed.

'It's gorgeous.'

'It matches your eyes.' From the folds of more paper Isabella extracted the scarf and a matching hat. 'You can wear it to lunch with your publisher.'

'Like hell I will. Why waste it on him?'

'Then you can wear it to lunch with me. At Lutece.'

For a moment Natasha stared at her silently. 'You're going out again?'

Isabella nodded. 'It's all right now. It's time.' Corbett had been right, she thought, her imprisonment hadn't lasted forever. Only ten months, though it seemed like a lifetime to her.

In the morning Natasha and the boys went back to East Hampton and Isabella went to work. Not on the phone to Rome this time, but with four real estate agents, who dragged her from one end of Park Avenue to the other, along the side streets, and up and down Fifth. In a week she had temporary office space, had hired five bilingual secretaries, rented mountains of office equipment, and ordered phones. It was barely more than adequate but it was a beginning.

At the end of the second week, she found what she was looking for. Atop one of the tallest skyscrapers in the city, two floors for the House of San Gregorio with a view of the entire city of New York.

Finding the apartment had taken her longer, but at the end of another two weeks of searching, she stood in a penthouse on Fifth Avenue, looking out at the view. There was the sweep of Central Park beneath her, the Hudson River in the distance, and the skyline of the city to her left, facing south. The apartment itself was spacious and lovely. There were four bedrooms – one for herself, one for

Alessandro, a guest room, and one she could use as a den – two maids' rooms, a huge dining-room with a fireplace, a double living-room, and a large hallway and foyer that reminded her vaguely of the house in Rome.

The real estate agent had watched her intently. 'You like it?'

'I'll take it.' There was an army of doormen and porters, even more than there were in Natasha's building twelve blocks south.

The next day Natasha came in from East Hampton to see it. 'My God, Isabella, look at that view.' Isabella stood proudly on her new terrace. There would even be room for the carousel, if it would survive the winter snows in New York. 'When do you move in?'

'Well, I called the movers yesterday. The ship gets in tomorrow. I was thinking of next Saturday. I have to get it over with, so I can get back to work.' Her henchmen from Rome had been arriving, and everyone was eager to settle down and dig in.

But Natasha looked suddenly unhappy. 'So soon?' Isabella nodded. 'That's awful. I'm going to miss you. And Jason says he'll be afraid to sleep alone in his room.'

'He can come to visit every weekend.' Isabella smiled at her.

'I feel as though I'm getting divorced again.'

'You're not.'

In the heat of the September afternoon the two women looked at each other, and Isabella finally decided to broach the painful subject. She owed it to her friend.

'I owe you an apology, Natasha.'

Natasha knew instantly what Isabella was speaking of, but she shook her head and looked away. 'No, you don't.'

'Yes. I don't understand what really happened. I was angry at Corbett. But I was wrong to lash out at you. I don't know if you tried to help him or not, but it doesn't matter. If you did it was out of good intentions. I know that. And I'm sorry for what I said.'

But Natasha looked at her intently now. 'You're wrong about him.'

'I'll never know that.'

'You could talk to him, let him tell you. You could at least give him that chance.'

Isabella only shook her head.

'Nothing lasts forever. Nothing good. Nothing bad. Corbett told me that in the beginning. He was right.'

'He still loves you.' Natasha spoke the words softly.

'Have you seen him then?' Isabella sought her friend's eyes, and Natasha nodded.

'He understands what happened. Maybe better than you do. He was afraid of that happening from the first. The only mistake he made was not telling you in the beginning.'

'It doesn't make any difference now. It's over.'

Unhappily Natasha knew that Isabella meant it. It was over for Isabella. But not for Corbett or the boy. But Natasha said nothing, and Isabella spoke no more of Corbett until that afternoon.

She was telling Alessandro about the apartment.

'You mean I can have my carousel?'

'Absolutely. I already called Rome.'

'Mamma! . . . Mamma! Wait till Corbett sees it.' His eyes glowed, and for an instant everything stopped.

Isabella looked at him strangely, then shook her head. 'He won't see it, darling.'

'Yes, he will! He's my friend.' Defiance blazed in Alessandro's dark eyes. No one had said anything to him, but he had sensed a rift between his Mamma and his friend. Alessandro didn't like it. Not at all. He could tell in the way Corbett now spoke of his mother. As if he were afraid of her. As if she were dead. 'I will invite him over to

253

see it.' He looked up at her, challenging, but her voice grew hard.

'No, Alessandro, you won't.'

'I will. I promised him this summer.'

'Did you? When?'

'When I saw him at the seaside. He was in East Hampton too.'

With that Isabella turned on her heel and marched off to find Natasha. Once again she found her in her office, with a cup of coffee in her hand, reading a fresh page. Isabella slammed the door hard behind her. Natasha jumped at the sound, then stared at her friend as though she'd lost her mind.

'What's the matter?' The look on Isabella's face was strangely familiar, but before Natasha could place it, Isabella began to rage.

'Why didn't you tell me? He was there in East Hampton all summer, hanging around Alessandro, trying to get to me again!'

Natasha stood up, hands on her hips. This time she wasn't giving an inch. 'Alessandro needs him, Isabella. And Corbett is *not* trying to get to you. Stop being so paranoid, for chrissake. What is it with you? You think everyone wants to steal your goddamn business, everyone is using you or your child.'

'They are, goddammit! They took my husband too.'

'"They" did. "*They*". People who were crazy, who wanted money. But that's over, Isabella. Over! No one is trying to hurt you now.'

'I don't give a damn. I don't want that man near him.'

'You're wrong. But tell him that, don't tell me.'

'But you knew it! You knew how I felt when I went back to Rome.'

'I thought you'd come to your senses, that you'd get over it.'

'I never will. I already came to my senses. The minute Bernardo mentioned his name. I don't want that man near Alessandro again.' With that she slammed out of Natasha's office, went to her own room, and with a trembling hand, picked up the phone.

He was quick to come on the line. 'Isabella? Is something wrong?'

'Very much so. And I want to see you. Now! Can you see me?'

'I'll be there in half an hour.'

'Fine. I'll meet you downstairs.' She didn't want Alessandro to see him. She watched the clock in her bedroom, and in twenty-five minutes she went down. Four minutes later the Rolls pulled up in front of the door. Corbett was alone in the car, driving. He got out and opened the door for her. She slipped into the car with him, but when he began to turn on the ignition, she quickly waved the hand wearing her new ring from Bernardo.

He noticed it and understood instantly what it was. He wanted to tell her that it was pretty, that she looked beautiful, that he still loved her, but she didn't give him the chance.

'Don't bother, Corbett. I'm not going anywhere with you. But I didn't want to speak to you upstairs where Alessandro could hear us.'

His face tensed with worry. 'What's wrong?'

'I want you to stay away from him. Is that clear to you? I want you out of his life, entirely, permanently, and completely. I've had enough of your games – working on my friends, my associates, my business, and now my child. The other you had a right to do; how you conduct your business affairs is up to you. But when you use me personally, or my son, Corbett, then you are engaging in a war you can only lose. If you come near him again, if you send him gifts, if you try to see him or call him, or if you let him call you, *I* will call the police and my lawyer. I will sue you for harrassment. I'll have *your* business, and I'll see you in jail. Molesting a minor, attempted kidnap, rape, call it anything you want to, but stay the hell away from my child!' She was screaming so loudly that the doorman would have heard her, if Corbett had not had the foresight to roll up the windows.

He looked at her for an instant, disbelieving what he was hearing. Then anger overcame him. 'Is that what you think I'm doing, Isabella?' he asked. 'Using the boy to get to you again? Is that what you think? Is it? How pompous, how arrogant, how incredibly stupid you are! I told you months ago that you should keep your business, I told you my offers had been withdrawn. I fell in love with you, and to tell you the truth I felt damn sorry for you. Locked up like an animal, afraid of everyone, trusting no one. You've had a bad break in life, Isabella. And so has the child. He lost his father; he's as lonely as you are. And you know what? I love him. He's a wonderful little boy. And he needs me. He needs a lot more than just you! You're a bloody machine. Your business, your business, your business! I'm sick of hearing about it. Now leave me alone and get the hell out of my car!'

Before she could answer him, he had jumped out, gone around the front of the Rolls, and was holding the door open for her, as, astounded, she stepped out.

'I trust I made myself clear to you.' She glared at him icily.

'Absolutely,' he said. 'Goodbye.' He got back in his car again, and before she had got back into the building, he was gone.

Chapter Twenty-Six

The apartment was looking lovely, the offices were working with the usual frenzy, and the carousel had just arrived. It was the end of September, and Jason and Natasha had come to the penthouse to try it out. Alessandro was jumping up and down, laughing and squealing, and Jason had decided that it wasn't 'bad at all'.

'Oh, God, I love it, Isabella. I want one too.' The two women smiled at each other, watching the children ride round and round. The first breeze of autumn had broken the spell of summer, and Isabella was stretched out on the terrace, outside her new home, pleased with her accomplishment.

The walls of the bedrooms had been covered in fabrics, there were wonderful curtains, and rugs on every floor. The bathrooms had already been done in marble when she bought it, but she had changed all the fixtures. Opening on to the terrace there were exquisite French doors.

'You're a genius,' Natasha said, looking admiringly around her.

'No. I'm a designer. Sometimes that helps.'

'How's the new collection coming?'

'Slowly.'

'So is the new book.'

'It takes me time to settle down every time I change location. But at the rate they're going on the new office space, I won't have to worry about that again till next year. It's taking them forever.'

'Baloney. How long have they been at it?' She grinned at Isabella. 'Two weeks?'

Isabella smiled back at her. 'Six.'

'Patience, patience!'

'A virtue for which I have never been known.'

'You're learning.' She had learned a great deal of that in the last year. 'How does it feel to go out again?'

'Heavenly.' And then she sobered. 'But a little strange. I keep waiting for it to happen. The awful. The inevitable. The press to flash lights in my face, and then the threats, the crank phone calls.'

'And does it?'

Isabella shook her head, smiling slowly. 'No, only the reporters from *Women's Wear* who want to know what I'm eating or what I'm going to wear. But it takes a long time to forget the nightmare, Natasha. A very, very long time.' At least she no longer waited for Amadeo to come home at night. It had taken a year. 'Which reminds me.' She turned her thoughts to something light. 'I want you to join me for dinner tomorrow night. Are you busy?'

'Of course not. The man I spent my energies on all summer just went back to his wife. The bastard.'

Isabella grinned, and they said it together: 'Nothing lasts forever.'

Natasha said, 'Shut up and tell me where we're going.'

The soft pink lighting warmed the familiar faces, faces one usually saw in fashion magazines or on the covers of *Fortune* or *Time*. Movie stars, moguls, publishers, authors, heads of corporations. The very good at what they did, and the very rich because they were. The tables were placed close together, the candles on the pink tablecloths danced in the soft breeze from the garden, and everyone's diamonds seemed to be glittering, as shining faces talked and laughed. Lutèce had never been lovelier.

They ordered caviar to begin with, and filet mignon and poached salmon for each of them. A half bottle of red wine for Isabella, and a half of white for Natasha's fish. The salad was hearts of palm and endive, and there were big beautiful strawberries for dessert. Isabella was looking comfortable and happy, when suddenly Natasha noticed her dress.

'What's the matter?' Isabella watched her, but her friend just sat and stared.

'For a whole year you look like a nun or a scarecrow and suddenly you don't and I didn't even notice.'

Isabella only smiled. The period of official mourning was over, and tonight, for the first time, she was dressed in the palest mauve and white. The underdress was a perfectly stark, white gaberdine of her own design, and over it she had worn a soft mauve cashmere tunic, with the amethyst-and-diamond ear-rings she had once lent to Natasha.

'Do you like it? It's new.'

'Same collection as my blue marvel?' Isabella nodded as Natasha leaned towards her to confess, 'I turned up the air conditioning the other day just so I could wear it around the house.'

'Don't worry. It'll be cold enough for it soon.' Isabella shuddered, already thinking of the long New York winter that would seem to go on forever.

'You look beautiful,' Natasha said. Still there was a glimmer of something very lonely in her friend's deep, onyx eyes. 'I'm glad it's over, Isabella.' She was immediately sorry she had said it, because in some ways she knew it was not. It would never be. The loss of Amadeo would always weigh on Isabella's heart.

'I can't believe that it's been a year.' Isabella looked up from her coffee then, a wistful look in her eyes. 'In some ways it seems as though he's been gone forever. In other ways it seems only yesterday. But it's easier for me here than it was in Rome.'

'You made the right decision.'

Isabella smiled again. 'Time will tell.'

They chatted on for another hour, and then they each went home, Natasha to what now seemed to her like an empty apartment, and Isabella to her new penthouse. She undressed quietly, put on her nightgown, went to kiss Alessandro, already sound asleep in his bed, and peacefully slipped into her own bed and turned off the light. It was six o'clock the next morning when she was awakened, startled, by the sound of the phone.

'Hello?'

'Ciao, Bellezza.'

'Bernardo! Do you know what time it is? I was sleeping. Are you bored already?' Bernardo had left for Corfu shortly after her own return to New York.

'Bored? *Sei pazza*. You're crazy. I love it.' His voice sobered quickly. 'Isabella, darling . . . I had to call. I have to go to Rome.'

'Already?' She laughed at him. 'Going back to work already? That was quick.'

'No, it's not that.' There was a pause as Bernardo steeled himself to tell her. He wished he were there with her, not thousands of miles away on an island, staring helplessly at his telephone. 'I got a call yesterday. I waited till they called me back this morning, until they were sure.'

'Who, for chrissake?' She sat up and yawned sleepily. It was Saturday and she had wanted to sleep till noon. 'You're not making sense.'

'They got them, Isabella.'

'Who got what?' She was frowning now, and her blood froze suddenly as she understood. 'The kidnappers?'

'All of them. There were three. One of them talked too much. It's all over, Isabella. It's all over, *cara*.'

Listening to him, she was suddenly crying and shaking her head. 'It was over last year,' she said. She didn't know if she was happy or sad now. It didn't make any difference anymore. Amadeo was gone. And catching the men who had killed him would not bring him back.

'We have to go to Rome. The police called me back this morning. They've got special permission to speed it up. The trial will be in three weeks.'

'I'm not going.' She stopped crying. Her face was deathly white.

'You have to, Isabella. You have to. They need your testimony.'

'Nardo . . . no! *Non posso. Non posso!* I can't.'

'Yes, you can. I'll be there with you.'

'I don't want to see them.'

'Neither do I. But we owe it to Amadeo. And to ourselves. You can't stay away, Isabella. What if something happens, if they are set free? Can you let this happen to someone else?'

At his words the events of a year ago rushed over her again. He had lied to her then, goddamn Corbett. It did go on forever. It would never be over. Never! She was crying again into the phone.

'Isabella, stop it. It's almost over now.'

'It isn't.'

'I promise you, *cara*. It is. Just this one last thing, and then you can put it behind you forever. The police asked me to call you, they thought it would be less of a shock if you heard it from me,' he went on. 'They don't think the trial will take more than a week. You can stay at the house.'

'I'm not coming.'

His voice was firm now. 'Yes, Isabella. You are.'

When she hung up, she sat in her bed. Seeing visions she had blotted from her mind for the last year – of waiting in the living-room in her green evening dress, watching the clock on the mantelpiece; of Alessandro and his handful of cookies that night. And then the phone call, the visit to Alfredo Paccioli to sell her jewellery, Amadeo on the phone telling her to be brave. She squeezed her eyes closed, trying not to scream. With a trembling hand, she reached for the phone again, dialled Natasha's number.

By the time a sleepy Natasha answered, Isabella was hysterical.

'What? Who is this? Isabella! What's the matter? Darling, talk to me . . . Isabella? . . . Please . . .' Natasha said.

'They've caught them . . . the kidnappers . . . and I have to . . . go to the trial . . . in Rome . . .'

'I'll be right over.'

Her face buried in her pillows, Isabella fled the visions and dropped the phone.

Chapter Twenty-Seven

They drove from the airport straight to the House of San Gregorio, speeding through Rome. It was that miraculous time of the year again, still sunny and warm, yet with cool breezes and blue skies and no clouds. Mid-October. It had once been her favourite time of year. She sat in the car in stony silence, wearing a grey suit and a matching grey hat. Bernardo could barely see her eyes beneath the brim, cast down towards her hands folded tightly in her lap.

'It starts tomorrow, Bellezza. You were right to come.'

She looked at him tiredly then, and he cringed at the pain he saw so sharply etched in her eyes. 'I'm tired of doing what's right. What does it matter now?'

'It matters, *bella*. Trust me.'

She took his hand in hers. After all this time, all the arguments and accusations, she did.

There were a few photographers waiting for her at the door, but Bernardo steered her through, and they passed rapidly through the house, to the penthouse, where he set her bags down, and poured them each a glass of wine.

'How was the trip?'

'It was all right.'

'And Alessandro?'

'Mad at me for leaving, but he's fine.'

'Did you tell him why you were coming?'

She nodded slowly. 'Yes, I did. I wasn't going to, but Natasha said I owed it to him to tell him. So he wouldn't be afraid anymore.'

'What did he say?'

She looked startled. 'He was happy. But he didn't see why I had to go. Neither do I.' She sipped at the wine again and looked at Bernardo, tanned and looking years younger after his month at Corfu.

'You did and you know it. What about the office?'

'Everything's fine.' For the first time she smiled at him as she pulled off the grey hat.

'What about you?' He looked at her sharply.

'What's that supposed to mean?'

'Are you seeing anyone? It's been over a year now. It's time you went out.' He had finally come to accept what would never be between them and cherish what they had.

'Mind your own goddamn business.' She looked away at the rooftops of Rome.

'Why should I? You don't mind yours. What about Corbett Ewing?'

'What about him?' Her eyes shot back to him, startled. 'How much do you know about us?'

'I figured it out eventually. Your violent reaction about F-B, and the way you sounded that day, when I mentioned Ewing to you on the phone. I've never heard you angrier.'

She nodded slowly. 'I have never been so angry. But I thought he'd seduced me on purpose, just to get his hands on San Gregorio.'

'Is that what you think now?'

She shrugged. 'It doesn't matter anymore. I haven't seen him at all.'

'Did he seduce you?' Bernardo's voice was very soft.

'That's none of your business.' Then she softened. 'For a little while I thought we were in love. But I was wrong, that's all. It would never have worked anyway.'

'Why not?'

264

'Because – oh, dammit, Bernardo, I don't know. Maybe we're too different. Maybe I'm married to the business now. Besides, it'll never be like it was with Amadeo. And I don't want to break my heart, or anyone else's, finding that out.' She looked at him sadly. He shook his head.

'So you waste yourself, is that it? At thirty-three you close the door. You lose Amadeo, and you give up.'

'I haven't given up. I have Alessandro and the business.' She stared at him defiantly, but he wasn't buying it.

'That's not much of a life. Did you at least give Ewing a chance to tell you what happened, to find out if what you think is true?'

'I told you, it doesn't matter. And yes, I saw him once when I got back from Rome.'

'And what happened?'

'Nothing. I told him to stay away from Alessandro. I found out that while I was here Natasha had let him see the child.' She sighed softly and smiled a bitter smile. 'I told him that if he came near us again, I'd call my lawyer and the police and have him arrested for molesting Alessandro – something like that.'

'Are you crazy? What did he say?'

'He told me to get the hell out of his car.'

'He was right. I'd have kicked you out. For God's sake, Isabella, what were you thinking of?'

'I don't know . . . Myself . . . Amadeo . . . something. I told you, it's over. It wouldn't have worked out.'

'Not if that's the way you've been behaving.' He poured himself another glass of wine.

'Natasha sees him of course. They're old friends.'

'Did she tell him about the trial?' Bernardo was looking at her strangely, but she only shrugged.

'I don't know. Maybe. In any case it was in the papers again the day before I left New York. Page nine this time; we're finally shrinking in importance again. I'll tell you.

265

I'll be damn glad when the only place I see my name is in the fashion section.'

'That'll come. After this week it'll all be over. Now get some sleep. I'll pick you up in the morning.' He kissed her cheek gently and left her sitting there, sipping the last of her wine.

Chapter Twenty-Eight

'*Va bène?*' Bernardo looked at her worriedly as she stepped out of the car. She had worn a black dress today, but no black stockings this time. It was a long-sleeved black wool dress, with alligator shoes and matching handbag, and her hat was discreet and small. She wore only her pearls and the ring Bernardo had given her the last time she'd left Rome.

'Are you all right, Isabella?' he asked. She was so pale that for a moment he was afraid she would faint on the courthouse steps.

'*Va bène.*' I'm fine.

He took her arm. In an instant the barrage began. Photographers, television cameras, microphones, madness. It was reminiscent of that whole ugly time. She clutched his hand tightly, and a moment later they were inside the courthouse, waiting in a tiny room adjoining the judge's chambers. He had made it available just for her.

They sat for what felt to Isabella like hours before a uniformed guard came in and beckoned to her.

Holding tightly to Bernardo, her legs feeling wooden, she followed him into the courtroom, averting her eyes from the long table where the defendants sat, trying not to look at them, not wanting to see. Bernardo could feel her trembling as she sat down.

The testimony was long and laborious: Amadeo's secretary, the doorman, and finally two San Gregorio employees who had seen the two men come in. The story about the car was explained, and Bernardo could see one of the men squirm. More testimony from the coroner, two minor officials, and then finally it was over; court would not reconvene after lunch. Due to the painful nature of the trial, and in consideration of Signore di San Gregorio's widow, the proceedings would be adjourned until the next morning.

The judge ordered the bailiffs to remove the accused. As they stood up, ready to be escorted away, Bernardo heard Isabella gasp.

They were ordinary men in plain clothing, men she had never seen, but suddenly they were there, before her, the men who had snuffed out Amadeo's life. Bernardo held her arm tightly. Isabella had turned whiter still.

'It's all right, Isabella, it's all right,' he said, feeling helpless to soothe her. She needed something more than even he could give her. 'Come on, let's go now.'

Blindly she let herself be led. In a moment they were being mobbed again on the front steps.

'Signora di San Gregorio, did you see them? . . . How did they look . . . Do you remember? . . . Can you tell us? . . .' A hand snatched off her hat. She was running and crying, protected by two guards and Bernardo, until at last they reached the car. She threw herself into his arms, sobbing all the way back to the house. He got her upstairs quickly and helped her to the couch.

'Do you want me to call a doctor?'

'No . . . no . . . but don't leave me . . .' she began as the telephone rang. She sat bolt upright with a look of terror in her eyes. She couldn't go through it again, couldn't bear it. 'Tell them to stop putting calls through.' But Bernardo had already answered it and was speaking in low tones. She could not hear what he was saying. Finally he looked at her, smiled, and nodded his head. And then, without explaining further, he handed her the phone and left the room.

'Isabella?' At first she didn't recognise the voice. Then her eyes grew wide.

'Corbett?' But it couldn't be.

But the voice answered, 'Yes,' adding, 'and don't hang up on me. Or at least not just yet.'

'Where are you?' Her face was expressionless; it sounded as though he were here with her, in the same room.

'I'm downstairs, Isabella, but you don't have to see me. If you want, I'll go away.'

'But why?' And why now of all times?

'I came to steal the business. Remember me?'

'Yes, I remember you. I – I owe you an apology . . . for what I said to you in the car.' She was smiling into the phone.

'You don't owe me anything. Not an apology, not the business, not anything. Nothing but ten minutes of your time.'

An idea occurred to her then, and she was astonished. Bernardo! Had he asked Corbett to come? 'Did you fly to Rome to see me, Corbett?'

He nodded his head and answered her. 'Yes. I knew what you must be going through. I thought that maybe you needed a friend.' Then, 'Isabella, may I come upstairs?'

A moment later she opened the door for him. She did not speak. Her eyes were dark and tired and empty. Slowly she put out her hand.

'Hello, Corbett.'

It was like the beginning. He shook her hand solemnly and followed her into the room.

'Would you like a glass of wine?'

She was smiling now as she looked at him, and it took everything he had not to take her in his arms. He shook his head and looked around the room. 'Is this your office?'

'No, it's an apartment we keep for important guests.

And then she looked at him unhappily and sat down with her head bowed. 'Oh, Corbett, I wish I weren't here.' He sat down next to her and watched her.

'I'm sorry you have to go through this, but at least they caught them. At least now you won't wonder what happened to them and if they'll ever strike again.'

'I suppose so. But I thought I had put it all away.'

He only shook his head. He didn't want to tell her that you never really can. You can't erase a memory. Or deny an irreparable loss. You could dull it, you could heal it, you could fill the void with something else. 'Isabella' – he paused for a moment – 'may I be there with you tomorrow?'

She looked at him, horrified. 'At the trial?' He nodded. 'But why?' Was he curious then? Was that it? Was he like all the others? Was that why he had come? She looked at him suspiciously, and he took her hand.

'I want to be there with you. That's why I came.'

This time she nodded, understanding, as her fingers tightened slowly in his grasp.

Chapter Twenty-Nine

The next morning she stepped out of the car with a guard ahead of and behind her, and with Corbett and Bernardo on either side. Together, they ploughed through the mob, her head bowed, her face hidden by a black hat with a brim. Moments later they were in the courtroom and the judge had entered and called Alfredo Paccioli, the jeweller, to the stand.

'And Signora di San Gregorio brought you her jewellery? All of it?'

'Yes,' Paccioli murmured.

'What did you give her in exchange for it? Did you give her anything?' The attorney was pressing, and again Paccioli said yes.

'I gave her all the cash I had in the office at the time. And I got another three hundred thousand dollars from merchants I know. I also promised to get her an equal amount the following week.'

'And what did she say?'

Corbett felt Isabella stiffen next to him, and he turned slightly to watch her. Her face was so pale, it was almost white.

'She said it wasn't enough, but she took it.'

'Did she tell you why she needed the money?'

'No.' Paccioli paused, unable to go on. When he spoke again it was almost a whisper. 'But I suspected. She she . . . looked . . . ravaged . . . broken . . . frightened . . .' He had to stop then as tears washed his florid face. His eyes met Isabella's. She was crying too.

The judge called a recess.

The testimony continued agonizingly for another three days. At last, on the fifth morning, the judge looked at her regretfully and asked her to take the stand.

'You are Isabella di San Gregorio?'

'I am.' Her voice was a tremulous whisper, her eyes almost larger than her face.

'Are you the widow of Amadeo di San Gregorio, who was abducted from his office on September seventeenth and murdered on —' The attorney checked the correct date. He supplied it, and Isabella nodded miserably.

'I am. Yes.'

'Can you tell us, in orderly fashion, what happened on that day? The last time you saw him, what you did, what you heard?'

Step by step she went through it: her arrival at the house that morning, the business they had discussed, Bernardo's warning, how she and Amadeo had been touched but had cast the warning aside. She looked briefly at Bernardo. There were tears in his eyes, and he looked away.

With anguish Corbett watched the proceedings, willing her to have the strength to go on. For days now he had watched her and listened, taken her back to San Gregorio each afternoon, and talked with her until night. But he had said nothing of an intimate nature, never touched her, except gently with his eyes. He had come to Rome as her friend, knowing that these days would be most painful, that in reliving it, at last she would be free. But knowing also that it might break her, that even if she survived it, she might want nothing from him. He had come anyway, he had been there, as he was there for her now.

'And when did you realise that your husband was late?'

'At . . . I don't know . . . perhaps seven-thirty.' She told of

272

being interrupted by Alessandro. And then, in agony, she explained further of calling Bernardo, of waiting, of suddenly being afraid. And then the phone call. She began to describe it, but she broke down and couldn't go on. She gasped for a moment, fighting for air and composure, but suddenly the tears were flowing from her eyes.

'They – they said they had . . . my husband.' It was a word strangled between a gasp and a scream. '. . . that they would kill him . . . and . . . they let me talk to him, and he said . . .'

Bernardo looked at the judge unhappily, but he only nodded. It was best if she got it over with all at once. They had to go on.

'And then what did you do?'

'Bernardo . . . Signore Franco arrived. We talked. Later that night we called the police.'

'Why later? Had the kidnappers told you not to?'

She took a deep breath and went on. 'Yes, later. But at first I was afraid that if I called the police, my accounts would be frozen and I wouldn't be able to come up with the money at all. And they were frozen, of course.' She sounded bitter as she said it.

'Is that why you tried to sell your jewellery?'

She looked at Paccioli, seated in the back of the courtroom, and nodded. He was crying openly. 'Yes. I would have done anything . . . anything . . .'

Corbett's jaw tightened, and he and Bernardo exchanged an anguished glance.

'And then what happened? After you got the money? Did you deliver it to the kidnappers, although it was less than they had asked?'

'No. I was going to. I was going to tell them. It was Monday night, and they wanted the money by Tuesday. But . . .' She began to tremble again. '. . . but they called . . . It was . . . it was . . .' A look of horror crossed her face, and

273

her eyes searched out Corbett and Bernardo. '*Non posso!* I can't go on!'

No one moved. The judge spoke to her gently and urged her to finish if she could. She waited a moment, sobbing, while the bailiff brought her some water. She took a small sip and went on.

'It was in the papers that I had been to Alfredo. Someone told them.' And as she said it she remembered the face of the girl. 'The kidnappers knew then that my accounts had been frozen. That we'd called the police.' She sat very still and closed her eyes.

'And what did they tell you the next time you spoke to them?'

She whispered, with her eyes closed. 'That they'd kill him.'

'Was that all they said?'

'No.' She opened her eyes again, as though seeing a vision, as though she herself were now very far away. The tears streamed down her face. She looked up at the ceiling. 'They said that I could . . .' Her voice was fading as she looked back again. '. . . say goodbye to Amadeo . . . And . . . I did. He told me . . . he told me . . . to be brave for a little while, that everything would be . . . all right . . . that he loved me . . . I told him I loved him . . . and then . . . .'

She stared blindly into the courtroom.

'And then they killed him. The next morning the police found him dead.'

She was lifeless as she sat there, recalling the moment, the feeling, and the last sound of Amadeo's voice, which seemed to fade as her own voice died away. Silently she looked at the three men accused of his murder, and still crying, she shook her head. The judge quickly signalled to Bernardo. Her part in the trial was over. He wanted her removed.

Bernardo got quickly to his feet, having understood, and Corbett followed him and the attorney to the stand, where they reached out to Isabella, who looked at them, uncomprehending. 'They killed him . . . they killed him . . . Bernardo . . .' Her voice was a hideous wail in the courtroom . . . 'He's dead!'

Her scream had carried outside the courtroom. As Corbett and Bernardo assisted her towards the doors, they burst open, and the photographers were unleashed into the courtroom.

'Come on, Bernardo!' Corbett was suddenly all action as he swept Isabella out in his arms. 'Stay away from her, you bastards.' Bernardo and two guards were ploughing ahead, as the judge shouted for order and deputies attempted to have the press removed. The courtroom was a shambles, and Isabella was crying, and the crowd watched them, stunned.

Somehow they reached her car at last, the doors closed, and the three of them pressed together in the back seat as the car sped away, the press still shouting, cameras clicking.

Isabella collapsed on Corbett's chest.

'It's over, Isabella. It's over, darling . . . it's over.' He said it to her again and again as, stricken, Bernardo watched. He regretted ever telling her to make the journey. He had been wrong, but Corbett's eyes didn't reproach him, even when they reached the fresh crowd of press waiting for them at San Gregorio.

Bernardo stared at them in horror as Isabella began to shed fresh tears. Corbett glanced at the crowd and quickly told the driver, 'Don't stop here. Keep going.' He looked at Bernardo. 'We'll take her to my hotel.'

Bernardo nodded savagely, thinking that the only intelligent thing he'd done lately was call Corbett Ewing and ask him to come.

They were in his suite at the Hassler five minutes later, and Isabella stared at them with a ravaged face.

'It's all over now,' Corbett said. 'You'll never have to go through anything like this again.'

She nodded slowly, like a child who has just seen her entire family die in a fire.

Bernardo looked at her sorrowfully. 'I'm sorry, Bellezza.'

But she was more herself again as she watched him, and she learned forward to kiss his cheek. 'It doesn't matter. Perhaps now it really will be over. What will happen to those men?'

'If they live long enough to get out of the courtroom, they'll be found guilty, and I assume they'll be sentenced for life.' Bernardo said it viciously, and Corbett nodded; he agreed. But he stood up then and walked quickly towards the phone. He spoke into it softly and returned a moment later to consult the other two.

'I think we should leave for New York on the next plane. Can you leave, Isabella? Or do you have business to do?' She shook her head numbly and then looked up at him.

'What about my things?'

But Bernardo was on his feet now. 'I'll go get them.'

Corbett nodded. 'Fine. Can you meet us at the airport in an hour?' Bernardo nodded in answer, stood up, and looked down at Isabella.

'Is that all right with you?'

'The trial is finished?' They both nodded. The essential testimony had been given and there had never been any real doubt about the outcome. It was a capital offence. The men who had taken Amadeo and killed him would be punished.

'It's finished, Isabella. You can go home now.'

Home. Bernardo had called New York her home. For the first time, she realised that it was. She didn't belong in

Rome any more. Not after today, after this week, after what had happened. Her eyes sought Corbett's after Bernardo had left them and Corbett had locked the door. She watched him as he closed his suitcase and then returned for a moment to sit at her side.

'Thank you for being here. I . . . it was so awful . . . I thought I was going to die . . . All that kept me going was knowing that I had to say it, had to finish it, and get it out . . .' She looked at him again. 'And I knew I could do it as long as you were there.' And then she had to ask him. 'Did Natasha send you?'

But he shook his head slowly. He wasn't going to hide anything anymore. 'Bernardo called me.'

'Bernardo?' She looked shocked and then she nodded her head. '*Capisco.*'

'Are you angry?'

Her voice was very gentle as she smiled at him. 'No.'

This time he smiled too. He looked at her for a long moment, sitting close to her on the couch. 'There are some things we need to talk about, but right now let's get to the airport and get on that plane. Do you have your passport? If Bernardo misses us, he can always send your luggage on the next flight.'

'My passport is in my handbag.'

'Let's go then.' He held a hand out to her, and they both stood up. The limousine was already waiting downstairs. There were no paparazzi. They had no interest in Corbett Ewing at the Hassler. They were too busy at San Gregorio.

Bernardo met them at the airport an hour later, five minutes before they had to catch their plane. Isabella clung to him tightly for a last moment. '*Grazie, Nardo, grazie.*' He held her tightly for a moment and then pushed her towards the plane.

277

'I'll see you in March!' were his last words to her, as Corbett waved to him and they boarded.

As Rome shrank beneath them Corbett watched her silently, staring out over the wing. Finally she turned to him and slipped her hand into his. But he couldn't wait any longer. He gazed at her with a worried look in his eyes. 'Is it too soon to tell you I love you?' His voice was a whisper that barely reached her ears.

The smile spread to her eyes slowly as she looked at him.

'No, darling, it was never too soon.' They kissed long and hungrily as the stewardess waited to serve them champagne. She poured the bubbling wine into their glass, and Isabella picked up hers and looked long and hard into Corbett's eyes. Then softly she whispered to him as she lifted her glass, 'Forever, my love' . . . as long as forever may be.

WANDERLUST

Danielle Steel

At 21 Annabelle Driscoll was the acknowledged beauty, but it was her sister Audrey – four years older – who had the spine and spirit. She had talent as a photographer; she had the restless urge of a born wanderer.

Inevitably it was Annabelle who was the first to marry, leaving Audrey to wonder if life were passing her by. The men she met in California were dull, worldly. Even in New York, they failed to spark her. Only when she boarded the *Orient Express* did she realise she was beginning a journey that would take her farther than she had ever dreamed possible . . .

STAR

Danielle Steel

Every dream demands a sacrifice

For Crystal Wyatt, growing up on a ranch in Northern California, Hollywood seems a million miles away. Bold, passionate and enchantingly beautiful, she knows her destiny is waiting for her.

But no one said it was going to be easy. Singled out for her devastating looks and captivating singing voice, Crystal soon embarks on the dangerous road to stardom. Her dreams are creeping closer, but then so are those determined to stop her. And when the darkest of scandals comes out, Crystal must face the challenge of her life.

In this wonderful novel, Danielle Steel tells the story of an extraordinary young woman and her determination to achieve her ambition – whatever the odds.

978-0-7515-0559-7

FAMILY ALBUM

Danielle Steel

Every choice has its price

Hollywood, 1945. Shipping heir Ward Thayer and screen star Faye Price are reunited after a chance meeting two years earlier. Unable to forget the connection they shared and helpless to resist it, romance quickly sparks.

But for Faye, daring and passionate, the life she's heading for with Ward is a threat to her ambition. How can she decide between Hollywood and motherhood? Is it right to choose fame over family? Faye is on the brink of an impossible choice that will shape her life – and the lives of those she loves – in ways she could scarcely have imagined.

In a novel that is filled with unforgettable scenes and a wonderful cast of characters, *Family Album* explores one woman's dilemma with sensitivity, compassion and warmth.

978-0-7515-0542-9

Other bestselling titles available by mail:

☐	Now and Forever	Danielle Steel	£5.99
☐	Going Home	Danielle Steel	£5.99
☐	Loving	Danielle Steel	£5.99
☐	The Ring	Danielle Steel	£6.99
☐	Palomino	Danielle Steel	£5.99
☐	Remembrance	Danielle Steel	£6.99
☐	Crossings	Danielle Steel	£6.99
☐	Full Circle	Danielle Steel	£5.99
☐	Golden Moments	Danielle Steel	£5.99
☐	Family Album	Danielle Steel	£5.99
☐	Star	Danielle Steel	£5.99

The prices shown above are correct at time of going to press. However, the publishers reserve the right to increase prices on covers from those previously advertised, without further notice.

————— sphere —————

Please allow for postage and packing: **Free UK delivery.**
Europe; add 25% of retail price; Rest of World; 45% of retail price.

To order any of the above or any other Sphere titles, please call our credit card orderline or fill in this coupon and send/fax it to:

Sphere, P.O. Box 121, Kettering, Northants NN14 4ZQ
Fax: 01832 733076   Tel: 01832 737526
Email: aspenhouse@FSBDial.co.uk

☐ I enclose a UK bank cheque made payable to Sphere for £ . . . .
☐ Please charge £ . . . . . . to my Visa, Delta, Maestro.

☐☐☐☐☐☐☐☐☐☐☐☐☐☐☐☐

Expiry Date ☐☐☐☐   Maestro Issue No. ☐☐

NAME (BLOCK LETTERS please) . . . .

ADDRESS . . . .

. . . .

. . . .

Postcode . . . . Telephone . . . .

Signature . . . .

Please allow 28 days for delivery within the UK. Offer subject to price and availability.